A KISS AT SUNSET BEACH

ROBIN JONES GUNN

A Kiss at Sunset Beach

A SIERRA JENSEN NOVEL

Robin Jones Gunn

A Kiss at Sunset Beach

Previously published in 2011 under the title, *Love Finds You in Sunset Beach, Hawaii* by Summerside Press.

ISBN 978-1-942704-44-7

Published by Robin's Nest Productions, Inc.

Cover Design by Rachel Schwartz

Interior Design by Ken Raney

❀ Created with Vellum

Somehow, the love of the islands,
like the love of a woman,
just happens.
One cannot determine in advance to love a particular woman
nor can one determine to love Hawaii.
JACK LONDON

CHAPTER ONE

Sierra Jensen stepped off the city bus and slipped her leather messenger bag across the front of her in a diagonal fashion. With quick steps, she turned uphill at the corner. A faint, sweet fragrance lingered in the warm November air.

When Sierra had first moved to Brazil from California, she thought the scent came from the vivid pink flowers blooming on the trees in this part of town. Her Brazilian friend Mariana set her straight and told her that the fragrance came from ethanol emissions—the sugar cane–based fuel that powered both cars and trucks. Mariana was also the one who urged Sierra to take the volunteer position at the after-school program where she was now headed.

The early afternoon sun came at Sierra from behind as she hiked up the hill past gated homes and security-locked fences. Here, below the equator, spring was giving a farewell curtsey as summer was about to make her grand entrance. Sierra knew that a bevy of long, sultry afternoons would be riding in on summer's regal train.

Scooting up to the school entrance, Sierra waved at the security guard, who reached over to press the buzzer to open the gate. As she waited, she held her wild, curly blond hair up off her neck. Once again, she considered the option of cutting her locks short. A shorter style might make her weekly visits to the *favelas,* or shanty towns, a less steamy experience this summer. Last December some of the women she assisted in the poverty-affected area of town teased her when she broke out in a pouring sweat as they worked together making beaded bracelets. They called her a *princesa* and sent their children to find pieces of cardboard with which to playfully fan their fair-skinned friend.

The gate buzzed, and Sierra reached to push it open. She glanced at the beaded bracelets on her wrist and smiled at the comforting clinking sound they made as they tapped against the row of silver bangles she loved to wear. This was familiar—bracelets, gauze blouses, and her unruly mass of curls. This had been her style for almost a decade, since the middle of high school. If she changed any of it now, she might not know who she was when she looked in the mirror.

Striding down the hallway, Sierra decided that the past year had been full of too many adjustments. Her life and her work with the mission organization had been in constant flux. Her hair and everything else about her needed to stay just as it was.

The principal's assistant at the front desk looked up as Sierra entered the office and greeted her in Portuguese. *"Boa tarde."*

"Boa tarde," Sierra replied. Her attempt to communicate further in Portuguese stopped there. The assistant nodded toward the principal's door and gave a hand motion indicating that Sierra should go in.

Sierra's dark-eyed, fashion-conscious friend Mariana was seated in one of the two chairs positioned at an angle in front of the principal's vacant desk. Mariana was shorter than Sierra but always sat with elegant posture. Her skin was a rich mahogany shade of brown, and her well-formed legs were one of her nicest features. She wasn't beautiful by model standards, but she was striking. Whenever Mariana entered a room, people took a second look.

"Hey, how's your day been?" Sierra asked.

"Not bad. How about yours?"

"Good. Busy." Sierra unstrapped her messenger bag and sat down.

"You do too many things, Sierra."

"Look who's talking."

"Yes, but I get paid for teaching here. You volunteer all over the place. You need a vacation. Both of us do. What do you think? We should go somewhere in January."

"In January I hope to be leading a summer program here for the high school girls. That's why I asked for this meeting with *Senhora* Almeida. I'd like to do a cooking class one day, a sports day every Friday, and maybe a drama program."

"Sierra, you do too much." Mariana leaned forward and put out her hand. "Come on, let's see your plan for this program."

"I haven't exactly written out a plan yet. I have all the ideas in my head."

"Of course you do." Mariana leaned back and gave Sierra a friendly smirk.

"What?"

"You have so many ideas. This is a good one, though, so I won't give you a hard time about it. For these girls, it would be wonderful."

"That's what I was thinking. Nothing else is like it that I know of in this area."

"I suppose you'll need an interpreter. And someone to write up the lesson plan and the proposal for you in Portuguese."

"Yes, as a matter of fact, I'm in the market for that sort of assistance." Sierra gave Mariana an appreciative smile. "You don't happen to know where I might find someone who would be able and willing to do that for me, would you?"

"Yes, yes, of course. I'll do it. I won't even make you beg this time. And I'll help you with the drama class. You know I'm good in that area." Mariana lifted the back of her hand to her forehead and struck a dramatic pose.

Sierra gave Mariana's elbow a squeeze. "You're so funny. Thank you, though. Again. I don't think I thank you enough for all you do for me."

"No, you don't thank me enough." Mariana grinned mischievously. "But do you see me complaining?"

Ever since Sierra and Mariana met at a fund-raising event almost three years ago, their friendship had remained steady. Mariana spoke perfect English and volunteered to serve as Sierra's translator whenever she needed one. The result was that Sierra could help others despite her seemingly futile struggle to learn Portuguese.

It also meant that the two of them spent lots of time together. The unique twist, from Sierra's point of view, was that Mariana accompanied her on many of the projects she did for the mission organization she worked for. Yet Mariana, in her own words, was "not among the faithful." Her goal in life was to be happy. And hanging out with Sierra, Mariana said, made her happy.

The side door to the office opened and Senhora Almeida entered with a serious expression on her face. She adjusted her dark-rimmed glasses and spoke in Portuguese before she even reached her desk.

Mariana translated. The words went in her ears in Portuguese and came out her mouth in English. This skill always amazed Sierra.

"Before you state your reasons for this meeting, Senhora Almeida wants you to know she has some difficult news to tell you. The decision has been made to cancel the after-school program for next year. She wanted you to know this right up front."

Sierra turned to Mariana, thinking her witty friend was playing a joke on her.

Mariana kept her eyes on the principal. Her chin was lowered in a somber expression. "She says she's very sorry. But the decision has been made. It has to do with the budget for the utilities and the extra hours for the security staff."

Sierra leaned back as if the metal chair were swallowing her.

Mariana gave Sierra a sympathetic look. "Everyone here has appreciated your work with these girls. She regrets that she is the one to tell you that your position has been terminated."

Terminated. The word pierced Sierra like an arrow.

"Senhora Almeida would like you to know she is very sorry. And what is it that you wanted to say to her in this meeting?"

Sierra rallied her emotions. "I wanted to see if we could do a summer program."

The principal looked surprised. Sierra didn't wait for her to reply. She went ahead and took a crazy chance, pitching her idea just in case something could be done.

The principal folded her hands on the desk and spoke in a decisive tone that told Sierra what she already knew before Mariana translated.

Sierra nodded that she understood. The budget. The many restrictions. Yes, she understood. Following Mariana's cue, Sierra rose from her chair since they apparently were being dismissed.

Offering her hand to the principal, Sierra said, "Thank you for letting me help out for as long as I did. I loved every minute of my time here. *Obrigada.*" Sierra added her thank-you in Portuguese and waited for the principal to shake her hand.

Instead of reaching across the desk, Senhora Almeida came around to where Sierra and Mariana stood. She opened her arms to Sierra in a motherly fashion, and when Sierra received the hug, Senhora Almeida kissed her lightly on the cheek. This was the kind of warmth and openhearted greeting Sierra had received when she first arrived at the school. It made her stomach do a flip-flop to now receive an equally tender yet bittersweet send-off.

Just as the buzzer sounded indicating the end of the school day, Mariana translated the principal's final words. "Please do not say anything to the girls about this decision. She will tell them before the end of the term."

Sierra agreed and walked with Mariana to the cafeteria where Sierra knew she had to appear upbeat during the next two hours with the seventeen girls who came each afternoon to practice their English.

"Not what you had hoped to hear," Mariana stated in a low voice, leaning close in the noisy hallway.

"No, not what I had hoped to hear."

"Let's go to dinner tonight. I'll meet you here when you're done, okay?"

Sierra agreed, even though she didn't have much of an appetite at the moment. She did like the idea of not going home to the tiny apartment she shared with a young married couple from Arkansas who worked for the same mission organization as Sierra and were going through language school.

They were a quiet and very busy couple. On the rare occasions they were home, they gravitated to their room and closed the door while normally gregarious Sierra was relegated to the lumpy foldout sofa that doubled as her bedroom. The arrangement was awkward but was the only one the mission organization could come up with three months ago when they started to restructure the ministry. Sierra and the young couple had fallen in the crevice between the way things had always been done and the way they would be done once the new administration passed its policies.

Mariana had invited Sierra to live with her in the apartment she shared with three other young women. Sierra would still have the couch as her bedroom, but as Mariana pointed out, at least she would have a social life. Sierra knew enough about her friend's social life to know that, in spite of Mariana's generosity, living with four Brazilian party girls was a bad idea.

Trying to breathe in a courageous attitude, Sierra opened the cafeteria door. The moment she saw the girls perched on the tables' edges, chattering like a bunch of colorful birds, she felt her throat tighten. Pulling up a small smile, Sierra blinked back the tears that rushed to her eyes. She knew that the next few weeks were going to be agonizing.

CHAPTER TWO

Jordan Bryce positioned his bare feet firmly in the cool sand at Goleta Beach and flipped his baseball cap on backward. He checked to make sure his camera was set on the lowest aperture and lifted the view-finder to his left eye. The big waves had arrived in Santa Barbara because of a mid-November storm, and today was the start of the promised surf-worthy swells.

First light had come, and dozens of surfers were already in the water. Jordan was one of only three photographers lining the far side of the beach. And he was ready.

Carefully adjusting the lens, Jordan focused on a lone surfer who had paddled out on an old-school long board. Jordan held his breath for just a moment and lightly pressed the button. He heard the magic *click-click-click* sound he so dearly loved, and a steady smile rested on his lips.

This could be it. Come on, Derek, come on. You got it. That's it! Yes!

Derek had pulled away from the other contenders. His dark wet suit blended with his Jamaican skin tone as he rode the charging wave like a jousting knight intent on toppling his opponent. Jordan shot every set of waves his old roommate managed to catch. The lighting was ideal—overcast skies and early morning sunlight illuminating his subject.

This could really be it!

The session lasted almost an hour before Derek paddled in and headed straight for Jordan, dripping and smiling broadly.

"Not bad, huh?" Derek shoved the end of his classic surfboard into the wet sand and slapped Jordan a watery high five.

"Ideal conditions." Jordan flipped his baseball cap back around on his recently cut mop of dark brown hair. "I got some epic shots."

"Let's see some of 'em." Derek stood beside Jordan as they peered at the digital screen on Jordan's camera. "Oh, nice. Look at that one. Killer. Did you capture the...yes! Excellent! Right there. That could be the one! Man, Jordo, you killed this session."

"Look who's talking. You were the one out there doing all the shredding."

"When can you have 'em ready?"

"Give me an hour. I'm heading back to my place now."

"This could be our day, Jordo."

"I know. I was thinking the same thing."

"Give me a call when you're ready to send them."

"I will."

"And listen, if I don't pick up my phone, call Mindy and let her know you're sending them."

"Okay. Got it." Jordan headed for his truck in the parking lot and realized for the first time how cold his bare feet had become while standing for an hour in the wet sand.

A few months ago he had adopted a strategy from a fellow photographer who specialized in winning surfing shots. The idea was to turn his solid five-foot-ten-inch frame into a fixed stand. In lieu of a tripod, he became the bipod that kept the camera steady. The trick, he was told, was to create the bipod barefooted so that each toe could act as a stabilizer in the sand. Then, once he had the distant surfer in view, he could line up the shot without a wobble. The stance resulted in clearer, steadier shots.

As well as cold feet. An inconvenience he considered well worth the payoff.

Jordan cranked up the heater in his truck on the drive home. His feet warmed up in no time. Fifteen minutes later, he turned into a long driveway that led to a five-thousand-square-foot estate. Jordan gave a wave to the gardener and slowly edged around the side of the six-car garage.

His five-hundred-square-foot bungalow, as well as his assigned parking spot, were in the back of the mansion by the tangerine trees. When he first moved into the detached guest-house more than a year ago, he was convinced it was all he needed. He had enough room for a bed, a refrigerator, a shower, and a corner to set up his computer and camera equipment. But lately Jordan was discovering that coming home to an empty space could be pretty lonely. He made sure he wasn't home very often.

Turning on his computer monitor now, Jordan pulled out the cable needed to load his photos to the computer. While the shots uploaded, he made coffee and poured himself a bowl of cereal. Then, sitting in his torn office chair, Jordan clicked through that day's catch, looking for the moneymaker.

There it was.

DS00547.

That was the one. Derek was in perfect position on his board. Across the crown of the silver wave, a glistening rooster tail sprayed. The inside curve bent just right in the belly of the curl to capture the crazy emerald and teal shades that came through when a wave was thin enough to let light in from both sides.

Jordan felt his heart pounding as he copied the file twice and sent a watermarked copy to Derek's e-mail. He called Derek while he clicked through the remaining shots.

"We got it," Jordan said the moment Derek answered. "I'm serious. We got it this time. I just sent it. Are you on your computer?"

"No. I can get on in five minutes. I'll call you back. You sound pretty sure of this one."

"Wait till you see it. I'm stoked, Derek. Seriously." Jordan paused and looked closer at the picture that appeared on his screen just then. "Whoa. We might have more than one. I haven't gone through all of them yet. This one is really nice too. Call me when you look at the one I sent."

"I will. Send me the other keepers too."

Jordan took his time going through the photos one by one. He saved to a separate file those that stood out. He had fourteen stellar shots. Fourteen. This was the best "catch" ever for him.

His cell phone buzzed. When he answered, Derek shouted, "Jordo, you did it, man. You did it!"

"I know, right?"

"Dude. Seriously. This is it. This is the one."

Jordan felt his smile tightening the dried sea spray still on his face. "You want to send them to Bill or should I?"

"I just called him before I phoned you. He's waiting for the file. You send 'em. All of 'em."

"Okay, I'll do it."

"You know what this means, don't you?" Derek asked.

"We're going to be able to eat next month."

"This isn't just grocery money, Jordan. You know how much *Surf Days Magazine* pays for a cover shot? And if they go for a spread, we're golden."

Jordan leaned back and let the early taste of success awaken his salivary glands. "What do you think? Billabong? Red Bull? Local Motion? Which one are you going to sign with?"

"Highest bidder, of course. Mindy's looking at the shots you just sent, and she says North Shore is a for sure now."

Jordan sat up straight, and his unstable chair wobbled precariously. "When?"

"Soonest I think we could pull it all together would be late December, early January. Once we get paid for these shots, all three of us can buy first-class airline tickets for Oahu."

"How about if we fly coach and use the rest of our funds to rent a place on the beach and to buy groceries while we're there?"

Derek laughed. "You're always thinking about your stomach, man. Oh, hey, Mindy says she'll work out the tickets and book the place for us. She has some connections. Happy New Year's to us, bro. Man, how many years have we been trying for this? At least six. We're finally going to do it. Have you sent the file to Bill yet?"

"No, I'll do it right now."

"I'm calling him," Derek said. "I want to be on the phone with him when he goes through these. I'll call you right back."

Jordan pressed SEND on his computer. The fourteen exceptional shots flung their way through cyberspace, headed for the desk computer of Derek and Jordan's mutual friend Bill Kempler, who had recently taken over as the editor of *Surf Days Magazine*. Bill's advice to the two of them during the surfing competition at Lower Trestles had been, "You get one exceptional photo, and I'll print it. After that, if you're willing to become your own publicists, I guarantee you'll see sponsorship offers coming your way. You bring me the best—you bring me 'the one'—and it'll all unfold from there."

Jordan had taken those words as a personal challenge. He wanted to capture the elusive photo for his friend. Since high school, Jordan's photography hobby had grown into a small side business. By the time he was twenty-one, he had shot three large weddings and had put up a photography website. His goal was to build his business in Santa Barbara and garner enough paying events to support him in his final year of college. To his parents' surprise and his, he met his goal.

In the four years since graduation, Jordan had lived out all the stereotypes associated with being a starving artist. He stocked shelves at the grocery store during the wee hours of the morning to pay for electricity and rent. He volunteered at his church with a mentoring program for young boys who didn't have fathers. And every chance he got, Jordan took pictures. Surfing shots were becoming his specialty, thanks to Derek's persistence.

The wind outside had picked up some muscle and was rattling the slatted shades in the bathroom. Jordan went to close the window and saw that it was raining. The drops were coming in at an angle, and the inside windowsill was dripping with the gathering intruders.

Jordan mopped up the moisture with a towel. He paused and thought about what Derek had said. Sunset Beach in January. Waimea, Pipeline. If Bill bought Derek's photo and liked the others, Bill might send Jordan to the North Shore on assignment for the magazine. It was too cool of a dream to dare to believe. And yet, Jordan knew he had captured "the one" for Bill today.

Jordan's cell phone rang. He rushed to grab it, feeling in his gut that his life was about to change.

CHAPTER THREE

Mariana's choice for dinner was for the two of them to drive across town to her favorite *churrascaria*. As she and Sierra left the school, Mariana said, "And I'm paying, so don't give me any complaints."

"No complaints," Sierra promised, even though she still didn't have much of an appetite. She knew she couldn't turn down the chance to eat at one of the nicer Brazilian steakhouses. Mariana grew up enjoying a lot of the finer things in life, and she knew all the best places to eat.

As soon as they had gone through the salad buffet line and sat at their table, Mariana said, "We need a vacation."

"You said that earlier today. In Senhora's office."

"I know. And you said you had plans for January. Only now, you—we—don't have any plans. So I think we should make some plans. We need to go somewhere exotic."

"Where do you want to go?"

By the way her friend narrowed her dark eyes and leaned forward, Sierra knew Mariana had already thought of some place, and Sierra had just stepped into Mariana's carefully laid net.

"Sunset Beach," Mariana answered confidently.

Sierra tried to remember where Sunset Beach was located. She had been to Copacabana and Ipanema, two popular Brazilian beaches near Rio de Janiero. She had never been to Sunset Beach. "Where is it? Near Rio?"

"No. Sunset Beach is in your country, not mine. It's in Hawaii."

"Hawaii?"

"Yes. Rodrigo went there last year, remember?"

Sierra vaguely remembered hearing about Mariana's cousin who had been in a surfing competition on the North Shore of Hawaii. "Is he surfing again this year?"

"No."

"Then why do you want to go?"

Mariana put down her fork. "Sierra, don't play sassy with me. You know I always win. I, or rather *we,* want to go to the surfing competition in Hawaii so we can see how beautiful it is there, and we can relax and learn about the wildlife."

Sierra speared a piece of cucumber with her fork. "I know what kind of wildlife you like to research on your trips." She bit into the cucumber with a crunch.

Mariana responded with an equally snappy crunch on a carrot stick. "What would be so terrible about meeting a good-looking surfer, falling in love, and spending the rest of our lives living on the beach?"

"In a little grass shack?"

"No, in a big mansion. See, this is your problem, Sierra. You don't dream. You have to dream, and when you dream, you have to dream big."

Sierra stayed focused on her salad, chewing slowly and not responding.

"What? What is it? I made you sad, didn't I?"

Sierra was thinking about the big dream that had brought her to Brazil. So much had changed since she had arrived as an energetic college student ready to change the world. Over the past four years, among other roles, she had been a soup kitchen cook, daycare assistant, construction worker, office administrator, medical clinic assistant, after-school program director, and craft instructor with the impoverished women who made and sold beaded bracelets. Even that work was winding down since all the distribution avenues were now in place, and the women were creating the bracelets without further help from Sierra.

"My dream was to come here and to make a difference."

"Well, you did, and you have. So now you need a new dream."

Just then a server appeared next to their table. He held a long skewer of sizzling hot beef from the fire pit where dozens of skewers of meat rotated over the flame. Pushing the half-finished salad aside, Sierra nodded, and the server used his carving knife to thinly slice the delicacy onto her waiting dinner plate.

"Here's what I think," Mariana said as the waiter served her next. "I think you need time away from here to think about what you're supposed to do next. Just a week. That's all I ask. We'll go to Hawaii, have some fun, break some hearts, and come home with ukuleles."

"Ukuleles?"

"You know, those tiny little guitars. Or we could bring home pineapples. Or hula skirts. I don't care. The point is, what good is it for me to have a father who works for an airline if I can't share his free airfare passes with my friends and go to interesting places every year?"

Sierra remembered how last year she had turned down Mariana's invitation to join her and two of her other friends for a six-day trip to Paris. The year before that the same trio had gone to New York.

"Why don't you go to Hawaii with your usual travel companions?" Sierra asked.

"Because I know I would have more fun with you."

Her answer surprised Sierra. It also touched her.

"And here is the important part. If I don't book a trip by December, the passes will expire. Don't you think that would be a terrible waste? We have free airfare waiting for us and probably a free place to stay, since my dad gets lots of discounts and he loves to spoil me."

Sierra slowly chewed her tender piece of flavorful beef. Another waiter came by with another long skewer and sliced roasted lamb onto their plates.

"You're not protesting," Mariana observed.

"I'm thinking."

"That's good." Mariana raised her eyebrows. "Wait. You wouldn't be thinking unless you were thinking of saying yes. You're going to say yes, aren't you? You're going to go to Hawaii with me. Say it."

Sierra nodded once and then kept nodding. "Yes. I'd love to go with you."

"I don't believe it! Okay, I'll start making all the plans as soon as I get home. This is going to be so fun. Sierra. You wait. You'll see."

After Sierra was back at her apartment and preparing for bed, she wondered if she had made a wise decision. She needed to let Mark and Sara know. They were the couple at the mission organization Sierra checked in with each month. With things being in such upheaval due to the reorganization process, she couldn't imagine that her leaving for a week in January would be a problem.

She pulled out her aged but trusty laptop and typed an e-mail to Mark and Sara. Part of her update was about the program at the school being terminated. She also let them know that the women in the favela were self-sustaining and that she was ready to be put to work in a new area wherever she was needed. At the end she added a note about going on vacation in January with Mariana.

Sierra sent the e-mail and then saw that she had an email from her brother Wes.

"Happy Thanksgiving! Remember the year you almost burned down Granna Mae's house when you forgot about the marshmallows on top of the yams in the oven? We miss you. Hope you can find someplace that will serve you some turkey and pumpkin pie for dinner."

Sierra leaned back. She had forgotten that today was Thanksgiving. In Brazil, it was just Thursday. At home, it was her favorite holiday, and she hadn't thought about it once until now.

Sierra put in her earpiece and dialed her parents' phone through her laptop. Calculating the time difference, she guessed they would just about be sitting down to Thanksgiving dinner.

Her dad answered, and Sierra visited with him as if she had remembered all along that it was Thanksgiving and had planned to call them. She stayed upbeat and bright and didn't tell anyone about the unhappy news she had received from the school that afternoon. She could update the family later in an e-mail so her dad wouldn't offer her advice over the phone. She loved her dad, but sometimes she felt as if he had too much advice to share.

Three of her four brothers took their turns saying hello. Her oldest brother and her sister were both married, but they and their families weren't with the rest of the crew this year. Only three of the six Jensen children would be sliding their feet under the family table. Sierra wished she could make it four children. She would love to see them all again. Especially Wes.

Her mom was the last one to come on the phone. Sierra wasn't sure why, but she choked up as she talked to her mom. Her voice was so comforting Sierra wanted to tell her everything she was processing. That, she knew, would be better to save for a more private conversation later.

"How are you doing, honey?" her mom asked.

Sierra put on the same brave demeanor she had worn for the girls that afternoon in the cafeteria and focused on the positive. "I'm good. I have some great news. Mariana invited me to go with her to Hawaii in January on her father's airline passes, and I told her I would go."

"That is big news. When are you going to be there? Will it be over New Year's?"

"I don't know the dates yet. It could be."

"Did you know that Tawni and Jeremy will be there over New Year's?"

"They are?"

"Wouldn't that be wonderful if you could see each other? Baby Ben is a year old already. He is the cutest little guy."

Sierra loved the thought of seeing her nephew for the first time. She and her sister had never been super close, but at this moment, she felt a deep longing to be with Tawni. "Where are they going to be? Which island?"

"I don't know. I can ask her. They're going for the wedding."

"Whose wedding?" Sierra asked.

"Paul's."

For the second time that day Sierra felt as if the chair she was sitting in was about to swallow her.

"Sierra, are you still there?"

"Yes, I'm here. I heard you. Paul's getting married." Sierra swallowed. "That's great."

"I'll tell Tawni to e-mail you with the details of where the wedding will be. I hope you can see each other."

"I do too." Sierra didn't think she wanted to see Tawni under those circumstances, but she didn't know what else to say. No one, not even her mother, knew that she still carried this single lit candle in her heart for Paul.

"We're about to sit down to dinner so I'll say good-bye for everyone. Happy Thanksgiving, honey. I love you."

"I love you too, Mom."

Sierra ended the call and let out a big sigh. Staring across the room she tried to accept the news her mom had so blithely told her.

Paul Mackenzie was getting married.

CHAPTER FOUR

The uniformed security personnel at the Los Angeles airport singled Jordan out of the stream of post-Christmas travelers and motioned for him to step to the side.

"Is this your bag, sir?"

"Yes, that's mine." Jordan watched as the heavy case was moved to a separate table.

"Okay if we open it for further inspection?" The rote question was delivered as more of a statement than something about which Jordan might have a choice.

"Sure. It's camera equipment."

The man put on thin ivory gloves and undid the clasps. He lifted from the customized, cushioned case each lens, filter, and light meter. "Are you a professional photographer?"

"Yes. I'm on assignment for *Surf Days Magazine*." Jordan realized he didn't need to add that bit of information, but it felt pretty good to say it aloud. Ever since he had picked up the call from Bill six weeks ago, Jordan's life had jumped onto the fast track. The photo he had captured of Derek was scheduled for the February cover of *Surf Days*, and Bill had hired Jordan to go to the North Shore on assignment the first week of January.

Derek and Mindy were flying over to Oahu to join him in three days, and as Derek kept saying, "We're finally livin' the dream!"

The guard closed up the case and motioned that Jordan could go to his gate. Jordan took his time, reopening the case, carefully checking and adjusting each valuable piece of equipment to make sure it was nestled in its proper place. Once he was satisfied, he closed the case, strapped it over his shoulder, and trekked through the airport.

Just as Jordan arrived at his gate, Derek called him.

"Hey, good timing. I'm about to board my flight." Jordan moved to the nearly vacant waiting area across from his gate so he could put down his heavy case and talk to Derek more easily.

"Mindy told me to call and say thanks again for being willing to go over early and shoot the wedding for her friend."

"Sure. No problem. I'm glad to do it. The extra job means a little extra money. You won't hear me complaining about that."

"She just told me this morning, though, that the wedding isn't on Oahu."

"Right. It's on Maui."

"I didn't realize that. So when you arrive on Oahu this afternoon, you're going to take an inter-island flight to Maui, is that how it works?"

"Yes, then I'll fly back to Oahu the same day you guys arrive. Your organized wife set it all up for me. I'll meet you at the place Mindy rented for us at Sunset Beach. I'll probably arrive before you and Mindy since I'm booked on the first flight out of Maui that morning. I told her I'd make a run to the grocery store so we have some food when you guys get there."

"At least you have your priorities in order."

"Right. Food first."

"If I was the first to arrive, I'm afraid I'd be in the water before I'd be at the grocery store. But, you know, I have to say, this isn't such a bad deal, is it? Your first trip to Hawaii, and you get to visit two islands, all expenses paid. In exchange, all you have to do is make good use of that new camera of yours and remember to grab yourself a piece of wedding cake."

"I know. It's not bad at all. And I do love free cake."

They talked a few more minutes about the latest surf report for the North Shore and Derek's new travel bag for his surfboard. Everything was looking good for a great week ahead.

"I'll see you in a few days then," Jordan said.

"You know it. Pipeline, Waimea, Sunset. It's all going to happen for us, Jordo. And, hey, if Mindy asks, be sure to tell her that I called and said thanks for doing the wedding photos."

"You got it." Jordan hung up just as two young women slid past him with their luggage and sat in the empty seats across from him. He glanced at the shorter, dark-haired woman directly across from him and then paused as he looked at the woman beside her. She had the hood of her sweatshirt up over her head and was wearing large, round sunglasses, which seemed odd since they were sitting indoors.

What caught his attention was the name of the university on her sweatshirt. Rancho Corona was a rival of the college he had graduated from. If Derek were here, he would have started up a friendly debate about which school was best.

Jordan wasn't the type to visit with strangers, though. He stood and headed across the way since boarding for first-class passengers had begun. Sliding past some of the waiting passengers who were using their coach boarding passes as fans, Jordan boarded as the announcement came for the business class group. The bump up to business was just one of the perks Bill had given Jordan on this trip.

"You know what the Good Book says, don't you?" Bill asked when he handed Jordan the ticket a few weeks ago. "It says that to the person who has been given much, much is required. The pressure's on. We're expecting a lot out of you, even though this is your first assignment for us. You make good on this one, and we'll keep you busy for a long time."

As Jordan located his seat on the plane, he thought about how much he would like for Bill to make good on that offer to keep him gainfully employed as a photographer. It was what he had wanted for a long time. All the hours of working as a late-night grocery stocking clerk were worth it if it meant he had broken through that invisible barrier all people in the arts seem to come up against. If he could be taken seriously as a photographer, he felt his future was finally opening up.

Stowing his camera case in the overhead compartment, Jordan took his seat. The extra leg room and wider seat were impressive. A flight attendant came by and offered him a cup of water or orange juice from a tray in her hand. Jordan reached for the orange juice and sat back, trying to appear as if this was the way he always traveled even though his last flight, more than two years ago, had been completely different.

On that trip, he and seven other singles from his church had flown to Costa Rica to help build a school in a remote village. Their flight out of LAX was delayed, which meant they missed their connecting flight in Guatemala City and were rescheduled the next day on a small, outdated plane with a carrier that went out of business soon after the bumpy ride into San Jose, Costa Rica.

The best part of that trip was being with Paige. He closed his eyes and remembered the great times they had had during the seven months they dated. Aside from a high school summer camp romance, brown-eyed Paige, with her little girl giggle, was his first serious relationship. The only problem was that she was more serious than he was at the time.

Jordan shifted in his seat, remembering how their relationship had ended poorly. He still felt bad about that. Not that there was anything he could do about it now. Paige had moved back home to North Carolina after she graduated, and Jordan had heard from friends that she was now engaged to a guy who had two little girls. He could see that being a good fit for Paige.

She would make a great mom. That was what she had wanted all along—the security of a husband, a home, and children.

Jordan felt as if he had more life to experience before locking into a thirty-year mortgage and making payments on a minivan. He told Paige he wanted to be "unencumbered" so that he could be available to help other people.

That's when their relationship came to an awkward halt.

Since then Jordan had become more cautious about using the word *unencumbered*.

Today, though, Jordan felt he was benefiting from the rewards of being unencumbered. He was living his dream.

During the flight, Jordan paid attention to how the other passengers pulled out their collapsible tray tables from the arms of their wide seats. He watched to see which button they pushed to recline their seats and how they started the entertainment selection that played on the individual screens built into the backs of the seats in front of them. This was nothing like his experiences flying in coach.

What he also noticed, as he observed those around him in business class, was that they were mostly couples. The older couple across from him kept smiling at each other. The wife slipped her arm through her husband's as he napped. Directly in front of Jordan, a young couple gave every indication they were on their honeymoon with their steady flow of touches, kisses, and cuddles. Everyone was happy to be headed toward Hawaii.

Jordan was too, but he had to ask himself the question that seemed determined to chase him all the way to the islands: what good is it to see your career dreams fulfilled when you have no one with whom to share your joy?

Gazing out the window at the endless stretch of thick white clouds, Jordan tried to ignore the fear that crept in every time he thought about getting married one day. A whisper came to him like a metallic-sounding wind chime, "It's too late, you know. All the good ones are taken."

Jordan wanted to believe, needed to believe, someone was out there, somewhere in this world, for him. He silently prayed and realized he sounded like Bill.

Lord, if You will bring me "the one," I'm willing to be my own publicist. Just capture the right woman for me and bring her to me, and I know everything will open up from there.

He wasn't sure if that was as honoring a prayer as it should be, but for right now, in this season of new beginnings for him, it was a start.

CHAPTER FIVE

Mariana's roommate drove them to the airport and spent the first ten minutes of the crawl through the heavy traffic giving Mariana a hard time for not inviting her along on the extravagant adventure to Hawaii.

"You went to Paris with me last year," Mariana said with her usual playful flippancy. "You have nothing to complain about."

"I know. I just wish I were going with you again." Aleen looked in the rearview mirror at Sierra. "I heard you're going to another island first so you can baby-sit."

Sierra shook her head at Mariana, who didn't turn around to accept her chiding. "No. Mariana is exaggerating again. I'm going to a wedding on Maui. My sister's brother-in-law is getting married, and she invited me to stay with her at the hotel. It's only for two nights. And I'll get to see my nephew for the first time."

"How old is he?"

"Fourteen months."

Mariana chimed in from the front seat. "We'll see if I exaggerated. I still think the only reason your sister asked you to come was so she can have a free baby-sitter while she's enjoying the wedding."

Sierra knew she should defend her older sister and say that Tawni wasn't like that. Tawni wouldn't have such an ulterior motive. But Sierra couldn't make that statement with confidence. Instead, she defended her place among the invited guests, adding that she had received an invitation and that she and the groom had been friends for a long time. Sierra stopped the explanation there and hoped Mariana wouldn't press for more details.

But of course she did.

"You said that to me before, about being friends with the groom for a long time. What kind of friends? You didn't explain that part."

"There's nothing to explain." Sierra guarded her words carefully. "We were friends when I was in high school. His brother married my sister. That's about it."

"If you say so." Mariana turned and scrutinized Sierra, looking for clues as to what had really happened.

That was exactly why Sierra had chosen not to say anything to Mariana about Paul. If she caught any hint about Sierra's long-harbored feelings for him, Mariana would have all kinds of advice and would quickly share the details with her roommates.

While Sierra appreciated Mariana's input in lots of areas in her life, when it came to advice on men and dating, the two of them disagreed. Mariana believed in stepping forward, pursuing the guy she was attracted to, and making her own "happiness," as she called it.

Sierra was determined to wait and see how God would lead in this area. Mariana seemed to enjoy pointing out that Sierra's method had produced zero relationships over the past few years. During that time Mariana had gone through three close relationships, with one of them ending in a painful breakup. She loved quoting, "'Better to have loved and lost than never to have loved at all.'"

Sierra had given up trying to find a quote to counterbalance Mariana's philosophy. All she knew was that the last time they got going on this topic, their friendly debate hadn't ended well. Sierra didn't want to invite that sort of tension and disconnect right before the two of them spent a week together in a small beach cottage.

"I have another question," Aleen said. "Mariana told me you're moving after you come back from Hawaii. Is that true?"

"Yes. It's not final yet, but it looks like I'll be moving to a village in the north."

Sierra had told Mariana about the new assignment as soon as the e-mail had arrived from Mark two days ago. Even though he was excited that the mission organization had found an ideal position for her, Sierra was less convinced. Although, when she told Mariana the news, she did so with an upbeat tone, as if the decision had already been made. That was obviously the way Mariana had presented the news to Aleen.

"I'm sorry you're leaving."

"Thanks, Aleen."

"Aren't you sad to be leaving?"

Mariana jumped in to answer for Sierra. "She's very sad, and so am I. It's tragic. And I don't want to talk about it. We're going to have a fun vacation, and that's what matters right now."

Sierra looked out the window at the dozens of beggar children dressed in ragged clothes. It was common at peak hours to see them threading through the slow moving rows of cars, offering to sell water, gum, and souvenirs to the travelers in the traffic jam. She remembered how she felt the first time she saw the children and how desperately she wanted to help them.

To the best of her ability she had done that. What she hadn't realized was the overriding impact of tradition and culture and how important it was that she respect the people she was trying to serve. Their society wasn't the same as North American society. She discovered that the first time she tried to convince one of the mothers in the favela to stop sending her son out to sell their bracelets in the street. Sierra had arranged for them to be sold in several shops in the city and was convinced this would allow the woman to send her son to school. The mother refused to let her son go to school, saying this was how it had always been for her family. The children supported the parents.

Mariana's cell phone rang. She answered and started talking in Portuguese.

Sierra took the opportunity to pull from her shoulder bag the printed copy of the e-mail Mark had sent her. She read it again, as if somehow the information had changed in the last two days. She knew the details hadn't sunk in yet.

We have some good news for you, Sierra.

A new ministry opportunity has opened up this week. I wanted to present it to you for consideration. We have a family who is requesting a teacher for their four children. They are in a remote area in the north, and therefore, if you take the position, your role will be twofold. First, you will serve as a teacher for their children, ages six, eight, nine, and eleven. Second, you will develop basic school curriculum that could be used with the children in the village. We're hoping that the lesson plans you put together will help us to initiate similar programs in other villages in the region.

We all agree that your willing spirit and energetic ability to spearhead new efforts make you ideal for this undertaking. The Board recently reviewed your history with us, and everyone noted that you have always demonstrated a superior ability to be flexible and live in meager conditions. That, along with your single status, makes you a great match for this position. I'm eager to know your thoughts on this.

On another matter, please pack up your belongings when you leave for vacation. We have a seminary student who will be moving into the apartment the day after you leave. We would like you to plan on returning to Rio and staying with us for the remainder of January.

I should add that, if you don't sense God leading you to take this new position, we currently don't have any other openings where we see you being a good match. We can evaluate what that means in terms of your future in Brazil once you return to Rio.

Please know that Sara and I are praying along with you in all this. You have some big decisions ahead of you.

With a heart for Brazil,

Mark

Sierra thought about the three boxes of her meager earthly possessions that she had taped up and left in a corner of the apartment that morning. Regardless of whether she took the position, she would be leaving Mariana and all that had become familiar over the past few years. She had jokingly told Mariana she was going to live a Brazilian version of "The Sound of Music" with the four children, except for the part about making them clothes from the curtains because she had a feeling they wouldn't have curtains. Mariana didn't think that was funny.

Sierra didn't think it was funny either. But she didn't know what else she could do at this point.

Returning the folded letter to her shoulder bag, Sierra pulled out her scratched-up pair of sunglasses and put them on. She didn't want to risk Mariana ending her phone call, turning around, and seeing Sierra in tears.

They made it to the Sao Paulo airport in time and caught the flight they were trying for with their airline passes. Sierra let the depression she was feeling be the sedative that kept her asleep during most of the trip. She was grateful she had pulled out her old hooded sweatshirt to wear on the chilly flight. Whenever she awoke, she noted that Mariana kept herself occupied by watching the in-flight movie, reading a magazine, and filing her thumbnail several times since it broke when she lifted her suitcase at check-in.

They were about to land in Los Angeles when Mariana leaned over and quietly said, "I'm sad too. But can we please make an agreement that we won't let your move ruin our vacation? I mean, we can talk about it all you want, and I think you should talk about it. Please don't turn into a... What are those sea animals that close up when you touch them?"

"A turtle?"

"No, those round things that grow on the rocks."

"A sea urchin."

"Is that it? I don't know. I've never heard that word. Let's just go with turtle. Don't become a turtle and close up in your shell. Get all your angry and sad feelings out with your sister, and when you arrive in Oahu, come prepared to have fun. Okay? Can you promise me that?"

Sierra wasn't sure she could make any promises at the moment. All she wanted to do was hide, as Mariana had noticed.

"I'll try," she said honestly.

"Good. Trying is a start. I'll take it."

Sierra kept her sweatshirt on as they went through customs and tromped through Los Angeles International Airport, heading for their connecting flight to Honolulu. Mariana kept a conversation going on the phone with her father. She was gathering the final details about the beach house he had graciously rented for them through one of his airline employee discount travel services.

They were almost at their gate when Sierra felt a surge of sadness sweep over her. This was the first time she had been back on American soil in four years. The announcements over the speakers were in English. The signs were in English. People looked, talked, and acted different than they did in Brazil. Everything around her was familiar, yet she felt so distant from all of it.

The US hadn't been her home for a long time. And now she wasn't sure how much longer Brazil would be her home. This change of position and location was going to be hard. She knew she could live in a rural village, but she didn't particularly want to. She also knew she could make new friends, but again, she didn't want to. She wanted to stay where she was and find new ways to serve there so she wouldn't have to leave all that had become familiar.

Pulling out her sunglasses again, Sierra shaded her eyes from Mariana's view or anyone else's who might notice her. To combat the chill that she still felt from the airplane and the strong air-conditioning in the terminal, she tucked back her hair and pulled the sweatshirt's hood over her head. She didn't care that as soon as Mariana finished her phone call she would inevitably tell Sierra that she looked like a turtle, and that was exactly what she had agreed to try not to become.

But for right now, that was what she needed. A sad little turtle.

CHAPTER SIX

When Jordan picked up his rental car on Maui, he had another unexpected traveling bonus. The car rental company had run out of the class of car he had reserved, and he was given a convertible at no extra charge.

Carefully storing his camera case in the trunk beside his suitcase, he hopped in the driver's seat and pushed the button that lowered the roof. The sun was directly overhead and began to bake the top of his head. Jordan went back to the trunk, pulled out his baseball cap, and was ready for the drive to the Wailea area where the wedding was scheduled to be held tomorrow afternoon. He was looking forward to diving into the water as well as knocking off some practice shots at sunset so he could get a feel for the best way to frame the photos for tomorrow's ceremony.

He turned on the radio and drove onto the main road that took him through Kahului. The dial was set to a station that played Hawaiian music. He kept it there, tapping his thumbs on the steering wheel. A local guy in a big truck pulled up next to him with the windows down. He looked over at Jordan and gave him a chin up nod and grin.

Jordan realized they were both tuned to the same radio station. That must explain why the guy had acknowledged him the way he did. Jordan didn't know any other reason why someone would be so friendly to a person who was obviously a tourist driving around in a convertible rental car. Or was it possible that the people on Maui were just that friendly?

The air felt hot and sultry until Jordan reached the open highway where there were fields as far as he could see on both sides. The breeze felt great as he sped along. He kept passing slow-moving cars and wondered if this was how slow everything was going to be on the island. He came up behind a rusted truck that had a big black dog standing up in the back and noticed the bumper sticker.

SLOW DOWN. THIS AIN'T THE MAINLAND.

Jordan was about to pass him, just as he would anyone driving that slow in California, but then he noticed the posted speed limit sign, and he understood. This road appeared to be the closest thing Maui had to a freeway and yet the top speed was forty-five miles per hour!

Jordan let up on the gas pedal and decided he better slow down. Why was he in such a hurry, anyhow? Rushing around had been the only speed his life dial had been set on during the past two weeks. He'd had a hard time keeping up with his job and his volunteer mentoring program while getting everything ready for this trip.

Now that he was here, he could slow down and take in the beauty all around him. Jordan gazed at the towering volcano that dominated the landscape on his left side. He had read in the in-flight magazine that the road went all the way to the observatory at the top of the ten-thousand-foot dormant volcano. The photos with the article made him wish he was going to be on Maui longer so he could go up to the summit and take pictures at sunrise.

Such thoughts used to make him dream even more intently

that one day he could become a professional photographer. Jordan realized that day had come. He had enough credibility now with the cover shot that he could pitch his work for a variety of other photo assignments while traveling to exotic locations for *Surf Days Magazine*.

Why not? All he had to do was put his portfolio together and submit his work to some airline magazines and tour companies.

Jordan let his imagination go as he drove through Kihei and soon rolled into the upscale, spectacularly landscaped area of Wailea. He easily found the five-star hotel where the wedding party was staying. Jordan took his luggage from the trunk and turned the car keys over to the valet. He registered at the front desk, once again having fun pretending that this was how he traveled all the time.

The lobby was a wide open space with a spectacular ocean view and an enormous bouquet of tropical flowers positioned on a large, round table in the lobby's center. Once he finished unpacking, Jordan planned to come back and snap closeups of the flowers to test his new camera.

He pulled out his phone to check the time and saw that he had missed a call from Derek. He listened to the message before calling him back.

"Jordon. Hey. Mindy was thrown from her bike by a hit-and-run driver. I'm with her at the hospital now. Say a prayer for us, okay?"

Jordan suddenly stopped in the middle of the lobby. He called Derek and waited for him to pick up. It went to voice mail.

"Hey, I just got your message. Is Mindy okay? Call me as soon as you can. I'm praying for you guys."

Jordan stood in the same spot for several minutes, numbed by the news and watching the screen on his phone, hoping Derek would call back.

Not sure what to do, Jordan kept his phone in his hand and

headed for the elevator. He waited for the door to open, silently praying for his friends. Just as the door opened, his phone rang with Derek's return call. Two other people brushed past him to enter the elevator. As Jordan moved aside, his arm swung out too quickly, and he bumped one of the women with his heavy camera case.

"Sorry," he said without looking at her. He was too intent on getting the phone to his ear. "Derek? How's Mindy? Is she okay?"

The elevator doors closed with the couple inside while Jordan stayed where he was, waiting for the report.

Sierra pushed the button, and the elevator door opened once more. She assumed that the guy who had just bumped her with his shoulder bag wanted to get in. The door opened, but the guy in the baseball cap stood in the same place, looking down as he spoke into his cell.

"Did they find the guy who hit her?" After only a moment's pause he asked, "What did the doctor say?"

Sierra took the cue that the poor guy was too distracted with what was obviously a difficult phone call. She pushed the CLOSE button, and the stranger beside her pushed the button for the third floor. She pushed the button for the fourth floor. The two of them rode in silence as she thought about how different this was from Brazil.

First, the hotel was like no place she had ever stayed. It was over-the-top amazing. And whether she should or not, she felt safe riding in an elevator with a stranger.

Second, everyone spoke English. Her overworked brain already felt as if it were on vacation. She was used to straining to listen to every conversation so she could catch enough words to manage to understand. Then her brain had to find a place to file the words away for later use. Here, she understood everything. Even the personal conversation of the guy on the phone outside the elevator.

It made her realize how much of life she had missed because she didn't understand the language. Sierra pondered, as she had many times before, why she wasn't able to capture the Portuguese language. If God had called her to serve the Brazilian people, wouldn't she be more effective if she could speak the language? If it hadn't been for Mariana, who was her constant, willing translator, Sierra had a feeling she would have given up a long time ago. She knew she was gifted in some areas, but language wasn't one of them.

She realized after the other passenger left the elevator that she was feeling a whole lot better than she had when she and Mariana had landed in Los Angeles. During their five-hour flight to Honolulu, Sierra had warmed up not only physically but also emotionally. Everyone on the flight seemed happy to be on their way to Hawaii, and that jovial attitude was contagious.

Somewhere over the blue Pacific, Sierra turned to Mariana. "I'm nervous about going to the wedding. I hope I made the right decision."

"Of course you made the right decision," Mariana told her. "You're going to see your sister and your nephew. I would have done the same thing. If I had a sister. Or a nephew."

Sierra was reminded, when she saw the look on Mariana's face, that ever since her mother died when she was eleven, Mariana had craved female company. She admitted early in their friendship that she needed to be around women who were sensible and moral like Sierra.

Mariana wasn't the only one who benefited from the relationship, though, as Sierra often reminded her. Both of them had strong needs for female companionship, and that need had been the cement that held their friendship together in spite of their cultural backgrounds and their long list of differences.

Sierra considered telling Mariana a little about Paul so she could understand the deeper reasons for Sierra's hesitancy. The words never quite formed in her thoughts or found their way to her mouth. Their flight landed in Honolulu, and Sierra's secret stayed with her.

They deplaned and walked as far as they could together in the large open-air terminal. Mariana was headed for the car rental desk, and Sierra had to catch the Wiki Wiki tram that would take her to the other end of the terminal for her interisland flight to Maui.

"Listen," Mariana said before they went their separate ways. "I know I complained at first that you were leaving me alone at Sunset Beach. And I may have exaggerated a little to Aleen. I know it's only for two nights. And it's okay. I found out where my cousin's friends are staying so I will hang out with them until you show up. It will be fun. You'll see."

Sierra had a pretty good idea why Mariana waited until the last moment to break this news to her. It left no room for Sierra to give Mariana a sisterly reminder of how things had gone the last time the two of them went to a birthday party at Rodrigo's apartment and a bunch of his surfer friends were there.

That party had been particularly distressing to Sierra because, to escape the craziness going on inside the apartment, she had gone to the swimming pool with Aleen and two other women. While they were calmly paddling around, Sierra had lost her necklace. She didn't realize it until an hour later when she took a taxi home by herself. It was a simple, one-of-a-kind necklace with an emblem in the shape of a daffodil.

Paul had given her the necklace when he had dubbed her the Daffodil Queen for the way she was bold and "blew the trumpet of truth." Even while he was away at school in Scotland, his letters said that she reminded him of the bright yellow daffodils that announced spring so brazenly.

The elevator door opened on the fourth floor, jolting Sierra back into the moment. She stepped out, checking her room number once again. 422.

Stopping in front of the hotel room door, Sierra stood quietly without knocking. She felt sheepishly hesitant and uncharacteristically shy. On the other side of that door were her sister, her brother-in-law, and her nephew. In that moment she realized how much she had changed—how much Brazil had changed her, how much God had changed her—over the past four years.

She was no longer the blaring daffodil, quick to tell everyone what they were supposed to do with their lives. Instead she had become a quiet, humble observer.

The funny part was that she had no idea what she was supposed to do with her own life, let alone advise others about theirs.

She had a feeling her sister would find that ironic considering all the free advice Sierra had dished out to her during their combative teen years.

Pulling her dormant courage to the forefront, she knocked softly on the hotel room door, drew in a deep breath and waited to see what would happen next.

CHAPTER SEVEN

Jordan trekked down the cement steps to the beach and wedged his bare feet in the warm sand. He still couldn't wrap his mind around the news Derek had given him less than an hour ago. Mindy seemed to be doing okay after being catapulted over the handlebars of her bike and landing in a grassy spot along the winding Santa Barbara hillside. They were waiting for some more tests to be run before she could go home, but Derek said she was telling everyone she felt fine.

Neither Derek nor Jordan mentioned how this turn of events might affect Derek and Mindy's flight in two days. It was best to wait and see what the doctor had to say.

Jordan surveyed the beach, looking for level spots for portrait shots. He noticed the finely ground sand had a much lighter ivory color than he was used to. That could affect the light reflection. The water, too, was a more turquoise shade than he expected. When he had viewed the hotel's website, he'd assumed all the photos of the ocean and beach had been retouched. Apparently color enhancement wasn't necessary. This cove really was as pristine as the promotional materials claimed. Already he was seeing that he would be working in conditions very different from where he was used to shooting on the beaches of Santa Barbara.

The angle of the light was what he had to worry about.

Jordan's creative eye lined up shots, as he took a series of sample frames to get a feel for the light and color. The more he worked, the more his confidence grew. This was going to be good. He could do this. He could pull off some spectacular shots that would be great for the bridal couple, but they would also provide a boon for the portfolio he needed to put together.

The background Jordan was most intrigued with was an outcropping of dark volcanic rock at the far right end of the beach. Bright green foliage grew in abundance and spilled over the lookout point. The vibrant green created a striking contrast to the rock's obsidian and the ocean's aqua. He decided to take the trail that led to the top of the lava flow.

Once he stood on the end of the outlook, Jordan tested his long-distance lens and was pleased to see how sharp the images were. With a few adjustments, he could clearly see the faces of people who were stretched out on the resort beach in lounge chairs. Pulling back the zoom, he took a series of shots of the beautifully manicured beach with the lined-up white lounge chairs and bright blue umbrellas. A yellow outrigger canoe was balanced halfway on the grass and halfway on the sand near a thatched-roof stand that bore a sign that read BEACH ACTIVITIES.

Next Jordan lined up some shots of an island that was in clear view across the ocean. He was feeling a lot more comfortable with the new camera and confident he could make use of all the lenses now that he had had a successful trial run. The only thing left to do was to meet the bride and groom at the gazebo before the rehearsal that evening at five o'clock. Jordan checked his phone again. No calls from Derek. But he did have enough time to return the camera to his room for safekeeping and return for a swim.

Jordan stepped out of the elevator on the fourth floor and ran the card key through the slot in his hotel room door. The small light turned red, not green, as it had earlier that afternoon when a swipe of the card had unlocked the door. He tried again. And a third time. Still no success. He wondered if the magnetic tape had been desensitized. He gave it one more try.

Then the door was yanked open from the inside. A young woman holding a naked, dripping wet baby in her arms looked up at him. Her face expressed the same startled surprise he felt. The toddler in her arms began to wail.

Jordan looked at the room number on the door. 422.

"I'm so sorry. I thought this was 424."

He turned and turned and hurried to his room next door before the startled young woman with the wild, curly blond hair had a chance to say anything over the din of the baby's cries.

Two images stayed in his mind as he ducked inside and closed his door. The first was the pudgy whiteness of the baby's bottom in contrast to the poor little guy's sunburned back. The second was the clarity of light in the woman's eyes. He couldn't remember exactly what color they were, but they had taken on a translucent luster like aquamarine in a stained-glass window at sunrise.

All Jordan could hope for was that the woman and her son weren't part of the wedding party. If by any chance they were, he would have to face them again in a few hours and hope she didn't recognize him without his baseball cap.

Sierra closed the hotel room door and tried her best to quiet her wailing nephew.

"It's okay, Ben. Shhh. It's okay. Back in the tub you go. We were having fun, remember?"

She lowered the sunburned little butterball back into the four inches of water and held out his favorite green truck. He stifled his cries with an involuntary shiver and took the truck from Sierra.

A few hours earlier Sierra had seen her nephew for the first time when she entered her sister's hotel room. It was her brother-in-law, Jeremy, who opened the door, gave her a big hug, and whispered that Ben was sleeping. Sierra glanced into the room and saw Tawni stretched out on one of the two queen beds next to the sleeping cherub. He was wearing only a diaper decorated with dancing penguins.

"He's adorable," Sierra whispered, barely making a sound.

Tawni managed to expertly extract herself from the bed and tiptoed across the room to offer Sierra a hello hug. The two of them slipped into the bathroom where the fan was running for background noise. They hugged again, and Tawni asked all the expected questions about how her flight had been and said how great Sierra looked.

Sierra told her sister she looked great, too, even though Sierra was surprised at how heavy Tawni was in the face. And in the bust and hips. Sierra realized that all the photos that had been posted online or e-mailed to her over the past year and a half were pictures of Ben. Very few had included Tawni. She remembered now how Tawni had frequently included lines in her e-mails about how her modeling days were over and how having a big baby had wreaked havoc on her body. Sierra thought Tawni was exaggerating, but now she realized how distressed her sister, who had been skinny her whole life, must be since she hadn't dropped the extra baby weight.

"It's so good to see you," Tawni said tenderly. She added a grimace and said, "And I hate to even ask you this since you just arrived, but I have an appointment for a manicure and Jeremy needs to go with Paul to pick up their tuxes. It's the only time I could get into the salon. Is there any chance you could watch Ben for us while he's sleeping?"

Sierra immediately thought of Mariana's prediction. She hated it when Mariana was right. And she often was.

"Sure, I'll watch Ben." She couldn't believe she had just said that with so little emotion.

"Jeremy and I are going to the rehearsal at five o'clock. Could you dress Ben and bring him down to the beach around five thirty? We'll meet you at the beach activities booth."

Tawni ran through the rest of the details, giving Sierra a quick tutorial on all things essential to caring for baby Ben.

"We really appreciate your willingness to do this for us," Tawni said. "Call my cell if you have any problems."

Three minutes later, Jeremy and Tawni were gone. Sierra stretched out on the bed next to her sleeping newphew. Ben roused but just enough to adjust his position in his sleep when Sierra's frame curled up next to him. His face was now turned to Sierra, and she had to smile. He was so cute. So, so cute. It took every ounce of self-control not to reach over and stroke his smooth skin or wrap one of his baby hair curls around her finger.

She loved listening to the steady little puffs of breath that flowed in and out through his puckered lips. He smelled like coconut-scented suntan lotion with a dash of grape jelly. Within minutes, the sight, sounds, and scents of irresistible little baby Ben had lulled her to sleep.

Sometime later, Sierra awoke to the sensation of a very small hand slapping her face. She pried open her lids to see Ben staring at her. He looked as if the shadow of fear clouding his face might bring a burst of tears any moment.

Sierra didn't move. She kept her voice low. "Hello, Ben. I'm your aunt Sierra. Did you have a nice nap? I sure did."

Ben didn't cry. He didn't move. He seemed unsure of what to make of this stranger in his bed.

Sierra smiled a gentle smile and hummed softly. She had been around so many babies in Brazil over the past four years she knew that every baby understands the universal language of a calm spirit and a soothing lullaby.

Ben blinked. He reached over, took ahold of one of Sierra's long curls, and gave it an exploratory tug. She gently removed his hand from her hair and offered her finger as a substitute for him to wrap his small fist around.

After pulling her finger to his mouth for closer examination, he let go, rolled over, sat up, and looked around the room. He spotted a plastic green truck on the nightstand and reached for it. A moment later Sierra had become the new highway over which the green truck traversed while Ben made a *burrr* sound.

"You like that green truck, don't you? Are you thirsty? Your mommy said you might be thirsty when you woke up."

The word *mommy* seemed to spark a primal alarm in Ben's memory. He let go of the truck, slid off the bed without assistance, and trotted across the room. He looked in the bathroom and then let out a wail that hit a decibel Sierra didn't think she had ever heard a baby hit before. And she had had her times with lots of wailing babies.

Going to him with her arms outstretched and a string of calm words, Sierra scooped him up to pat his little back. He let out an even louder wail right by her ear. She could easily guess what that squeal was about. His back felt warm to the touch and was most likely sunburned even though she couldn't get a good view of it as he reared back in her arms.

"Let's put you in a cool bath. Would you like that?" Sierra balanced Ben on her hip, cooing comforting words to him as she ran the water in the tub and carried him back to the bed for his green truck. As soon as he had the truck in his hand, the wailing stopped.

Three minutes into his bath, Sierra heard someone trying to use a key to enter the room. "Maybe your favorite people in the world are back early," she said to Ben. When the sound of the key in the door continued without the door opening, Sierra tried to remember if she had bolted the door. She knew she couldn't leave Ben in the tub, so she scooped him up without bothering to reach for a towel and went to open the door.

A guy in a baseball cap stood there, looking as stunned to see her as she was to see him. As soon as he said, "Sorry," she recognized him as the distraught vacationer by the elevator because his *sorry* sounded the same way it had when he had apologized for bumping her with his bag.

Ben wailed his opera singer wail, and the guy left. Sierra returned her little pudge-ball nephew to the tub where once again the green truck calmed him down. Ben was happy to be back in the water, splashing everywhere. She managed to spray the soothing sunburn gel on his back and arms.

Next step was to dress him in one of his dancing penguin diapers. Sierra checked the top dresser drawer where Tawni said Sierra would find his special rehearsal dinner outfit. It was a classic little navy-blue sailor suit with shorts and heavy fabric top with a wide collar and tie down the front.

"You are going to roast in this. Wait. I have an idea." Sierra opened her suitcase and looked for her smallest T-shirt. She found a white one that she usually wore as a camisole under a button-up shirt because the T-shirt was too short and tight to wear by itself.

"Come here, little sailor. How about if you wear this to keep you cool until it's time for pictures?"

Ben made no objections to the airy T-shirt that came down past his knees. The short sleeves hung past his elbows. He trotted around the room, flapping his arms as if he had just discovered the wind beneath his wings.

"Okay, now I have a big problem. How am I going to shower

and dress but still watch you?" Sierra checked the clock. She had only twenty minutes before she was supposed to take Ben down to the beach.

Collecting every toy she could find in the room, she lured Ben into the bathroom and closed the door. As he sat on the floor in a puddle of toys, she took the fastest shower on record with the curtain halfway open. Just as Ben discovered that he could make a loud noise if he lifted and dropped the toilet seat, Sierra stepped out of the shower and slipped into in an aqua-colored, V-neck sundress. The lovely dress was a hand-me-down from Mariana, but Sierra didn't mind that a bit. It fit her nicely, and since it was Mariana's, she knew it was a well-made dress. It could even be a designer dress.

"Ready?" Sierra scooped up her nephew along with the diaper bag where she had put the sailor suit and the canister of sunburn relief. With her free hand, she grabbed the room key from off the dresser along with her sunglasses. Since she hadn't had time to wash her hair, she had pulled it back in a clip so that all the wild curls cascaded down her back.

Before she had even made it to the elevator, Ben gave her hair a tug. One of the tucked back curls was pulled out of the clip and set free to bounce to its own tune on the right side of Sierra's face. Next he went for her sunglasses.

"You have busy hands, don't you, Ben Boy. Go ahead, you can play with my sunglasses. They're all scratched up anyway."

The two of them were the only passengers in the elevator as they rode to the ground level. Sierra tried not to feel too wistful as they made their way past a swaying hammock that was occupied by two giggling little girls in pink ruffled bathing suits. That's where she would like to be right now, lounging in the tropics with a fruity beverage in her hand, complete with a tiny umbrella.

Instead she was on baby duty.

Trying to not get too upset about the arrangements, she noticed that Ben was gnawing on her sunglasses.

"That can't possibly taste good. Why don't you try wearing them instead of eating them? Like this," She placed the large, bug-eyed glasses on his face. All the way to the water he held the glasses in place with his pudgy hand and looked right and left, checking out the change in scenery.

Not until Sierra slid her feet out of her sandals and her toes touched the warm sand did the kaleidoscope of upcoming events fully hit her. Any minute she would see Paul Mackenzie. She needed to think of something to say when she saw him. Something calm and polite and friendly.

Settling Ben in the sand at the designated meeting spot by the beach activities booth, Sierra pulled his favorite green truck out of her tote bag. She carefully lowered herself beside him in her lovely turquoise dress.

Her heart was racing.

I never should have come.

CHAPTER EIGHT

Showered, dressed, rested, and ready, Jordan collected his camera gear and headed down toward the grassy area where the bride, Kinsey, had asked to meet him before the rehearsal.

He loved the feel of the warm trade winds that met him as he made his way past the pool to the manicured lawn. Under a gathering of coconut palms was an outdoor dining arrangement the hotel staff were setting up. Tiki torches circled the private circle of four round tables covered with white tablecloths that were flapping in the breeze. In the center of each table were outdoor lanterns with fancy metalwork topping each one, and at each place was a dinner service of china and crystal.

"Excuse me," Jordan said to one of the uniformed wait staff who was arranging the silverware beside each place. "Is this for the Mackenzie wedding party?"

"I'm not given those details. Would you like me to find a manager who can assist you with that information?"

"No, that's okay. Do you mind if I take a few shots?"

"Go ahead. Those two tables are done."

Jordan found the best angle for the fading afternoon light and snapped a dozen shots, just in case this was where they would be sitting. The surroundings and the great colors in the grass and foliage made it impossible for Jordan not to frame a bunch of great shots.

Turning toward the ocean, Jordan walked closer to the sand and took a couple of shots of the cloud bank over the neighboring island. He focused his viewfinder toward the beach, adjusted his position, and tried to capture the best angle of the outrigger. He took one shot and then checked it on the screen. The most amazing lighting trick had occurred in the shot. He didn't see it while taking the picture, but there it was in the frame.

Just beyond the outrigger a young woman was seated in the ivory sand. She wore a turquoise dress that created a stunning contrast to the green grass, the canary-yellow outrigger, and the stretch of sand and sea in the background. All those elements were striking enough to line up a second shot.

He snapped several photos and found that with each of them the lighting phenomenon wasn't with her colorful dress or graceful posture but with her enchanting tangle of golden hair. The woman's back was to him and she had amazing hair that fell like a waterfall of long blond curls down her back. She was positioned so that streaks of afternoon light escaped the buffer of clouds and reflected off the sand and through her hair in a way that gave her an angelic glow.

Jordan couldn't snap the series of photos fast enough.

Then, just as quickly as the rays of light had fallen on her, the cumulus curtain was drawn tight and the radiance faded. Jordan knew he had captured some stellar shots. He was eager to download the photos so he could see the details and try to figure out what elements made the shot line up so perfectly. He didn't usually take pictures of random people; he considered it a violation of their privacy. But this woman's face wasn't turned to him so he thought it was okay this time.

Making his way across the grass back to the gazebo, Jordan spotted the group gathering for the rehearsal. He checked his phone to see if he was late and saw a text from Derek.

Call me soon as you can.

Jordan wanted to stop to call Derek right then but saw that he was already a few minutes late. Not wanting to start off on the wrong foot with the bride and her family, he sent a quick text and hurried over to the group.

To his relief, the bride seemed calm, and so did her mother. He expected a little more tension because the marriage plans had been changed fairly recently. Mindy had told him that the couple originally planned to get married in San Diego, but Kinsey's father had been diagnosed with cancer and was undergoing treatment. Since her parents lived on Maui, the bride and groom had decided less than two months ago to move up the wedding date and hold it here so her father wouldn't have to travel. Part of the fallout of the adjusted schedule and location was that they couldn't book a photographer on such short notice. That's why Mindy had recommended Jordan.

As soon as the introductions were made, Jordan stepped back and went to work, capturing candid shots of the rehearsal while staying as concealed as possible. He caught several great shots of Kinsey talking with her mom as they stood outside the gazebo. The rest of the wedding party headed for the dinner, which was ready to be served at the outdoor tables. Kinsey turned to Jordan and motioned for him to closer.

"I'm not sure if you heard us giving the update to everyone earlier." Kinsey's mom reached for a folder inside her beach bag and pulled out a printed sheet of paper. She handed it to Jordan. "This is the schedule for tomorrow. Everything will go in the same order except the wedding is going to start at eleven."

"Eleven?" Jordan asked.

"We had to make the adjustments for my dad," Kinsey said quietly. "He's doing okay. Not great. The treatment he's going through makes him exhausted in the afternoons. He's completely zonked out right now. We realized that if we kept the afternoon time slot for the ceremony, my dad wouldn't be able to walk me down the aisle. He might have to do the honors in a wheelchair as it is. But he's better in the mornings."

"I'm sorry to hear that."

"Thanks. We're really grateful the hotel allowed us to change the ceremony time. We'll still be here, in the gazebo. They'll put up a canopy on the grass for the guests to sit under. Then we'll go right from the wedding to the luncheon reception. We would still like to have some photos taken at sunset tomorrow."

"Okay. Sure."

"I hope this doesn't throw you off too much," Kinsey's mother said. "I know that lighting and time of day are important to photographers, and we've changed all that."

Jordan appreciated that she was aware of the position he was in. Most people didn't. But it was his dilemma, not hers. She had plenty of other things to worry about.

"It'll be fine." He gave her a reassuring smile. "I can adjust to whatever you would like. My job is to make myself invisible and capture all the memories I can for you and your family."

Kinsey and her mother seemed to sigh in unison. Jordan knew he had said the right thing.

"We should head over to the dinner." Kinsey's mom glanced at her watch. "Have we covered everything?"

"I think so," Kinsey said. "Don't worry about being late, Mom. Paul had to go back to his room to pick up the gifts for his groomsmen."

Turning to Jordan she said, "Did you see where the rehearsal dinner is set up?"

"Yes, I did. I'll be right behind you guys. I want to grab a few pictures of the gazebo while it's vacant and the light is nice and muted."

Kinsey and her mom headed toward the tables on the grassy area by the beach. A moment later, Kinsey hurried back to the gazebo. "I thought of one more thing. I don't know if I told you, but Paul will be wearing a kilt for the wedding."

"Okay." Jordan worked hard to respond with a straight face.

"I just thought I should tell you that. And the other thing is that we'll have bagpipes for our recessional. So that should make for some great shots."

"Yes. Definitely."

"Okay. Well, I just thought you should know so you can be ready for everything tomorrow."

"I'll be ready." Jordan hoped he looked professional.

Apparently Kinsey caught a hint of his surprise because she added, "It's a tradition. Paul's family is from Scotland. Well, not his parents but his grandparents. You probably guessed that with a last name like Mackenzie."

Jordan couldn't keep his smile repressed now. He had to say her new name aloud. "Kinsey Mackenzie."

"Yes. And please don't ask what everyone else has already asked."

"What's that?"

"Will we name our first daughter Lindsey?"

Jordan laughed, and Kinsey gave him a great smile.

"Hold that." He lifted his camera and snapped three shots of her with the sky blushing in the background. "Nice. You're very photogenic. I think you're going to be really happy with how your photos turn out."

"I'm sure we will be." Kinsey turned to go. Over her shoulder she called back, "Be sure to tell Mindy I said hi and thank her for recommending you."

Jordan almost told Kinsey about Mindy's bike accident, but he held back. He didn't have any specifics to report on Mindy's condition. Plus the bride had enough to think about with her wedding being moved up to eleven and her father being too weak to attend the rehearsal dinner.

Jordan snapped a dozen shots of the gazebo in the fading light and then pulled out his phone to call Derek.

CHAPTER NINE

Sierra gazed at the ocean and was certain she had never seen such vibrant colors all in one place. The azure blue of the sky and the turquoise of the ocean blended with perfect harmony. To her right was an outcropping of petrified black lava rock that had raced to the sea eons ago and instantly cooled to form a jagged peninsula that closed off that side of the beach. Over the obsidian rocks tumbled a trailing vine the color of an exotic, green-chested Brazilian bird.

Still balancing baby Ben on her lap, Sierra held him as he kicked his bare feet in the lumpy, soft white sand. She hoped the sand wouldn't harm her nice dress. Mariana had given her two hand-me-down dresses, insisting she would need one for the rehearsal and a different one for the wedding. This was the nicer of the two, and already Sierra regretted that she hadn't saved it for the wedding and worn the black-and-yellow dress tonight.

Ben leaned way over and tried to pick up a fistful of sand.

"Where's your green truck? Here, play with this." Sierra delivered the favorite toy at just the right moment. She thought the way he made a vibrating sound with his mouth whenever he held the truck was adorable. He was such a good little guy. She was smitten with him, which helped her to overlook the scattering of sand now embedded in the beautiful blue-green dress.

Sierra looked up to see Tawni and Jeremy strolling hand-in-hand through the sand. She felt a momentary boost of satisfaction, knowing that by watching Ben she was providing the two of them a chance to be alone and enjoy each other in this gorgeous place. The sky was fading to a soft apricot shade now that the sun had slipped behind the ruffle of clouds lining the top of the island that was across the sea. This was an evening made for couples to stroll barefoot in the sand.

Tawni and Jeremy waved and came toward Sierra. Her sister was only a few feet away when she said, "What is my son wearing?"

"It's a T-shirt. He was so hot from the sunburn I was trying to keep him cool as long as possible."

"Where's his sailor suit?"

"It's right here in the diaper bag. I thought it would be better to wait and not get him all dressed up until he needed to look dashing."

Jeremy leaned down and lifted Ben. "How are you, buddy? Were you a good boy for your aunt Sierra?"

"He's been a very good boy, haven't you, Ben?"

Tawni looked toward the grassy area. "I think were supposed to be over there where the tables are set up. Let's go ahead and dress Ben now."

The trio went to work. Sierra pulled the sailor suit out of the diaper bag, and Jeremy knelt beside Ben. He pulled the T-shirt over his son's head while the clever little waif tried to toddle off to the water wearing only his diaper.

"Oh, no you don't. Come here." Sierra captured him and planted a kiss on his sandy belly. As she spit out particles of sand, Ben fought a good fight and wailed a piercing wail. Not even the green truck pacified him this time.

In the end, he was dressed as cute as could be and still exercising his lungs to their full capacity. Jeremy took the properly adorned sailor boy down toward the water in an effort to divert his attention. Tawni gathered up Ben's toys and shook off the sand before returning them to the diaper bag.

A woman's voice called to Tawni from the grass area. Sierra looked up at the young woman who was waving, and Sierra's jaw went slack. She couldn't believe her eyes.

The woman was wearing the same blue dress Sierra had on.

"Is that Paul's fiancée?"

Tawni looked up and waved. "Yes, that's Kinsey."

Sierra looked at her sister as if she didn't believe her. "Kinsey Mackenzie?"

"Yes. Didn't I tell you that was her name?"

"No." Sierra wondered what other details her sister hadn't mentioned in her e-mails about the wedding.

"Don't run off yet. She's heading this way with her mom. You need to meet her."

"I will as soon as I change."

"Why are you going to change?"

"Tawni, we are wearing the same dress."

Her sister looked at Kinsey and then back at Sierra. "You are. I didn't even notice. Do you want to borrow something of mine to wear?"

Before Sierra could manage to make her exit, Kinsey had approached with a wide, engaging smile. "You must be Sierra. Tawni told me you were coming. I'm Kinsey. This is my mom, Joan."

They exchanged hellos, and Kinsey reached over to hold onto Sierra's forearms in a warm gesture usually reserved for close friends. Looking Sierra in the eye, she said, "I've been looking forward to meeting you. Paul's mom told me about how you prayed faithfully for him when he was going through a really rough stretch in his life a few years ago. His mother and I both believe your prayers for him made all the difference in his life. For a long time I've wanted to meet you and thank you for praying for my future husband."

Kinsey's words hit Sierra in an odd way. She had friends who had prayed for their own future husbands. One friend, Christy, even wrote letters to her future husband. This was a twist. Sierra had prayed her little heart out for someone else's future husband. She didn't know how she felt about that. She also didn't know what to say.

"So thank you." Kinsey gave Sierra's arms a squeeze and pulled back. As she gave Sierra a more thorough looking-over, her lips formed a silent "Oh." Apparently Kinsey had just noticed their matching dresses.

"I know. Crazy, huh? I'm going back to the room right now to change," Sierra said.

"I think it looks better on you," Kinsey said. "Maybe I should go change."

Kinsey's mom and Tawni offered the appropriate sort of twitter of laughter at the bride-to-be's suggestion, making it clear that the bride should have first dibs on everything. Especially wardrobe selection.

"No, I'm going to change," Sierra said decisively. "I'll be back in ten minutes."

Kinsey's mother's face went flat. She quickly looked at Kinsey and then at Tawni with a hint of panic in her eyes. The unspoken SOS that went around that Bermuda triangle was clear. Sierra wasn't on the guest list for the evening events.

She had assumed she was, based on the information Tawni had given her in an e-mail saying that Sierra should be at the hotel in time for the rehearsal dinner.

"You know what?" Sierra said, quickly trying to save face. "I'm so tired, with the jet lag and everything, I was thinking of just excusing myself and seeing all of you at the wedding tomorrow."

Kinsey looked at her mom with an uncomfortable expression. "You know, with Dad not being able to come to dinner, we could..."

"No, I..." Sierra held up her hand before Kinsey tried to slide Sierra into her father's place at the rehearsal dinner. "I really need to go back to the room. My stomach is a little upset."

That statement was true. Sierra did have an upset stomach. Not because of the awkward moments she had experienced in meeting Kinsey but because of the inevitable moment she wasn't ready for. She wasn't ready to see Paul. Not yet.

Sierra picked up her sandals, feeling like an odd variation of Cinderella who was about to flee from the festivities.

She had begun to walk away when Kinsey's mother said, "Sierra, one quick question." She had her planning folder out and was running her finger down a list. "What is your last name, dear?"

"Jensen."

Without looking up, Joan pulled out a pen to make a note. Obviously the name "Sierra Jensen" was missing from the wedding guest list.

Feeling at a loss as to what to do next. Sierra offered one final attempt to dose off this encounter with something positive. She turned to Kinsey. "Congratulations, by the way, in case I don't have a chance to tell you tomorrow. I'm really happy for you and Paul."

"Thank you, Sierra. That means a lot." In a lowered voice Kinsey added, "And honestly? The dress really does look better on you."

CHAPTER TEN

"She's pregnant?" Jordan leaned against the side of the gazebo and switched his phone to the other ear, repeating the question as if he hadn't heard Derek correctly. "Mindy is pregnant?"

"Yes. Believe me, it's a surprise to both of us. She started hemorrhaging, and they ran a simple test. That's how we found out."

"Is the baby okay? And Mindy, is she okay?" Jordan asked.

"They let us know that she could easily miscarry." Derek's voice was low and tight with tension.

"Oh, man. I'm so sorry, Derek. So sorry for you guys."

"Mindy's sleeping right now. She seems okay, from what all the tests showed. No concussion, which is a miracle. I'm going to go find something to eat. This has really come at us hard and fast."

"Is there anything I can do?" Jordan realized how pointless such a question was, but he had to ask.

"No, you're where you're supposed to be. Just pray for us, will you? I'll keep you updated."

"I will be praying. And if you guys need me there or whatever, just let me know. "I'll come back."

"No, don't start getting all heroic on me. You stay there and do what you need to do. I'll let you know how things are going here. We'll just take this as it comes."

"Okay. Well, call me anytime, all right? Sorry I couldn't grab your calls earlier today."

"Don't worry about it. I'll text you if I can't reach you. I just didn't want to text about the baby."

"I understand."

"Thanks, Jordo. I'll talk to you later."

Jordan stood beside the fairytale-like gazebo surrounded by striking, tall red ginger plants and rich green ferns. He looked out at a picture-perfect peach and rose-colored sunset. All he could do was blink and swallow the lump that had grown in his throat. He couldn't imagine what Derek and Mindy must be going through. Here he was, in paradise, and their lives had gone into a dark place.

He prayed fervently for their child's life, for Mindy's healing, and for Derek as he tried to hold it all together. Even though Jordan couldn't do anything, he still wished it were possible for him to drive to the hospital right now, be with them through the night, and then come back to shoot the wedding in the morning.

Jordan remembered that he was supposed to be taking pictures now at the rehearsal dinner. He drew back his shoulders and filled his lungs with the salty air. Trying to clear his thoughts so he could focus on the work ahead of him, he headed toward where the group was gathering.

In the soft twilight shades, the area prepared for the lawn party looked enchanting. Flickering tiki torches surrounded the clutch of people while the evening breeze ruffled the white tablecloths' draped edges like a flock of roosting doves. The mellow sounds floating from a musician playing a slack key guitar stretched out beyond the circle of tables and drew longing gazes from visitors passing by.

Thoughts about Derek, Mindy, and their unborn child followed Jordan down from the gazebo. All this beauty fell flat on his spirit. Moments like this were meant to be shared. Life was meant to be shared. He suddenly felt like he was very much the outsider at this event, alone, and not connected to anyone. He was simply commissioned to capture the magical moment for others.

Jordan told himself that he couldn't do anything for Derek and Mindy, but right now he could do this. He could capture a beautiful moment for someone else. That reminder was enough of a shake to bring him back to the moment and set to work.

Sierra opened her eyes in the darkened hotel room. She was alone in her queen-sized bed. Last night she had fallen asleep with her arm around Ben and vaguely remembered Tawni and Jeremy returning to the room, taking Ben, and wedging him in between them in their bed. After that Sierra knew she had fallen into a deep sleep, relieved not to be dozing with the subliminal awareness that she mustn't let Ben roll onto the floor.

The digital clock on the nightstand said it was 5:44. Outside their closed sliding glass doors the first streaks of morning were lightening the sky. Sierra rolled over and thought of how her appreciation for mothers everywhere had elevated.

Last night Jeremy had brought Ben back to the hotel room only half an hour after Sierra had returned and changed out of the blue dress into a pair of shorts and a T-shirt. He said Ben wouldn't calm down enough to sit with them at the rehearsal dinner, so Jeremy was going to try to get him to eat something in the room and then see if he could take Ben back.

"Jeremy, let me take care of him," Sierra offered over Ben's continuing tantrum. She was pretty sure all he needed was to get out of the itchy sailor suit and be allowed to romp around in his diaper while his sunburn calmed down.

"No, I can't ask you to do that. You've done enough already, Sierra."

"Jeremy, this is your brother's rehearsal dinner. You need to be there. Go. Seriously, I'll take care of Ben."

Sierra's prediction was right. Once she had Ben stripped down to his diaper, she sprayed his back with the sunburn soother, and he was a different boy. She ordered room service, found some soft Hawaiian music on the clock radio, and the rest of the night was a breeze.

That was, until Sierra tried to get Ben to go to sleep. His fascination with Sierra had worn off after she changed his diaper for the fourth time that day. He kicked, squirmed, and found great delight in trying to run away from her.

How her mother had managed to raise Sierra and her five siblings without experiencing a nervous breakdown was beyond Sierra. She had a feeling that the nicest thing she could do for Jeremy and Tawni was offer to be on baby Ben duty for the next twenty-four hours so they could be free to fulfill their roles at the wedding.

That meant that if Sierra was going to have any time to herself today, it had to be now while everyone else was still sleeping. Stealthily she pulled her new bathing suit out of her suitcase along with a wraparound sarong. Changing quickly and quietly in the bathroom, she left a note saying she had gone swimming and would be back before eight o'clock.

Then, grabbing her flip-flops and closing the door with extra care, Sierra made her way down to the beach where the new day was beginning to show its shining face. Her bare feet hit the cool sand and she lifted her chin to feel the fresh breath of the trade winds scrambling her unbrushed hair. She wasn't the only early bird out on the beach. Her original thought had been to take a walk along the shore and then swim in the spacious hotel pool. As soon as her feet slid into the water at the shoreline, she knew the ocean was the spacious pool she wanted to swim in that morning.

Sierra slowly walked into the calm morning swell and lowered herself into the cool saltwater, feeling her skin tingle. The gentle plunge woke up all her senses. With long strokes she swam as if she were heading for the island she could see across the wide blue expanse. Once she was far enough past where the small waves were breaking, she swam parallel to the shore.

Behind the hotel, farther inland, the green slopes of the huge island volcano blushed with the new day's golden glow. As Sierra swam, she watched the sun rise from behind the volcano, accompanied by a fleet of thin clouds the shade of pink rose petals. It was going to be a beautiful day for a wedding.

She continued to float and paddle about, watching the shore as a few more eager vacationers came down to the nearly vacant beach. One of them, a dark-haired guy, caught her attention. He was tall but not too tall. His build was solid but not too muscular. She liked the way his hair seemed to be styling itself in the breeze, sticking straight up in the front.

As Sierra watched with her chin just above the water's edge, the guy pulled off his shirt, tossed it on the sand not far from Sierra's clothes, and walked straight toward the water. Without hesitation he strode into the ocean and dove into the curling wave that met him head-on. He came up on the other side of the foamy wave with a shake of his head that scattered the salty droplets. Then, to Sierra's surprise, he let out a whoop that could only be a cry of delight.

From her viewpoint, it didn't appear that he had noticed her bobbing along about twenty yards from him. His shout to the new day seemed to come from a spontaneous heart, and the expression made Sierra smile. She wanted to relax and enjoy that same sort of lighthearted interaction with this spectacular place, and more importantly with the One who had created all this beauty.

The guy swam parallel to the shore in the opposite direction from where Sierra was treading water. He made purposeful strokes all the way to the outcropping of dark volcanic rocks.

Sierra felt a little shiver. She wanted to swim after him, as silly as that sounded. She wanted to ride in the wake of his energizing motions and feel her spirit lighten the way it had when he had let out his joyful holler. Sierra knew Mariana would tease her if she ever told her what she was feeling right now. She called Sierra an "eternal optimist" and the one who brought sunshine to every situation. Mariana would never believe that Sierra was in need of cheer or that she wanted to swim after a guy just to be around him. In Brazil, Sierra would often go in the opposite direction whenever outgoing, boisterous guys were around. Marianna knew that.

But this morning, as she floated in what felt like a dream, everything inside Sierra was urging her to swim as fast as she could to catch up to the joy-bringer who had brought a smile to her face.

Giving in to the impulse, Sierra swam toward the rocks. She kicked like crazy and scooped fistfuls of water as her arms carried her forward. She had no idea what she would say if she caught up with him. If she could turn invisible, she would. All she wanted was to share this moment with someone else.

That's when it hit her how alone she felt.

Even in Brazil with Mariana and all the supportive people from the mission, she was on her own, disconnected from home, family, and all that had been familiar while she was growing up. Being back in the US made her realize how cut off she had been. It also struck her that, even though she was reconnected with part of her family for the wedding, she was still the odd-numbered adult.

Of course Aunt Sierra would watch Ben. She was single. She

had no one to sit with at the wedding or the reception. What was it that Mark had written in his e-mail about why she was so well suited for this new position with the family in Brazil? It was her single status. She was easy to relocate because there was only one of her.

With each arm stroke, Sierra fought internal waves of discouragement. She was young. She was using her life to make a difference. She needed to appreciate that she was in Hawaii. *Come on, Sierra. Don't get discouraged. Chin up. Be grateful. Trust God.*

Just then the guy turned around and started to swim in her direction. Sierra had to make a quick decision. He was less than thirty yards away. Should she swim back to shore and scamper off to her room? Or should she stay and wait out the moment?

Just then the most unexpected thing happened.

CHAPTER ELEVEN

"Did you see that?" Jordan called out to the woman who was in the ocean not more than twenty yards from him. He paddled over closer to her. "Did you see the whale that just jumped?"

"No, where was it?" She swam closer to him.

"Straight out toward the island at about two o'clock. I saw a big plume of water from a whale spouting. Look! There! Do you see it?"

Across the great expanse of water a huge white puff rose from the surface. A moment later an enormous whale came out of the deep blue sea and breached in a wide arc, splashing on his way back into the watery depths.

"Whoa!" The woman gave a spontaneous laugh of awe and delight.

"That's incredible, isn't it?"

"There's another one!" The woman pointed to the left of where he had sighted the first whale.

A second great beast leapt from the ocean and curved as it returned to the sea with such a splash that Jordan wished he had his camera. "Unbelievable!"

"This is so amazing."

As they watched, the whales continued to breach and make fabulous splashes in the water. Jordan thought it seemed as if the whales were frolicking like kids in the water on a summer day.

As quickly as it had started, the flurry of marine activity ended. He didn't know enough about whales to estimate if or when the pod might surface again and go about their enormous somersaults. Jordan looked more closely at the young woman who was the only other early-morning swimmer and now was just a few feet from him. Her long, wet hair was slicked back from her face. She had a fresh, clear-eyed look and lovely eyes. He guessed she was about his age. Something about her seemed vaguely familiar.

Still looking at where the whales had been, the woman said, "That was amazing. Like Genesis chapter one all over again."

As soon as the words were out of her mouth, she turned to Jordan. It seemed she hadn't meant to say that aloud. Either that or when she turned and looked at him, what she saw startled her.

Then Jordan realized where he had seen her. She was the mom who had been holding the baby when he accidentally tried to enter her room yesterday.

"Were you the one who opened the door when I . . ." Jordan paused.

"Yes. I thought I recognized you."

"In case I didn't say it yesterday, sorry about that."

"Don't worry. I understand completely. It's confusing. All the doors look alike,"

"Yes. Well, again, sorry."

"No problem."

Neither of them seemed to know what to say next. They floated in an awkward silence until Jordan finally said, "I should probably get back."

"Me, too,"

They faced another awkward moment when they swam together toward the shore. It would have felt even more uncomfortable to Jordan if he had hung back and let her swim in first because then it might seem as if he were watching her. If he swam ahead of her, it would seem rude somehow.

Maintaining their synchronized pace, they arrived onshore and seemed to be trying not to look at the other as they went for their abandoned clothes. Once again, they were in tandem since their clothes were tossed on the sand only a few feet from each other.

"I would have brought a towel if I had known I was going to swim," the woman said.

"Me too."

They pulled their clothes on over their wet skin. She gave her long hair a twist and wrung out the saltwater.

"I think they have a shower up there by the pool." Jordan wasn't sure why he said that

"I'm going to wait until I get back to my room."

"So am I." Again, he could have smacked himself for the way this conversation was going. The worst part was that he was having a hard time not stealing glances at her. Yes, she was very attractive, but he shouldn't be looking because she was married and most likely her husband was waiting for her back at the room with their baby.

"Well, I hope you have a good day." Jordan gave a funny wave. He was certain that the look on his face was equally idiotic.

"You too."

She had the sweetest smile. And just a sprinkling of freckles across her nose.

Jordan turned away from her and headed toward the hotel through the garden area. He didn't look back. Several trails led to the hotel lobby and elevators. He hoped she wasn't following him but was taking a different route. He would feel even more ridiculous if they ended up in the same elevator since they were on the same floor.

To guarantee that they wouldn't meet up, Jordan headed for the espresso bar he had seen the night before that was located next to the gift shop. A morning cup of coffee sounded great, and he could hide out long enough to avoid meeting up with her again.

Jordan wound his way through the lobby and pulled open the door to the small espresso bar. Only two people were in line, which was good. But *she* was one of them.

Two things happened before Jordan could quietly back away. First, when he saw her standing in line with her long hair cascading, he knew that she was the mermaid in the turquoise dress he had captured in his lens last evening.

Second, as soon as he set one foot inside, she turned to look at him.

Going with the flow, Jordan gave her a half smile to acknowledge the obvious and then stepped over to the shelves as if he were in the market for a new Hawaiian coffee mug with the word *Wailea* in bright pink letters. Picking up a mug as if he were examining it, Jordan tried to catch glimpses over his shoulder so he would know when she was gone.

He listened for her voice to determine when she had completed her order. That was when he realized he was dripping water from his swim shorts. Glancing at the door, he knew he should go, no matter how strange his exit might seem, before he left a puddle on the tile floor.

The door swung open just then and the groom from the wedding walked in. Jordan turned back to the mugs and closed his eyes, trying to remember the guy's name. He remembered the last name, Mackenzie, but couldn't recall the groom's first name.

Before he could say anything, he overheard the guy say, "Sierra?"

Glancing over his shoulder, Jordan watched as his mermaid turned and faced the groom with a look of mixed trepidation and tenderness.

"Paul. Hi."

They moved toward each other awkwardly, the groom making a noble effort to give her a hug or perhaps a kiss on the cheek.

She leaned forward to receive his gesture at first but then quickly pulled back saying, "I'm still dripping with saltwater. Sorry." Her laugh sounded nervous.

"Early morning swim with the dolphins?" Paul asked.

"Whales, actually."

"Hey, listen, Kinsey told me about the misunderstanding on the arrangements for dinner last night. I'm really sorry, Sierra. I heard that you and Ben ended up in your room ordering room service."

Sierra. Her name is Sierra and she's with some guy named Ben.

"It was fine. Really. Don't worry about it."

"You'll be at the ceremony, though, won't you?"

"Yes, definitely. And congratulations, Paul. I'm really happy for you and Kinsey. She seems like a wonderful person."

"She is. And thank you. Sierra. That means a lot."

The barista asked, "Did you want to order something?"

"Yes," Sierra said. "I'd like a peppermint tea. Medium."

"Still drinking tea, are you?" Paul asked. "I thought all the time in Brazil might have turned you into a coffee drinker." Now he was the one who seemed to have a nervous laugh. "I also half-expected to see you show up in your cowboy boots."

"I have them with me, so be careful what you wish for."

"Anything for you?" the barista asked Paul.

Jordan realized this was his chance to make a swift escape. He slid out the door and went the shortest route to the elevator, thinking about the curious bits of information he had picked up.

Sierra was probably a relative or a wife of a relative based on what he'd picked up from the people he'd met at the rehearsal dinner last night.

What intrigued him was that Paul indicated that Sierra had spent a lot of time in Brazil. Brazil was on Jordan's short list of places to go to one day. He'd always wanted to see the Christ statue in Rio de Janeiro. Capturing an angle no one else had yet caught would be a great photo challenge.

Thoughts of travel and Brazil reminded Jordan of Costa Rica, and Costa Rica always reminded him of Paige. Jordan unlocked his hotel room door and headed for the shower. He wondered what his life would be like if he had gotten serious about Paige when she was ready to be serious. Would they be married now? Would he still be able to have the dream career opportunities he was experiencing now if he were married?

Jordan thought about how Mindy had only improved Derek's career. She was vested in his success while still pursuing her own interests. To Jordan, Derek and Mindy were the ideal couple. If he could find a woman like Mindy, he'd be golden.

Earlier that morning, Derek had sent another text asking Jordan to "pray like our child's life depends on it because it does."

With all his heart, Jordan prayed again for Mindy, Derek, and their unborn child.

CHAPTER TWELVE

Sierra took a sip of her peppermint tea and waited as Paul paid for his cappuccino. She wasn't as flustered as she thought she would be when she saw him for the first time. She had felt more flustered during the encounter with the guy in the water this morning. They had shared such an incredible experience as they watched the whales. But as soon as he realized he had tried to open her hotel room door with his key, he seemed skittish. Sierra noticed that he had entered the espresso café right after her. Was that a coincidence, or did he know she was there? She hadn't seen him leave the café or order anything to drink. It was kind of strange.

Paul motioned toward one of the small tables outside that had two chairs. "Do you have a minute?"

"Sure."

Sierra was glad for the warmth of the tropical weather outside. The air-conditioning inside the café had chilled her with her wet swimsuit and dripping hair. Now that she was sitting across from Paul and not feeling as jittery about the guy from the beach, she noticed how much Paul had changed. His wavy brown hair was longer than she had seen him wear it before.

In the same way that his brother Jeremy had filled out, Paul also had become more solid through the shoulders. Both Jeremy and Paul were built like their father, who was a large man with broad shoulders. With Paul's solemn mouth, long hair, and slightly crumpled white shirt with rolled-up sleeves, he reminded Sierra of an actor who played a Victorian poet in a film she and Mariana had seen right before Christmas. It seemed a fitting look for Paul since he was a writer.

She took another sip of tea as Paul pulled his chair over into the shade. She remembered the many long, handwritten letters he had sent her from Scotland while he was going to university. She had read his letters over and over and had prayed many heartfelt prayers for him during her last two years of high school while he was going through rocky times. His life started to turn around and to Sierra's delight, they finally shared a few promising, hand-holding months after her returned to the U.S.. They agreed to take it slow to see if anything more than friendship developed.

From Paul's perspective, nothing did. Their casual dating relationship slowed to a crawl and came to a stop during Sierra's first year of college. To intensify the blow, Paul's brother had fallen in love with Sierra's sister. All the family support and happiness on both sides were focused on Tawni and Jeremy while Sierra quietly buried her still-warm feelings about Paul and waited.

Now here she was, face-to-face with him after all these years, and nothing was as it seemed it would be when she saw him again. Sierra thought she would feel her heart race at the sight of him. She thought seeing him would make her melt or cry or at least feel some of the old attraction she had experienced when they had first met at Heathrow Airport in London.

None of that accompanied her thoughts and feelings this morning.

"I read your updates about Brazil," Paul said. "It sounds like you've had some amazing experiences, Sierra."

"I have. It's been good."

Paul tilted his head. "Have any interesting Brazilian men captured your heart?"

"No." She felt funny confessing this truth to him. He was getting married in a few hours. She was an unattached nomad at the moment and didn't want to be reminded of that uncomfortable fact.

"I'm surprised. I thought you would have gotten married long before me."

Sierra wasn't sure how to take his statement. Did he somehow see her as pushing for a marriage commitment when they were quasi-dating? Or was he trying to make a guy sort of compliment, meaning that she was worthy or being pursued by some eligible bachelor? Sierra decided the only way to find out what he meant was to ask him.

Paul leaned back. "I just meant that you were more relationship-minded than I've ever seen myself being. You always go after what you want. At Jeremy and Tawni's wedding, you seemed like you wanted to be the one to walk down the aisle."

"That's not true. To be honest, I wanted you to notice me that day. I was still thinking our relationship might have another final round to go before it was all over."

Paul laughed.

Sierra remembered that laugh. It came across somewhat condescendingly in a friendly way but mostly as an attempt to camouflage his sense of being caught off guard.

"You haven't changed when it comes to your zeal for the truth, Sierra."

She was glad to hear that. With all the other ways she had

changed over the last four years, she liked knowing that Paul still saw her as a bit brazen when it came to speaking her mind.

"You can relax, though, Paul." Sierra added a coy smile the way Mariana had taught her by example. The softened expression and merry twinkle had allowed her to charm her way out of a possibly awkward moment more than once. "I didn't come to this wedding with the same objective."

"Well, that's good to know." Paul added his own twist of a grin to his reply. He sipped his cappuccino as Sierra tried to think of what to say next.

"So, now I'm curious," He said. "Did you really think at Jeremy and Tawni's wedding that you and I would start dating after we saw each other? Because I thought we had given our relationship as much of a chance as we could back when you were at Rancho Corona. Did I give you the wrong impression?"

Sierra felt cornered. She had found herself in that spot more than once with Paul. Her lips parted but no words tumbled out.

"Is that how you felt, Sierra?"

She crossed her legs and leaned back. "Here's how I felt. I felt as if I had invested a lot of time, prayers, and thoughts into the possibility of our relationship going somewhere deeper than it did. I felt as if you pulled back and decided it was over before I had the same understanding."

"Did you want me to prolong the inevitable breakup?"

"No, of course not. I'm just saying that you reached the ultimate conclusion before I did. That's all."

"And you would have liked it if we had kept up a front for everyone a little longer. Is that it?"

"No. I didn't want to be fake about it. I was just . . ." the word that came out surprised her. "Sad. I was sad that nothing came of us."

Paul leaned back. He didn't seem as if he had been very sad. She could see the wheels of his logical male mind spinning as he took a slow, deliberate swig of his drink.

"And are you still sad?" he asked.

"No." Sierra shook her head and answered with an honesty that felt good to hear resounding in her heart "Not at all. I'm not sad. I think everything turned out the way it was supposed to for you. For both of us. I did wonder for a long time if maybe both of us had changed enough over the years that, should we meet up again, we would click, you know what I mean? Like the many jagged pieces that never fit together in our puzzle would have rounded off at the corners so they could be connected."

"And we're still jagged, aren't we?"

Sierra nodded. They were as jagged in their connection as they had always been. That was as evident to Sierra now as it must have been to Paul all those years ago. "Kinsey is a great fit for you, Paul. I meant it when I said I'm really happy for you both."

"Thanks. I'm glad I ran into you and we had this chance to talk, just the two of us."

"Me, too."

"So, are we good?" Paul asked. "Is there anything I should apologize for?"

"No, of course not. If anything, I probably should be apologizing for keeping you. You do have a wedding to get ready for."

Paul laughed again. "True. I'm glad you haven't changed, Sierra. That's a good thing. I hope you never change." He looked at his watch. "I need to get going." He grinned in a way she had never seen him grin before. "I don't want to keep my bride waiting."

Sierra smiled back. What she felt for Paul right then was the best sort of sisterly affection. This was where she had always hoped her emotions would end up toward him. But on their own, her feelings had always gone to a sad place. This encounter changed everything. She finally felt as if the closure was solid.

With clarity in her spirit, Sierra said, "God bless you on your wedding day, Paul Mackenzie."

He stood, leaned over, and kissed her on top of her salty wet head. "And God bless you, Daffodil Queen. I look forward to going to your wedding one day so I can see your face looking as happy as I feel right now."

He strode across the courtyard and headed for the row of oceanfront suites.

Sierra lingered, swinging her crossed leg as she thought about what had just happened. It was fun to see Paul so in love.

She listened to the birds twittering in their hidden spots in the beautiful green foliage and hoped his final blessing would come true. She did hope that he would come to her wedding someday and that she would be as happy as he was today.

She just didn't know how that was going to happen while she was teaching four children in a rural village in Brazil.

Maybe a relationship that leads to marriage isn't in my near future.

Sierra let out a long sigh.

Then why is it that I so dearly desire to fall in love with the right guy and share my life with him? Are my priorities messed up?

Pushing back from the table, Sierra decided to head back to the hotel room before her spirit had a chance to fall into another pocket of sadness. She knew she needed to make the big decision as to whether she was going to accept the teaching position. She just didn't want to make any decisions until she had had time to think and pray it through.

But today was not the day for any more contemplation or decision making.

CHAPTER THIRTEEN

"Let's try to get a few more shots before the sun goes down all the way." Jordan framed the happy couple with the neighboring island in the background and gave way to a slow grin. The timing was just right because the island appeared to wear a gathering of pink, lacy clouds like a flowery wreath around its highest point. Trailing from the clouds were vivacious streamers of mango-shaded light.

The sun had just begun to slip behind the ruffled clouds when, just as had happened that morning when he was swimming, across the wide expanse of blue, a whale breached. Without telling Paul and Kinsey what he had seen, Jordan said, "Can you move a little to the left? A little more. There. Perfect."

Holding his arm as steady as he could, he hoped to catch the whale's next splash in the upper right corner of the photo. Now, if the great beast would only cooperate and breach again.

"Keep those expressions," he said calmly. "Hold that pose for me. Yes, just like that. You got it."

Kinsey was standing barefoot in the sand, holding up the train of her satin wedding gown. Paul was in his kilt. They were turned toward each other with the fading sunlight on their faces. Jordan planted his feet, held his breath. . .and there it was! The perfect setup.

He snapped, catching a dozen shots in succession as the whale rose up out of the water behind them.

"Got it! Terrific. I think that's it, unless you wanted any other specific poses." Jordan decided not to mention that he hoped he had captured the breaching whale in the shots—just in case they didn't turn out. He had been with the couple all day and knew he had taken plenty of good photos.

The couple rubbed noses and kissed, lost in the moment. They looked over at Jordan as if they were surprised he was still there.

"I'm sorry," Kinsey said. "Did you ask us something?"

Jordan smiled at the loving couple. "Nope. That's it. I think you're going to be happy with what we got."

"Thanks again." Paul extended his right hand and gave Jordan a strong-fisted shake. "We appreciate your doing this for us."

"Of course. It was my pleasure. By the way . . ." Jordan hesitated. He'd been wanting to ask Paul a question for a few hours but didn't want his inquiry to come out the wrong way or to seem unprofessional.

"Yes?" Kinsey asked.

"I was wondering. . . " Jordan tried to sound casual. "It's about one of the guests. She had long blond hair and had a little boy with her. Is she part of your extended family?"

"That's Sierra," Paul said. "Her sister is married to my brother."

"Oh. Okay."

"We included her in some of the family group shots," Kinsey said. "Didn't we? I thought we did."

"Yes. I think you did." Jordan didn't just think they had—he knew they had. He had paid attention to where Sierra was and who she was with throughout the day. He noticed that whoever the "Ben" was that she had gone back to her room with last night to order room service wasn't at the wedding ceremony. The gathering was small, and most of the time Sierra was by herself with the baby in her arms.

Jordan carefully asked, "And so was Ben in the wedding party? I just wanted to make sure we got all the family in the shots you wanted."

"Ben was in a lot of the pictures," Kinsey said. "Hopefully, you got a few when he wasn't crying."

Jordan made the connection. "Oh. So Ben was the little boy."

"He's my brother's son. My nephew," Paul said.

"My nephew, too." Kinsey smiled at Paul.

"*Our* nephew," Paul agreed. He leaned in to kiss his new wife.

Jordan made his exit, allowing the happy couple their chance to enjoy their wedding sunset moment in private. As he headed to his room he let the news sink in that Ben was Sierra's nephew, not her son. His first thought was that if he had known that earlier, he would have said something to her at the reception. He didn't know exactly what he would have said. Something that would have opened up the free-flowing dialogue they had experienced that morning in the ocean before the awkwardness set in.

But then, she still could be married. Or engaged.

Jordan stopped at the outdoor shower by the pool to rinse the sand off his feet. He waited his turn and noticed that Paul and Kinsey had followed him. She demurely slid in front of Jordan and turned on the lower fawcet.

Jordan couldn't help but snag one more shot. The contrast at the shower stall made for a great photo composition. On one side was a skinny boy with red hair rinsing off his Boogie Board. He was staring at Paul in his kilt. Paul was helping to balance his bride. Kinsey wore a wreath of flowers around her head and held up her elegant gown while pointed her bare toes in the directed spray. Jordan snapped ten more photos from two different angles.

"Those will be fun to add at the end of our album," Kinsey said. "Thanks again, Jordan."

The three of them said their good-byes again. As Jordan strolled through the hotel grounds, images from the wedding flipped through his thoughts. He remembered the way Sierra looked, dancing with the little baby in her arms, making him laugh. She was the most intriguing, watchable woman he had seen in a long time. Nothing about her seemed common or predictable.

Stopping by the pool, he put down his heavy case and pulled out his camera. Jordan stretched out on a lounge chair, turned on his camera, and flipped through the shots from the wedding reception until he found a photo with Sierra sitting at a table during the reception. Zooming in on her hand, Jordan found what he was looking for.

She's not wearing a wedding ring.

He checked more closely in two other shots. Nope, no ring. Leaning back, Jordan let the information settle in. Maybe she was available. He should try to find out. But who would he ask now?

It would be ideal if he could bump into her again casually and they could start a conversation. He would be able to tell a lot about her if they could have a chance to talk face-to-face. He knew what room she was in. Maybe he should casually knock on the door and . . .

What's the point? I'm leaving for Oahu on the first flight in the morning. How can I even think about a relationship when my career is beginning to take off? That's where I need to focus my attention.

Jordan was pretty sure he would regret his decision not to initiate a connection with her that evening. To settle his thoughts, he repeated something he had told himself many times over the past decade. *The timing isn't right. When the timing is right, God will bring the right woman my way.*

Closing his eyes, he listened to the lilting Hawaiian music piped into the pool area. Then, pulling out his phone, he checked his messages and made the difficult call to Derek that he had been dreading.

Sierra leaned her elbows on the edge of the hotel pool and rested her chin on her folded arms. Slowly fluttering her legs in rhythm with the soothing Hawaiian music that came through a concealed speaker behind her lounge chair, she thought about the position that had been offered to her in Brazil.

An hour earlier she'd been in the hotel room sitting on the bed with her sister. Tawny was rocking Ben in her arms and sincerely expressing her appreciation to Sierra.

"Thank you for taking care of Ben during the wedding, Sierra. I didn't mean for you to end up with him all day. He certainly seemed happier with you than with anyone else."

"He's a doll, Tawni. You and Jeremy are so blessed."

"Thanks for saying that. I need to remember that. He's a good baby most of the time. It's just been such a huge life change for me."

"I can imagine."

"What are you planning to do now?" Tawni looked like she was ready to jump at the chance to leave if Sierra offered to baby-sit again.

That's when Sierra decided she was ready for a break from baby Ben. "I'd like to go down to the pool and do some thinking. I'm in the middle of some big life changes as well."

Tawni didn't ask Sierra what those changes were. That was typical of their relationship. In a way, Sierra was glad Tawni hadn't asked for details. She wanted to process the decision about the open position without a lot of outside influence.

"If Jeremy comes back, I think I'll join you."

"Good. I'll stick around by the pool, then." Sierra gathered her beach clothes and went to the bathroom to change. When she was ready to leave, she saw that Tawni was stretched out next to Ben, and both were sound asleep.

The time Sierra had spent at the pool napping and swimming had relaxed her. But the solitude hadn't produced any answers to her dilemma. Instead of focusing on whether she should accept the position to help the family with the four children, Sierra was thinking about the photographer at the wedding.

She had found out from Kinsey's mom that his name was Jordan. He lived in Santa Barbara and was a sought-after professional photographer whose photos were on magazine covers. He had agreed to shoot the wedding because a mutual friend had made the connection for them.

Kinsey's mother seemed friendly and eager to offer Sierra any information or assistance she could. She said she thought he was single but offered to make sure, if Sierra wanted to know. Sierra had brushed off the offer and switched to talking about how beautiful the wedding had been. She wondered if the excessive helpfulness was compensation for the uneasy moments on the beach the night before.

Sierra kicked her feet in the warm saltwater pool and wondered if she would see Jordan again before she left on a midmorning flight for Oahu. If she did, would he be as reserved as he had been during the wedding? She had a feeling that if he was unattached and if he by any remote chance had a glimmer of interest in her, then he would have said something at the wedding. He would have made the first move.

As it was, all she and Jordan exchanged during the lively

festivities were a few glances. Nothing worth building a dream on.

Scolding herself for letting her thoughts wander off and not staying focused on the decision at hand, Sierra climbed out of the pool. She wrapped up in her towel and settled onto the lounge chair. The sky turned a deep shade of amethyst as the clouds took on a peachy color around their ruffled edges. Sierra watched as a palm tree swayed in the evening breeze, looking like a hula dancer.

She lowered her gaze and her breath caught in her throat. Jordan was coming into the pool area. He was still dressed as he had been at the wedding and was carrying his camera and case.

Sierra watched as he took a seat on one of the lounge chairs on the other side of the pool. He pulled out his camera and seemed to be viewing the images. Pushing her wet hair back over her shoulders, Sierra adjusted her position just in case he looked across the pool area, noticed her sitting by herself, and came over to talk to her.

Sierra waited. She watched him. He didn't look up.

He had such a great presence. Strong, broad shoulders; steady posture. She'd noticed at the wedding that he had a quiet sort of self-assurance. Sierra thought he was handsome. He exemplified the true All-American kind of guy she had missed being around while she was in Brazil. His light brown hair and wide smile gave him the look of someone who enjoyed the outdoors, as she had witnessed that morning in the ocean. All he needed was a baseball cap and he would fit in with all her favorite college guys she had left behind when she moved from Southern California to Brazil.

Sierra continued watching Jordan across the pool and wondered what part of Santa Barbara he was from. When she saw him pick up his phone and hold it to his ear with a serious expression, she had a feeling he wasn't going to look in her direction or entertain any thoughts about striking up another conversation.

He could be calling his girlfriend or his wife, for all I know. What am I doing?

Sierra gathered her things and headed back to the room. The sun had set, and a hotel employee trotted past her with a lit torch in his hand. He was wearing only a wraparound skirt made from Hawaiian fabric. As he touched the torch to the first tiki light at the edge of the pool area, he lifted a large conch shell that he was holding in his other hand. He put the shell to his lips and blew into it so that a long, low, melodic note sounded.

The day that had begun with breaching whales and was punctuated by the stirring call of bagpipes and wedding vows was now coming to a close with a clarifying sound of the islands.

Sierra took one last look over to where Jordan sat with his head down, caught up in his phone conversation. She knew better than to let her emotions get away from her, but for some reason, she didn't want to walk away. This guy had really gotten to her.

Willing herself to release any of the whimsical thoughts she still held since spotting Jordan that morning, Sierra whispered her own farewell to the day and to the island of Maui. Tomorrow she would be on Oahu with Mariana. Things would be back to the way they always were.

She hoped that when that happened she could come to a conclusion about what she was supposed to do next.

CHAPTER FOURTEEN

On Jordan's early-morning flight to Oahu, the passenger next to him was an older man in a colorful, floral print shirt wearing a shell lei. He was eager to make small talk about all the facts he knew about Pearl Harbor and how he was going to "hit the beach at Waikiki" and load up on mai tais while he watched the hula dancers. He suggested that Jordan join him, but Jordan politely turned him down, saying he had other plans.

"But you're on vacation, aren't you? Us single guys gotta stick together. I'll be your wing man."

Jordan declined the offer once again. He had to smile to himself, though, because the man reminded him of his grandpa Jack. Not because of his crude demeanor but because of his looks. Jordan's grandfather had thick white hair like this man and also had an outgoing personality. He, too, would start up conversations with strangers. Grandpa Jack had been a phys ed coach for decades. He often had told Jordan and his two brothers, "Grow up. Be a man. Take the hit and get back in the ring."

This morning Jordan wished his grandpa Jack were sitting next to him, coaching him on staying in the fight, rather than this guy who said he was looking for the nearest bar as soon as they landed. Jordan needed some encouragement after the big hit he had taken last night during his phone conversation with Derek. As Jordan had sat by the pool, he had tried to say all the right things to Derek. But he still hadn't come to terms with what Derek had told him.

The flight was short, and when they landed in Honolulu, the man across the aisle said to Jordan's seatmate, "Did you hear about the storm coming in? I heard on the news last night that they're expecting some forty-foot waves at Waimea."

"Maybe I should head on up there," the eager tourist said. "I'll hang ten with the natives."

Jordan moved past the two men to deplane. He had heard the same weather report in his room last night on the news. All the predictions pointed toward the big waves rolling into the North Shore before the day's end. That meant the Triple Crown surfing competition would be on. It also meant Jordan would catch the cover-worthy photos he had come for. The weather was just what Jordan and Derek had hoped it would be when Mindy booked the flights for all of them to be on the North Shore this week.

Yet Jordan was here alone. And Derek and Mindy wouldn't be coming.

Jordan focused his attention on locating his luggage at baggage claim, picking up his rental car, and inputting into his phone's directional program the address of the rented house at Sunset Beach. Once he was on the road, he thought again about the conversation he had had with Derek the night before at the pool. It had been difficult to hear the latest update.

Mindy was still under careful watch and needed to stay at the hospital another day or two. The good news was that she hadn't miscarried. The difficult part was the way Derek was processing the fact that he wouldn't be surfing in this week's competition. This had been Derek's dream as much as it had been Jordan's, and they both held out for the slight possibility Derek could come in a few days.

The only way that would happen would be if Mindy went home from the hospital today and if her mom could come from Arizona to be with her. Derek could catch an early flight the next morning and hopefully still have a chance at keeping his spot in the lineup. If not, it was all over for him.

Jordan was pretty sure he and Derek both knew it wasn't going to happen. He just didn't want to be the one to say it out loud. What mattered, and what both he and Derek kept repeating, was that Mindy and the baby were okay.

As he drove into the Sunset Beach area he wondered if what he was feeling was some sort of survivor's guilt. Derek would have been stoked to see this sleepy town with all the tall palm trees growing beside houses that looked as if they had been built forty years ago. People were riding beach cruiser bikes down a long, winding walkway. Dogs were crossing the street in between the backed-up cars at the stoplight. Chickens gathered in a park on the right side of the road and pecked at the grass under the shade of a row of trees.

In every direction there were people. Girls in bikinis, guys with sun-bleached hair, each carrying a surfboard under one arm and waving to somebody with the other. Tourists and locals blended in colorful groups as they headed for the beach that lined the left side of the road for miles.

Jordan stopped at the first grocery store he saw and filled his shopping cart with essentials to stock the refrigerator. As he reached for Derek's favorite cereal, Jordan knew it was going to be rough living out his half of the longtime dream without having Derek and Mindy there. Even if Jordan managed to get some epic shots, celebrating their publication would be a one-sided victory.

The beach house was not far from the grocery store and it was nicer than Jordan thought it would be based on the price they were paying. Mindy had set it up through her mom who worked in the travel industry. Jordan parked the car at the back of the two-story blue house and carried his luggage up the stairs to the converted apartment on the top floor. He walked to the front of the large, open room and looked out the wide, front window. The view of the beach and outstretched ocean was amazing. The swells were rising, and the waves were building as a slow drizzle of rain began to come down.

Returning to the car, he brought in the groceries and noticed the wind had picked up. The predicted storm was on its way, and he had made it just in time.

For the next two hours the storm's momentum grew as Jordan sat at the kitchen table and kept his eyes fixed on his laptop. Since no heats were scheduled for that afternoon, he thought it would be a good idea to do as much on the wedding photos as he could before he needed to edit and send off the surfing shots he would be taking over the next few days. The wedding shot he had taken of Kinsey and Paul at sunset with the whale breaching wasn't as great as he had hoped.

One of the best shots, in his opinion, was when Kinsey was rinsing the sand from her feet and the young boy was watching with fascination. The angle was just right to catch the fading light on her dress and the look on the boy's face.

Some of the others weren't as great as he had hoped his new camera would deliver. He began to have some qualms about his zoom lens and wasn't sure it was going to work the way he had hoped to capture the long-distance shots he needed of the surfers.

Any feelings of being a professional faded. He knew the sort of telescopic lens he should have bought, but he hadn't spent the huge amount of money on the right lens when he had the chance. Now he was regretting that decision.

As he clicked through the wedding photos, a picture of Sierra appeared on his screen. He paused and studied her face.

Everything about her appealed to him—her natural beauty; her clear, blue-gray eyes; her soft expression. And that hair! She was beautiful. He wondered when she had been to Brazil, as Paul had mentioned in his greeting to her in the café. What was she doing there? Where did she live now?

Once again, Jordan regretted a decision he had made. Last night he could have taken a risk and tried to connect with her somehow. But he didn't. He let the thin sliver of opportunity slip past him and now it was too late.

Opening another file on his desktop, Jordan pulled up the photo he had taken of Sierra on the beach in the shimmering aqua dress. He looked at the shot for a moment, still not sure how he had captured the angles the way he did. In terms of composition, it was a significant shot. That's why he would keep it as his screen saver. The photo was worth studying, no matter who the subject was. With a few clicks, Jordan set the mermaid photo as his screen saver.

In an attempt to keep his mind occupied with something other than his regrets, Jordan went to the small refrigerator and pulled out a carton of orange juice. He returned to the table with the juice and clicked open the music file on his computer. Music always helped him to stay on task when he had a large project. He selected a playlist he hadn't listened to for a while, and as soon as the first song started playing, Jordan went back to work, editing Kinsey and Paul's wedding photos.

The wind had kicked up, and now the palm tree beside the house was scratching its jagged fronds against the side window. Jordan thought he heard someone calling out. He went to the window at the back of the house and noticed that another car was parked next to his rental car. He knew the lower portion of the house had been rented out to someone else that week, but he hadn't seen anyone come or go from there. He watched the rain pelting the side of the neighbor's house. The palm trees that grew between the two driveways bent in an unnatural way under the wind's commanding force. He had never seen a storm like this in Santa Barbara.

From the other side of the upstairs apartment he could hear the stairs rattling.

Man, it's really starting to shake out there. I hope this old place holds together.

Jordan heard a pounding sound at his side door. At first he thought the wind was doing the knocking, but then he heard a muffled voice calling out what sounded like, "It's me." He went to the door and pulled it open.

There, on his doorstep, stood a surprise that took his breath away.

CHAPTER FIFTEEN

The warm tropical rain hit the windshield of Sierra's rental car at an angle. The weary windshield wipers seemed unable to work fast enough to clear the pane so she could see the road. She realized she should have taken the advice that had been given to her forty minutes earlier when she was handed her car rental agreement and a driving map of Oahu.

"Do you know where you're going?" the rental agent asked her.

"Sunset Beach." Sierra opened the driving map. "Can you show me the best way to get there?"

The woman marked a red line on the map. "If you want some advice, I'd say you would be better off going to the Moana Shopping Center first and treating yourself to a matinee at the movies."

"Why is that?"

"It's going to start raining any minute. You might as well wait it out."

Sierra thought the woman was kidding. This was Hawaii. The weather had been gorgeous on Maui when she left that morning. A little "liquid sunshine," as the shuttle driver had called the rain that morning, wasn't going to slow her down.

Now that she was driving through the storm's onslaught, Sierra was having second thoughts. She remembered how her interisland flight that morning on the small plane had been bumpy, and the pilot had announced something about the winds. Again, she had only the gentle trade winds in mind when she headed for the North Shore.

The movie back in Honolulu was sounding like a very good idea about now. But it was too late. She was committed. And by her calculations, she was more than halfway there.

She thought about the wedding the day before and how Paul had pulled off wearing a kilt as if he were born to wear one. Actually, with his heritage, he was. The ceremony was beautiful, and Kinsey was a gorgeous bride. She clearly loved Paul, and he gave every evidence that he was crazy about her.

At the point in the ceremony when they held hands and repeated their vows, Sierra watched Paul's expression. He wore a look of commitment mixed with heady infatuation. It was a look Sierra had hoped he would one day give to her. But that would never be.

She was okay with that. Better than okay. Sierra felt as if she had closed the door to the room in her thoughts where she had tucked many quiet ponderings about what might happen with that relationship. Now she knew. He was in love and married to Kinsey Mackenzie.

The playful name still made her grin.

Sierra thought about what else she had learned at the wedding. She had discovered she could never expect her sister to be anyone other than who she was, and that meant Sierra and Tawni would never be the sort of sisters who sat on the bed and shared their secrets. Somehow Sierra had hoped that might have changed since their growing-up years. But Tawni was as private as ever. Still, it had been good to see her, and very good to have some time with baby Ben.

Sierra remembered how Ben had cried that morning when she gave him her good-bye hug before heading for the door with her luggage. He toddled across the room to her and raised his arms, begging to be picked up. She bent down to give him one more cuddle and a kiss. Then she slid out the door and hurried to make it to the airport shuttle. All the way to the elevator she could hear his wails.

Sierra grinned when she remembered how Ben had wailed when the bagpipes started at the end of the wedding ceremony. He had been settled comfortably in her lap, almost asleep in the warm lull of the repeating of the vows and the exchanging of the rings.

Then the bagpipe recessional began.

Ben sat up straight, looked Sierra in the face, and wailed louder than the piper, if that were possible. She slid out the side and took Ben to the pond on the other side of the lobby where he could watch the large, orange koi fish swishing in between the floating lily pads.

When Sierra returned to the reception, Ben was eager to go to his dad. That left Sierra free to mingle. The only problem was, there was no one to mingle with. The guests all seemed to know each other already and all of them seemed to be sitting together in pairs. So, she found a seat and watched the photographer. That's when Kinsey's mom had leaned close and provided the interesting data on Jordan.

Not that any of the information was needed. The two of them had shared one extraordinary moment in the ocean watching a whale breech but nothing else.

Sierra didn't want to get hung up on thinking about Jordan now. It was pointless. She didn't want to get hung up on anything while she was in Hawaii. Her place was back in Brazil.

Or at least that's what she told herself. If God had different plans for her, He would make that clear, wouldn't He?

Sierra's thoughts were distracted by the sight of so many open fields on either side of the road as she drove through the rain. Based on pictures she had seen of Waikiki and Honolulu, she had pictured Oahu as a fully populated island. But the area she was driving through made it clear that hundreds of acres were still being used for agriculture. On the right she passed a sign for a coffee plantation and kept on going, heading for a town called Haleaiwa.

The rain continued to come in at an angle, and out the front windshield she could see the palm trees bowing to the powerful wind that was demanding allegiance. She kept going on the two-lane highway and focused her attention on following the directions Mariana had given her to reach their rental house. Sierra poked her way along, she found the street sign with the word KAIWAHINE and turned left onto the short street that led to the beachfront house matching the address on Mariana's papers.

Relieved to be done with the drive, Sierra parked beside another small car and felt a sense of accomplishment to have arrived. She waited in the car a few moments before jumping out. The rain was coming down hard. She didn't have an umbrella, and her hooded sweatshirt was packed in her suitcase in the car's trunk.

When it seemed the rain was letting up just a little, Sierra used her driving map as a covering for her head and dashed to the house's side door. She knocked quickly and called out, "Mariana, are you there? It's me."

No one came to the door. Sierra tried to peer inside through the slatted shades' but she couldn't see anything. She knocked again and called out more loudly over the sound of the wind.

Knocking a third time and calling out without a response, Sierra shook her bare arms and sent a slide of raindrops scattering off her soaked skin. In desperation, she tried the doorknob. It was locked. She ran around to the oceanfront side of the house in hopes of finding another door. She had no success but became even more drenched.

She noticed that the house had an outdoor staircase on the far side that led to the top floor. With nothing to lose at that point, she dashed up the rickety stairs to the second floor as the wind twisted her hair every which way. The rain doused her with another attack as the stairs beneath her feet gave an agonizing moan. She felt them sway and grabbed the splintered handrail for support.

At that moment, Sierra knew that a tropical storm wasn't something to be taken lightly. She wished she had stayed back in Honolulu by the airport until this severe winter system had moved through.

Her drenched hair was plastered against the right side of her face. Her shorts and top were dripping wet. The soaked driving map she had used as her only covering was ripped from her hands and carried off by the frenzied wind.

The door opened, and Sierra let out a gasp. She was so buffeted by the ferocious wind that she stumbled back against the unsteady railing.

The handsome face that greeted her reflected equal astonishment as her name rolled off his lips. "Sierra?"

She staggered, but the quick, open arms of the upstairs occupant reached out to take her as if she already belonged here with him.

CHAPTER SIXTEEN

The name that had been on Jordan's mind for the past hour sprang from his lips as he opened the door. "Sierra?"

She was soaking wet and looked just as startled as he was. Sierra toppled backward against the railing, and Jordan lunged forward to grab her. His arms were around her in an instant. He could feel how rain-soaked she was.

"Are you okay?" His mouth was against the side of her drenched hair.

She pulled back and stared at him as if she couldn't speak.

"Come in." Jordan kicked the door back open with his foot while still keeping a protective arm around her shoulder. "Come on. It's treacherous out here." He closed the door, locked it, and looked at her again to make sure he hadn't dreamed this up.

Gathering his wits as quickly as he could, he pulled his arm back. "Let me find you a towel. Wait there. Don't go anywhere." He laughed a nervous laugh on his way to the hall closet and added, "Not that you would want to go back out there. They're saying this is going to be quite a storm."

"So I heard." Sierra's voice seemed to tremble.

Jordan pulled a clean towel from the closet and hurried back to hand it to her. She put the towel to her face, and he realized he had given her a hand towel. "Wait, I'll get you a bath towel."

"This is fine," she said.

He returned with a larger towel anyway and felt his heart still racing. "What else can I get for you? Do you want some dry clothes? A shirt or something?"

Sierra looked down and seemed too befuddled to know how to reply. She patted down her bare legs with the towel and looked up at him. "How did you know my name?"

"Your name?"

"You said my name when you opened the door."

"Paul told me who you were."

Her expression softened. She pulled her wild tangle of hair over her shoulder and patted it dry with the towel.

"I'm Jordan, by the way. Jordan Bryce," He extended his hand instinctively, as if just remembering all the manners his mama had taught him.

"Sierra Jensen. Nice to meet you." She slipped her small hand into his and smiled cordially.

The feel of her hand in his gave him a shiver up the back of his neck. She pulled her hand back too soon in Jordan's estimation and looked down at the tile floor where they were standing.

"Do you need another towel? I'll find you another one." He hurried back to the hall closet and pulled out a bright orange and yellow beach towel, feeling like an idiot for not grabbing this one first. She had progressed from a hand towel to a bath towel and now a beach towel when this was what she needed all along.

"So what are you doing here?" Jordan blurted out.

Sierra stood on the bath towel and wrapped the beach towel around her shoulders. With a tilt of her head she said, "I was going to ask you the same thing."

"I'm staying here. I'm on assignment. For a surfing magazine. And you?"

Sierra brushed her hair back from her face. "I'm staying downstairs with a friend of mine. I mean, I think this is the place she rented. The address matches the information she gave me. I just got here, but she's not downstairs. At least she didn't open the door when I knocked."

"I haven't heard anyone down there since I arrived a few hours ago. I didn't see any cars either. Do you want to wait here until she comes back?"

Sierra looked out the wide front window at the furious storm now raging at full force.

"I think maybe I better. I checked the door downstairs, and it was locked. I guess I could get some dry clothes from the car and wait up here until she comes back."

"Let me get your suitcase for you. Is the car locked?" Jordan still couldn't believe this was happening.

"You'll get drenched, too. It's okay. I can get it,"

"No, you're almost dried off now. Let me get it for you. I have to make sure the windows are rolled up on my car anyhow." He was pretty sure his windows were closed, but it was the best excuse that came to him at the moment.

She hesitated before agreeing and handing over the car keys from the pocket in her shorts. "Thanks. I appreciate it."

"No problem." Jordan reached for his keys on the kitchen counter. "I'll be right back. Make yourself at home."

He headed toward the door, and just before he opened it, he turned to look over his shoulder to make sure she was really there. She was.

Jordan paused long enough to give her a grin.

She grinned back.

"This is crazy," he said. "The storm, I mean."

"Yeah. It's wild."

Bustling down the stairs, Jordan barely felt the onslaught of the driving rain. All he could think about was that she was there on Oahu, standing in his apartment.

Okay, God, I get it. I'm supposed to pay attention to this one. So, what happens next?

~

I can't believe this is happening.

Sierra stood with a beach towel around her shoulders and her feet on a bath towel in the middle of Jordan's apartment. She was still dripping and shivering slightly, waiting for him to return with her suitcase. Her heart pounded, and her hands were quivering.

This is crazy! It's too much of a coincidence. Somebody had to have set this up.

Sierra thought about how Katie, one of her friends from Rancho Corona, would have called this a "God thing."

Just then she noticed the song that was playing on the laptop across the room was a favorite of hers and one she hadn't heard since leaving the US. Sierra glanced at the laptop and then looked again. She went closer for a better look.

The picture on Jordan's laptop screensaver was of her.

Why does he have a picture of me on his laptop?

Although, she reasoned that it wasn't exactly of her. It was of the beach, the outrigger canoe, and the water. It just happened that the back of her head was in the shot. The picture was beautiful, with the evening light coming through her long hair, giving it an airiness that created an unreal celestial glow.

She chose to believe that Jordan didn't know she was the woman in the photo but that he had pulled it up as a favorite for the lighting and composition.

Another gust of wind shook the windows. She had never seen a storm like this before. The sky had grown dark from the invading clouds, and the view of the ocean out the window displayed waves bolting to shore at a powerful pace. Sierra couldn't imagine anyone attempting to surf those screamers, and from where she was standing, she couldn't see anyone trying.

She wondered if Jordan was having trouble getting into her car. He had been gone awhile. It seemed like enough time to grab her suitcase and return.

Sierra heard the sound of feet tromping up the stairs on the side of the house and could tell by the stomping sounds that he was almost to the small landing at the top. She left the beach towel on the floor and went to open the door for him. As soon as she did, a huge gust of wind blew from behind the house and the rickety wooden steps cracked loudly.

Jordan had just reached the top step and put Sierra's suitcase on the landing when a second crunch sounded.

"Look out!" Sierra cried.

The wooden planks broke loose just four steps below where Jordan was standing.

"Go inside!" he yelled at her as he lurched up onto the landing.

Instead of retreating, Sierra instinctively reached for him and circled her arms around his middle. He wrapped his arms around her in response, and for a moment they clung to each other in the rain, watching the stairs crash to the cement walkway below.

"Quick! Get inside." Jordan pushed Sierra into the apartment and followed right behind her with her suitcase. He slammed the door and stood in front of her, dripping wet.

For a few seconds neither of them spoke. They stared at each other, blinking.

"Are you okay?" Jordan wiped back the rain from his face with the wet palm of his hand.

"Yes, I'm fine. Here, this towel is fairly dry." She handed him the beach towel. "Are you all right?"

"Yeah." He blinked. "Wow."

"I know. Wow," Sierra repeated.

"I better call the rental agency and see if they can get somebody over here to fix that."

"They'll probably tell you to wait until after the storm has passed."

"Right, but did you see how much of the stairs broke off? We can't get up or down until that's fixed."

They stared at each other again as the reality set in. They were trapped together and had to wait out the storm.

"Do you have any more towels?" she asked, not knowing what else to say.

A crooked smile rose on Jordan's face. "I think we're down to two washcloths and a pineapple-shaped pot holder."

Sierra loved his quirky comment. "I'll go with what we have then. Mind if I use your bathroom?"

"Go ahead. It's through the bedroom."

He followed her, carrying her suitcase inside the small bathroom and ducking out quickly to give her privacy.

Leaning against the back of the closed bathroom door, Sierra shut her eyes. Her heart was beating in a steady rhythm. Outside the storm was raging. Inside this small space and inside her heart, she felt an unusual sense of calm, as if she were in a hurricane's eye.

And Jordan Bryce was in that place with her.

CHAPTER SEVENTEEN

Grabbing a dry T-shirt and pair of shorts, Jordan took them into the kitchen to change while Sierra was in the bathroom.

I can't believe she just showed up on my doorstep! Stuff like this doesn't happen.

Jordan went on a hunt for his cell phone so he could call the property management company. It took him a few seconds to scout around and find that he had left it on the table by his laptop. He scrolled through his address book, found the number, and placed the call.

Then he looked at his laptop and saw the screen saver.

Oh no. I hope she didn't see that picture. What would she think?

While the call was ringing through to the property management company, he quickly changed the screen saver back to the previous one, which was the prize photo he had taken of Derek last month.

A recorded message played, stating their hours on the mainland and that, if callers reached their number after-hours, they should call 911 for an emergency or leave a message.

Jordan left a message but had no hope that anyone would listen to it or call him back that day.

As soon as he hung up, he looked online for any sort of construction or handyman service he could find on the North Shore. Jordan was into his third unproductive call when he heard the bedroom door open. He turned to see Sierra walking toward him. Her hair was down, and her curls formed a dozen blond ringlets that fell over her shoulders. She was wearing a pair of jean shorts and a navy-blue hooded sweatshirt with the words RANCHO CORONA UNIVERSITY on the front.

Jordan put down his phone and tried to remember where he had seen someone else dressed in a Rancho Corona sweatshirt.

"At the airport," Jordan said partly to himself and partly to Sierra. "It was you."

She gave him a confused look.

"Sorry." Jordan ran his hand over the top of his hair, shaking out the last of the rain. "I thought I saw you at the airport"

"Which airport?" Sierra pulled out a chair beside him to sit down.

Jordan caught a whiff of coconut-scented lotion. She was so alluring to him in her casual simplicity. He wanted to lean over and kiss her right then and there.

Dragging his thoughts back to reality, Jordan said, "I saw someone in Los Angeles at the airport the other day. She had on the same sweatshirt and was wearing large sunglasses."

"That was probably me. I was with my friend Mariana. She's the one I'm meeting here."

"By any chance was your friend speaking a foreign language? She was on her phone and I noticed. Her voice was kind of loud."

"Yes, that's Mariana. She was speaking Portuguese. She's from Brazil."

Jordan realized how little he knew about Brazil. "Is Portuguese the national language?"

"Yes."

"Interesting. I would have guessed Spanish."

"No. I wish it were, I know a little bit of Spanish from high school. I've live in Brazil for over four years, and I still can't speak Portuguese."

"Four years?" Jordan was even more intrigued with Sierra. "What have you been doing there?"

"I've been working with a Christian mission organization."

"Really? I'm a Christian, too." Jordan wasn't sure why he felt he needed to make that clear. He quickly asked, "What exactly have you been doing in Brazil?"

Sierra looked down. "I've done a variety of things, helping out wherever they need me. At the moment I'm in a transition."

"That's never fun." Again, he wasn't sure why he said that.

She looked up and added, "I'm supposed to be here on vacation, relaxing and thinking so I can figure out what's next."

Jordan nodded, trying to take in what she was saying and appear interested instead of popping off with comments to everything she said.

"What about you?" Sierra asked. "Have you been a photographer for a long time?"

Jordan still couldn't believe he was marooned in the middle of a tropical storm with this amazing woman.

"Ah, well, I've been pursuing photography as a profession since I graduated from college, but this is actually my first paying assignment."

"Nice."

"Yeah. It's my big break." He looked out the window at the driving rain.

"Not exactly how you expected it would be," Sierra said.

"No. It's not. It's . . . " Jordan made a quick decision to not tell her about Derek and the struggle he felt about being here without him.

Changing the subject, he said, "I went to Westmont College,

by the way, so I guess that makes us rivals." He knew that anyone who had gone to Rancho would recognize the name of another Christian college in California. He also thought it might help her to feel a little more at ease to be able to talk about something they had in common.

Sierra's expression brightened. "You did? I have friends who went there."

She named a few people. Jordan didn't know them. She narrowed her eyebrows and lowered her voice, "I have to ask you something."

"Sure."

"Does any of this seem bizarre to you?"

"What do you mean bizarre? Don't you hang out in rickety apartments in the middle of hurricanes with people you've never met? And with broken staircases? I mean, what's bizarre about any of that?" Jordan hoped he was coming off sounding clever.

Sierra laughed, as he hoped she would.

"Well, there is that. But I mean, here we are with all these overlapping pieces in our lives. We were both at the wedding, and now we're renting apartments at the same house. I've never been in a situation like this."

"Neither have I."

"Doesn't it feel like too many coincidences?"

Before Jordan could stop himself, he popped out the thought that came to mind. "Not if God is trying to tell us something."

Her eyebrows rose and their gazes met. Jordan felt an unexpected confirming sense of certainty. He couldn't remember feeling this sort of calm assurance with any woman. Something inside him rumbled a defining thought as he looked at her. It was as if heart was saying, *it's you.*

A gust of wind rattled the windows on the back side of the house, and both of them turned that direction, even though they couldn't see the windows that were being affected. The rattling broke the intense moment between them and prompted Jordan to remember the project before him of finding someone who could fix the stairway.

"By the way, I called the property management company," he said, lifting his cell phone. "But they only have a recording; so I'm trying to hunt down someone local who can help us out."

"Have you had any success?"

"Not yet. I have a few more numbers to try."

"Is there anything I can do?" Sierra asked.

"I don't think so." Jordan felt the awkwardness returning like he had felt when he was fumbling with all the towels just after Sierra showed up. He made another attempt at being hospitable. "Are you hungry? Would you like something to eat?"

She seemed to think for a moment before she said, "Yes. I am, now that you bring it up. How about you? Are you hungry? I could make something for both of us."

"Sure, I could eat something too." At the moment Jordan wasn't sure if he was hungry. Giving her something to do while he made the calls seemed like a good idea. "There's a few groceries in the kitchen. Not a lot. Are you sure you don't mind?"

"No. I don't mind a bit. I like having something to do." She got up and added, "Any food allergies I should know about? Do you like the crusts cut off your bread?"

Jordan liked her playfulness. "No, I'm not particular. Except for corned beef and cabbage. I can't eat that. I can't even stand the smell of it. My grandmother used to make it, and when I'd go over to their house and she had it on the stove. . ."

"Pretty bad, huh?"

"Yeah, pretty bad."

"I'm guessing you didn't buy corned beef and cabbage when you went to the grocery store." Sierra was grinning at him.

"No. I didn't."

"That's good."

In an attempt to explain why he'd tossed out the corned beef comment, Jordan said, "Yeah, corned beef is my grandfather's favorite so it seemed to be on the menu every time we went there for his birthday or any other holiday."

"Was your grandfather Irish by any chance?" Sierra washed her hands in the sink and looked around.

"Yes, he is. Are you looking for a towel?"

"Hard to believe that I need another towel, isn't it?"

Jordan jumped up and opened the cupboard underneath the sink. "I got some paper towels. Here. I don't know why I put them away instead of leaving them out"

Sierra opened the wrapper and pulled off a towel. Jordan opened the refrigerator, giving a verbal summary of the inventory. "Sorry that I don't have a lot to choose from. If you want, I could make us some eggs. I don't make very good omelets, but I'm not bad at scrambled with a little cheese on top. I think I bought cheese."

"I can do this if you'd like to get back to the phone calls. I don't mind at all. Honest."

"Right. Okay. I'll leave you to figure out what to make and I'll see if I can get somebody over here." He returned to the table and positioned himself so that he could nonchalantly watch Sierra in the kitchen as he made his calls. She had an elemental sort of gracefulness to her movements. Just as it had been yesterday at the wedding, he couldn't take his eyes off her.

When he had been in Costa Rica, he remembered watching the local cook as she worked in their rudimentary, camp-style kitchen. She worked with the same uncomplicated motions, as if she didn't require a lot of sophisticated cookware or ingredients to prepare a meal.

Jordan remembered how he had taken pictures of the woman in Costa Rica as she stirred sauce in a blackened pot and patted tortillas with her hands. The lighting wasn't good, and none of the shots had turned out well. He kept them because they reminded him of the cook's contentment in the kitchen as she worked. He liked the photos because the cook, in her simplicity, reminded him of his mother.

He saw that same effortlessness in motion as he clandestinely watched Sierra.

The ringing he had been listening to on his cell phone while lost in his thoughts was interrupted by a voice on the other end. "Hello?"

Jordan sat up and looked at the computer screen to remember whom he had called. "Hello. Is this Island Fix It Man?"

"Yeah."

"I'm at Sunset Beach in a rental, and we just lost the stairway that leads up to the apartment where I'm staying. I'm wondering if you're able to come fix the stairs."

"Whoa! You lost the whole stairs?"

"Yes. All but the top three or four steps, and the landing by the door still is attached. We're trapped upstairs here. There's no other way to get in or out"

"Auwee! You got big problems, brah."

"Yes. Exactly. Can you help me out?"

"Not today. Not in this storm. You gotta' wait it out. Give me your address. I'll come in da morning."

Jordan gave him the address and asked, "What time do you think you can be here?"

"In the morning." Then he hung up.

"Did you find someone?" Sierra asked.

"I think so. He was the last one on the list, but at least he answered."

"Sounds promising."

"There's one problem, though."

Sierra turned her full attention to Jordan.

He tried to deliver the news casually. "He said he wouldn't

come during the storm. We need to wait it out. But he can be here tomorrow morning."

Jordan watched Sierra carefully. For a moment she didn't move. Then she picked up the spatula and turned back to the stove to flip what looked like French toast. "These are almost ready. Would you like to eat at the table or here at the counter?"

Jordan decided that her response was a good sign. She was flexible in the midst of an inconvenient situation. She didn't freak out. And the French toast smelled amazing.

If his brain hadn't yet issued the obvious command, his heart was now repeating it loudly so that he could feel a ringing in his ears.

Whatever you do, don't let this one get away.

CHAPTER EIGHTEEN

Sierra drizzled the thick coconut syrup over the sliced bananas on top of her French toast. She adjusted her position on the counter stool where she sat only a few inches away from Jordan. Everything about this moment felt surreal, and yet at the same time it felt natural, as if she had cooked lots of spontaneous meals in this tiny kitchen.

The familiarity could have something to do with the compact space, which was similar to the places she had lived in during the last few years. It wasn't unusual for her to meet new people and share meals with them. But the string of people she met in Brazil were rarely Americans, were hardly ever good-looking guys to whom she was attracted, and never once did she calmly eat beside a stranger in the middle of a tropical storm while unable to exit the building.

"Wow, this is good. Where did you find the coconut syrup?" Jordan asked.

"In the refrigerator next to the ketchup and mayonnaise."

"It must have been there from the last tenant."

"That was convenient." Sierra took another bite. "This did turn out pretty good."

"You sound surprised."

"I haven't made French toast in a long time."

"I can't say that I've ever made French toast, so thanks for getting creative with the limited resources."

Sierra knew Jordan was looking at her, but she kept her attention on her breakfast, cutting small pieces of the toast and chewing them slowly. She had been aware of his long gazes from the moment he had opened the door to her. As crazy as the situation was, she still felt calm.

Sipping her orange juice, Sierra thought about how Jordan had said these circumstances weren't such a coincidence if God was trying to tell them something. Could that be true? What exactly was God trying to say?

"So, you went to Rancho Corona," Jordan broke into her thoughts. "And you've been in Brazil for four years. I'd like to hear more about what you've been doing there?"

For some reason the answer to this question embarrassed Sierra. She hadn't done much of anything measurable, in her estimation. Her last few years had been filled with a lot of this and that and serving wherever she could, but she hadn't accomplished anything noteworthy.

Taking her time to chew the French toast, Sierra considered how to frame her answer. "I worked in a couple of different cities. The headquarters for the ministry are in Rio de Janiero so that's where I spent most of my time."

Sierra tried to describe some of her various experiences to Jordan. He seemed interested in what she had to say, so she kept talking, telling him about the different churches she had been connected with, the girls group at the school, the women who were now making beaded jewelry and the administrative office position she held a little more than a year ago.

"Not exactly a one-page résumé," she joked.

"It sounds like you're an entrepreneur."

Sierra gave Jordan a skeptical gaze. "Is that what I am? I've been trying to figure that out."

"From what you said, you enjoy helping to start new projects and doing what it takes to keep them going."

"I guess you're right. I don't think I've ever broken it down like that before. I was really bummed when one program I was helping to develop at a school was discontinued. It had so much potential to expand, and it was providing lots for the teen girls. I'm still sad that it was cancelled."

"It sounds like you're a motivator too."

Sierra thought about that description as well. "I do like to encourage people and motivate them to find ways to help themselves."

She tried to imagine how those strengths would be used if she accepted the new "Maria von Trapp" position as a teacher.

Sierra stood and automatically headed toward the sink to rinse off her plate. At the apartment where she lived they had a continual problem with tropical bugs and tiny ants. Everyone washed all dishes right after they were used and took out the trash every evening.

"Why don't you let me clean up," Jordan said, getting up. "You cooked. I'll clean."

"I don't mind. There's another piece of toast here. Would you like it?"

"Do you want to split it?"

"No thanks. It's all yours."

Sierra watched as he harpooned the piece of cooled French toast and put it on his plate.

"Do you want it warmed up?" She asked.

"No, this is fine." Jordan poured some syrup over the top and broke off a corner piece with his fork. Leaning against the counter he said, "So you're here in Hawaii to take it easy and make some decisions about what's next. Is that what you said?"

Sierra nodded. She felt a bubble of tears rise to her throat.

Her feelings rose right to the surface every time she thought about returning to Brazil. She loved living there and knew that the new position as a teacher was where she was needed. It was just harder than she thought it would be to visit the US and glimpse what life would be like if she stayed there.

She really did not want to talk about her life anymore. Her stomach still felt a little fluttery being around Jordan. She hoped it would make her feel less jittery if she didn't feel like her life was up for evaluation right now.

"What about you?" Sierra asked. "You said you're here on assignment. How did you get this job?"

Jordan finished the last bite and came over to the sink next to Sierra where he rinsed his plate. "Are you sure you want to hear the whole story?"

"Sure." Sierra offered a small grin. "I'm not going anywhere."

Jordan grinned back at her. "Apparently not."

He put away the syrup as the wind continued to roar, rattling the windows and howling through the crack under the front door. Heading over to the couch by the front window, Jordan sat down as he talked.

Sierra wasn't sure if she should sit next to him or sit in the chair on the side. The couch looked much more comfortable than the wicker chair so she sat on the other end of the couch and listened to his story about the photo he had taken of his friend Derek and how it was slotted for the February issue of *Surf Days Magazine*.

"Would you like to see the picture? It's right here." He stood and brought his laptop to her.

Sierra noticed that the photo of her on the beach was no longer the screen saver. It had been changed to a picture of his friend, and the shot was amazing.

"Wow, the water looks translucent, and your friend is right at the peak of the wave. This is the picture that's going to be on the cover?" Sierra asked.

"Yes. Hopefully. I mean, it's scheduled, and they paid for it, but things can change. Things change a lot, don't they?"

"Yes, they do." At first Sierra took the comment to mean changes in the variety of ways she had served the ministry in Brazil. But then she looked at Jordan and sensed that something was weighing on him when he made the comment. Perhaps he was in the midst of changes as well.

A strong gust of wind caused the palm tree at the side of the house to bend so that the soaked palm fronds slapped against the window.

"It's still howling out there," Sierra said.

Jordan put the laptop on the coffee table and stretched his arm across the back of the couch as they watched the effects of the wind and rain.

"I'm so glad this storm didn't arrive yesterday," Sierra said. "Can you imagine if it had been like this at Paul and Kinsey's wedding?"

"I hadn't thought of that. It was perfect weather for them, wasn't it?" Jordan turned toward Sierra. "I have to show you a photo I caught of them at sunset."

He opened a file on his laptop and clicked through to the picture of the whale breaching in the background as Paul and Kinsey kissed on the sand.

"That's amazing!" Sierra leaned closer to take a better look. "I can't believe you caught the picture at just the right moment. They are going to love this. That could be another cover shot for a magazine."

"It's not crisp enough for that. But as a wedding photo, it's got to be one of their best."

"I wonder if it's the same whale we saw when we were swimming yesterday morning."

"Could be. Here's another shot I really liked." He flipped to the one of Kinsey at the outdoor shower with the curious boy.

"Oh, that's perfect. Jordan, these are so good. Would you

mind showing me the rest of the photos? You don't have a privacy agreement or something, do you?"

"No. Of course I can show you. Are you sure you want to see all of them? There's more than you might imagine."

Sierra grinned. "Again, I'm not going anywhere."

Jordan grinned back. "Then we might as well start at the beginning with the rehearsal dinner."

"Good. I missed that."

"I know." Jordan looked at her out of the corner of his eye as if he hadn't meant to say that.

Sierra didn't reply. She felt her heart beat a little faster. Maybe he had noticed her earlier and had taken the photo of her on the beach on purpose. She wasn't sure what to think about that.

Jordan moved closer on the couch so they could both look at the laptop screen more easily. Sierra leaned in as he pulled up the file of pictures he had taken of the ocean and the landscape when he first arrived at the hotel.

She watched his hands as he tapped the keyboard, and she remembered how it felt when they shook hands earlier. Jordan's hands were strong, his handshake decisive. Her thoughts easily flitted to how it had felt when he had grabbed her on the landing and pulled her in out of the storm. At the moment she was too startled to think about what was happening, but now that she'd had time to reflect, the memory of the unexpected sensation of Jordan's arms wrapped around her warmed her from the inside. She felt herself blushing as she remembered the way he had sheltered her and pulled her in from the landing.

In barely a minute Sierra composed an entirely new scenario in her thoughts of what the next season of her life could be. She could move to Santa Barbara and find a job at a restaurant. Her parents had a friend who owned an Italian restaurant there. Surely he would be willing to hire her. She could be near Jordan, and they could take their time getting to know each other to see if there really was something that God was trying to tell them, as Jordan had said.

As quickly as that lovely dream floated into her thoughts, Sierra blew it away. She barely knew Jordan. She had a position waiting for her in Brazil. Santa Barbara wasn't where she belonged. She needed to pull her priorities back in line.

"That's pretty," Sierra said, commenting on a nice shot of the beach with the white lounge chairs lined up and the blue beach umbrellas providing bright polka dots of shade.

Jordan adjusted his position so that the laptop was balanced on his crossed leg. When he moved, their shoulders touched. Sierra felt herself warm again at his closeness. She sat still, unaware of what photo was showing on the laptop at the moment. She knew that what happened next could change oh so much. She waited to see what he would do.

Jordan didn't move away.

And neither did Sierra.

CHAPTER NINETEEN

The closeness of Sierra—her voice, the fragrance of her skin, her perceptive comments about his photos—had a mesmerizing effect on Jordan. When he had leaned in while he showed her the photos from the wedding, she had responded just right. She stayed close, as if she were at ease with him. Jordan felt at ease with her too.

When he clicked on a photo that was composed well, she commented with an insightful and artistic eye. She praised his work, but she didn't gush. He liked that too. Several of her comments were helpful on which photos she thought Kinsey would like the most. Sierra pointed out two shots that Jordan would have disregarded. She said she liked them because of the expression on Paul's face, and that would be more important to Kinsey than a slightly blurry background.

When Sierra made a comment defending Paul's Scottish heritage, Jordan ventured to ask how well she knew the groom. Jordan still hadn't sorted out what it had meant when he watched the two of them meet with such a mixture of hesitancy and familiarity at the hotel espresso bar.

"I take it you know a lot about Paul, or at least you've known him a long time."

Sierra paused before answering with a single word. "Yes."

"I didn't mean for that to come across as invasive."

"No, it's fine. It's an odd relationship." Sierra pulled her long hair over her shoulder and held it in a bunch with both hands before she lowered her voice and said, "I guess you could say I had a thing for Paul in high school."

"A thing?" Jordan paused the slide show and put the laptop on the coffee table. He wanted to convey to Sierra that she had his attention. "Did the two of you date during the same time his brother was going out with your sister?"

"No, it wasn't like that I met Paul at the London Heathrow Airport. He borrowed some money from me. We ended up sitting beside each other on the flight back to Portland. He was going through a lot at the time. He had just been to his grandfather's funeral. We started to write letters to each other. No e-mails. Handwritten letters." Sierra turned away. "I don't know why I'm telling you this."

Jordan was even more intrigued. He picked up on the Portland comment, thinking it would give her an out if she didn't want to say anything else about Paul. "So you lived in Portland?"

"Yes. My family moved there from a small town in Northern California. We moved into a big, old Victorian house where my grandmother lived. That's another whole story."

It was quiet for a moment. Jordan took a chance and opened up the subject of Paul in case Sierra had anything else she wanted to say.

"So, you and Paul got to know each other through your letters, then."

Sierra nodded. "And then his brother met my sister and they got married and now Paul is happily married and it's all good."

Jordan read in her expression that she was telling the truth.

He could understand the slight awkwardness when he observed their encounter at the hotel.

Jordan got up. He headed for the refrigerator. "Would you like something to drink? More orange juice?"

Sierra joined him in the kitchen. "I think I'll make some hot tea. I saw some in one of these cupboards." She reached behind Jordan and pulled out an opened box of mango mint tropical tea.

She lifted the lid, and as Jordan watched, a huge cockroach scampered out of the box and got as far as Sierra's wrist before she shook it off onto the floor and let out a muffled squeal.

Jordan quickly reached for the frying pan that was drying on the counter and managed to smash the two-inch-long intruder.

He looked at Sierra, amazed that he had been fast enough to kill it.

She gave a shiver and scrunched up her nose. "That was impressive."

"You mean the size of the cockroach?"

"No, your speedy reaction."

"I was impressed that you didn't freak out."

"I've seen worse."

"In Brazil?"

Sierra nodded. "Comes with the tropics. Love the weather. Not quite as crazy about the bugs."

Jordan cleaned up the flattened pest with a paper towel. Sierra handed him the box of tea. "Here. This can be his final resting place." Jordan carted off the box and bug to the trash while Sierra washed the bottom of the frying pan.

"So, what do you think?" Jordan asked. "Orange juice?"

"Sounds great."

The wind rattled the window in the bedroom, and Sierra said, "I hope Mariana is all right. She said she was going to spend time with friends who were staying at a place called

Turtle Bay. I hope she's there and not stuck somewhere on the road."

"Why don't you call her?"

"I don't have a cell phone."

Jordan wasn't sure he heard her correctly. "Is it still in the car?"

"No. I don't own a cell phone."

Jordan tried to mask his surprise. He didn't know anyone who didn't own a cell phone.

"When I said earlier that my lifestyle in Brazil was pretty minimalistic, well, that means no extra money for a cell phone."

"You can use mine."

It took the two of them several minutes to figure out get the number entered correctly so it would go through. When it rang, Jordan handed the phone to Sierra. He could tell by the way she was talking that she was leaving a message.

"Not answering, huh?"

"No. But if anyone can fend for herself, it's Mariana." Sierra returned to the couch and tucked her feet underneath her as she sipped the orange juice.

"Do you want anything else to eat?"

"No thanks."

Jordan opened the refrigerator, not sure what he was looking for and not even sure he was hungry.

"I take it the French toast didn't fill you up."

"No. I mean, yes. It did fill me up. It was good, too, by the way. I'm just checking to see what's in here."

"You sound like my brothers."

Closing the refrigerator and ignoring his urge to nervously nibble on something, Jordan returned to the couch. "How many brothers do you have?"

Sierra pulled back her hair from over her shoulders and wrapped it in a circle at the base of her neck. "Four. Two older, two younger. I only have one sister, Tawni. She and I are in the middle. What about you? Any brothers or sisters?"

"Two brothers. I'm in the middle."

"I love being in the middle, don't you?"

"For a long time I wished I was the oldest, but I think you're right. Being in the middle is good."

"What about your parents?" Sierra asked. "Are they still together?"

For the next hour and a half they talked nonstop on a variety of topics. Twice Sierra told him how fantastic it was to talk to someone in English and to relate immediately on subjects that would only mean something to someone who grew up in the US. They went through preferences on music and movies and even landed on their favorite chapters in the Bible. This wasn't like any conversation Jordan had experienced with any other girl. Ever.

Earlier, when Sierra was making the French toast, she had taken off her hooded sweatshirt. She had on a white, short-sleeved shirt with dark blue embroidery around the top. Jordan liked the way it looked on her. More than that, he liked her look. She reminded him of a beachy sort of flower child. He had seen old photos of his mom when she wore the same sort of gauzy shirts with cutoff blue jeans, and secretly he had thought he had the coolest mom.

Sierra was asking Jordan about his new camera when his cell phone rang. "Could be your friend," he said, looking at the screen. "Oh. No, actually it's my friend. I need to take this."

Sierra headed for the kitchen while Jordan answered the phone. "Hey, Derek. How are you guys doing?"

"A lot better. I got your message earlier this morning. Thanks for checking in."

"Of course. Are you guys still at the hospital?"

"No, we're home now. Mindy's on complete bed rest for a

week. Then she'll go back to the doctor, and we'll see how it's going."

"So, that's good news, right? The baby is doing all right?"

"For now, yes. That's what it looks like."

"Glad to hear that." Jordan had been watching Sierra out of the corner of his eye. She was pulling out a box of microwave popcorn, apparently in response to his unproductive search for something else to eat. "What about you? What's the plan for the competition?"

"We're going to get through tonight here at home and see how everything goes before making a final decision in the morning. I can still be there by tomorrow afternoon, so we'll see."

"All right. Sounds good. I can call you in the morning. Or you can call me."

"I'll call you. Were you able to get some good shots today?"

"No. We're in the middle of a huge storm. It's not like anything I've ever seen before. We lost the stairs to the apartment."

"What do you mean you lost them?"

"They broke off. We're stuck here until the repair guy can come in the morning."

"That's crazy!"

"I know."

"Wait. You said 'we're' stuck. Who's with you?"

Jordan paused. He realized that while it seemed natural to have Sierra with him, it was going to be hard to explain to Derek.

"Jordo? You still there?"

"Yeah. I'm here."

"Who's there with you?"

Jordan quickly said, "A friend."

There was a pause, and then Derek said, "Dude, you have a girl there with you, don't you?"

"Yeah. Definitely." Jordan was trying to play it cool.

"Seriously?"

"Yeah. You know how I am." This was way too much fun, just giving Derek clipped answers and making him guess.

Jordon could hear Derek saying, "Mindy, he's got a girl at his place. No, at Sunset Beach. Of course I'm sure. Hey, Mindy wants to know what her name is."

Jordan tilted the phone down away from his mouth and cleverly said, "Hey, Sierra, I think you'll find a big bowl for the popcorn in the cupboard next to the oven."

"Oh, okay. Thanks," she replied.

"Dude, I heard her! I heard a female voice coming from your apartment. Jordo! This is epic. You're not just playing with us, are you?"

"No, absolutely not."

"Okay, then you have to call us as soon as she leaves."

"Right. Like I said, I'll call you in the morning." Jordan loved ending the call with the sound of his friend railing in the background and Mindy's voice saying, "What? What happened?"

As soon as Jordan hung up, Sierra pushed the button on the microwave. She turned toward him, seemingly oblivious to the conversation he had just had about her. "Do you want something to drink?" she asked.

Just then the microwave went out with a *phist* sound, and all the lights went out. The only light in the apartment was an emergency style nightlight plugged into the wall by the front door and the screens on Jordan's cell phone and laptop.

"I hope I didn't just do that," Sierra said.

Jordan turned on a flashlight app on his cell phone and headed for the window in the bedroom. "I don't think it was the microwave. I think all the power went." He looked out the window. "The neighbor's house has gone dark as well."

"I found a flashlight," Sierra called from the kitchen. "And some matches and candles."

Jordan joined her in the kitchen. Together they lit three candles and placed one on the kitchen counter and the other two on the small coffee table in front of the couch. Sitting back down on opposite ends of the couch, they listened to the howling wind as it roused the palm tree and scraped its tousled fronds against the window.

Outside night had fallen. All was dark.

CHAPTER TWENTY

Sierra folded her arms across her stomach at her end of the couch and tried to decide if she was more touched by the soft beauty of the candlelight or more freaked out by the moaning wind and the palm fronds scratching at the wall, as if they wanted to get in.

Just then Jordan's cell phone rang, causing both of them to jump. He reached for it and held the phone close to the candlelight to see the screen.

"Looks like it's your friend this time. I don't recognize the number."

He handed Sierra the phone. As soon as she answered, Mariana let out a scramble of words in Portuguese that were so loud Sierra held the phone away from her ear.

"Mariana, where are you?"

"I'm at the apartment where Tianna is staying. Do you remember her?"

Sierra wasn't sure if she remembered Tianna. At the moment, it didn't matter.

"I left you a note, Sierra. You were supposed to come over

here. Didn't you see my note? It was on the door. I taped it to the door."

"The wind must have blown it off, Mariana. I didn't see any note when I arrived this afternoon."

"Well, then where are you? Were you able to get inside the house?"

"No. Well, sort of. I'm upstairs."

"But we didn't rent the upstairs. We only rented the downstairs."

"I know. But I'm here, and it's fine, and I'll explain everything later. Are you coming back to the house now?"

"I don't know. This storm has been so bad. I was thinking of staying here. I don't like to drive in bad weather. Did your electricity go out?"

"Yes. Did yours?"

"Yes. Spooky, isn't it?"

Sierra looked at the flickering candles on the coffee table and the way they gave the room a romantic, cozy glow. She didn't think the power outage was spooky at all. But she couldn't confess that to Mariana.

"Are you safe where you are?" Sierra asked.

"Yes, of course. What about you? It's boring being in that house by yourself, isn't it?"

Sierra wanted to say that she wouldn't know about that, but again she didn't want Mariana to catch a hint of Jordan being there with her. She glanced over at him and then looked back at the candle. "I'm doing fine."

"Then we should both stay where we are and see each other in the morning."

"Yes, let's do that," Sierra agreed.

"Be safe."

"You too."

Sierra hung up the phone and handed it back to Jordan. It struck her as ironic that now he was the one listening in on her phone conversation after she had picked up all kinds of details from the call he had just finished with his friend.

"Is everything okay with your friend?" He asked.

"Yes."

"I noticed you didn't tell her about the collapsed stairway."

"I had a feeling if I did she would try to drive over here tonight. It seemed better to wait and fill her in on the details in the morning."

"I take it you and Mariana are pretty good friends."

Sierra gave Jordan a summary of how her friendship with Mariana had grown over the years and how Mariana had been the initiator of this vacation since her father worked for an airline and got a good deal for them.

"My friends' wife has a connection like that through her mom. She's the one who booked this place for us."

Jordan rested his bare foot on the coffee table. "I sure hope Derek can make it over here, but the possibility is slim. If he can't catch a flight in the morning, I'm thinking he won't make the lineup for the rest of the week. I don't know all the qualifying details; Derek does. I just know that it isn't looking good."

Sierra had picked up a few details about Derek and his wife from catching bits of Jordan's conversations. She wasn't sure how much she was supposed to know so she asked a broad question. "How is his wife doing?"

Jordan explained about the bike accident, the tests at the hospital, and the surprise discovery of the pregnancy.

"I'll be praying for them," Sierra said.

The expression on Jordan's face softened in the candlelight. "Would you? That's awesome, Sierra. I really appreciate that. It seems like that's about all we can do now. It's down to the wire."

They talked for another hour about friends and college days and how much things had changed for both of them over the years since they had left college. To her surprise, Sierra opened up to Jordan more than she planned to. She even confided in him how difficult it had been living in an apartment with a married couple and never having her own space since her bed was the sofa.

"That settles one decision for tonight," Jordan said. "Whenever you're ready to go to bed, you get the bedroom."

"I wasn't telling you about my previous living setup so that I could call dibs on the bed."

"I know."

"I'm quite at home on the couch."

"I know."

"You're not going to argue with me, are you?" Sierra asked.

"Not yet." Jordan smiled. "I'll wait until something comes up that's really worth arguing about."

"Sounds like a good idea."

"Okay. So we're agreed. When you're tired, you take the bed; I'll take the couch."

Sierra agreed, but she didn't move. She was enjoying being with Jordan too much to be the one to close out the night.

"You know," Jordan said, "even though the lights went out, we could still watch a movie on my laptop. I have extra batteries for it."

"Sure, that sounds good."

Jordan went to his camera bag from which he pulled out an extra battery. "I don't know what you would be interested in watching. I don't have a lot on here. There is one surf movie that you might want to watch. I don't know. I loaded it because I was going to study how the waves come in at Sunset Beach and see how the lighting is."

"Sure, we could watch that."

"You wouldn't mind?"

"No. I think it would be interesting."

Jordan seemed to like her comment as he set up everything. He positioned the laptop on the coffee table and clicked through to start the film. At first they were both sitting at opposite ends of the couch. Jordan made the first adjustment and slid toward the sofa's center, turning the laptop more toward Sierra. "There, can you see it better now?"

Sierra did something that was daring for her. She moved over just a little so that she felt she was close enough to Jordan to appear friendly but far enough away to show that if anything was going to happen between the two of them, it would be through a series of baby steps.

The pillow from the end of the sofa somehow ended up making the move with her, and she held it over her stomach. Slouching down, Sierra rested her head against the back of the sofa. For an old couch with a big bird of paradise print on the cushions, it was pretty comfortable.

"Are you doing okay?" Jordan asked.

Sierra glanced at him in the glow of the candlelight mixed with the blue haze of the computer screen. In a low, contented voice, she answered. "Yes, I'm okay. How about you? Is this comfortable for you?"

He seemed to interpret her signal as an indication that an invisible line needed to be drawn between them tonight. He leaned back. "Yes, this is good."

Sierra agreed. This was good. Part of her wanted him to reach for her hand or lean closer so that their shoulders touched. But he stayed right where he was, close but not touching. This was just right.

The movie rolled, and they watched by candlelight. If Sierra had been asked to come up with a scenario for a dreamy first date, this would have been it. Tropical storm, collapsed staircase, and all.

CHAPTER TWENTY-ONE

Jordan heard what sounded like a heckling chuckle.

He opened his eyes and tried to focus in the dim light of the new day. On the edge of the coffee table perched a small, pale green gecko—the source of the noise. The lizard-like creature ran off as soon as Jordan sat up and looked around. Two small candles had burned down to their bases. His laptop was closed. And he was alone on the couch.

Sierra.

Jordan stood and stretched his stiff shoulders. He tried to focus on the clock on the microwave in the kitchen, but it was flashing all eights. Or maybe it was threes. It was too dark to know for sure. The bedroom door was closed, and he hoped his footsteps wouldn't wake his guest. Reaching for his cell phone, he saw that the time was 4:37.

Too early.

He plugged in his phone. Apparently the electricity had been restored during the night because it showed that the battery was charging. That's when he noticed the quiet. The wind had changed. The storm had subdued. He opened one of the slatted windows on the side of the house, and as he cranked the lever, he felt a rush of cool air enter between the levers. The air was fragrant and refreshing so he went to the other side of the upstairs apartment and cranked those slatted windows open as well. A beautiful cross wind blew through the rooms, and with it came the crashing roar of the waves.

As Jordan stood by the window straining to see the size of the swell in the darkness, he tried to remember when Sierra had gone to bed last night. He recalled telling her that he was falling asleep somewhere during the middle of the lull-inducing surf movie. Sierra had replied that she was falling asleep too. He was pretty sure that's when she shuffled wearily into the bedroom.

In the early morning light, Jordan returned to the sofa and plugged in his laptop. It made all the usual start-up sounds before he turned down the volume and quietly went to work, editing and organizing the wedding photos since there wasn't much else he could do until the Island Fix It Man showed up.

Fifteen minutes into his work session the bedroom door creaked open. Jordan turned and saw Sierra padding toward him, wrapped in the thin yellow blanket that had been folded up at the end of the bed.

"Morning, Did I wake you?"

With a sleepy gaze she said, "No, the birds did."

Jordan listened and heard a distant chittering of tropical birds. "Did you notice that the storm has passed? And we have electricity."

Sierra flipped a switch, and the kitchen light brightened the whole room. She let out a groggy moan. "How about if I make us some coffee?"

"Sounds great."

Jordan watched as Sierra shuffled into the kitchen with the end of the blanket trailing behind her. She used one hand to keep her cocoon in place and the other hand to pull a bag of Kona coffee from the cupboard.

"Are you cold? I could close the windows."

"No, the fresh air is nice. I can put my sweatshirt back on. How do you like your eggs?"

Jordan smiled. "Breakfast too?"

"Why not?" Sierra yawned and reached for her sweatshirt that she had left on the counter. She pulled it over her head and yawned again.

"Are you awake yet?"

"Not quite."

"You would think the time difference would be working in your favor so you wouldn't be so jet-lagged."

"It's not the jet lag. I'm just not much of a morning person. If given the choice, I'd sleep in till noon every day."

"Is that what your schedule is like in Brazil?"

"No. Rarely. I'm usually up by seven."

"I have you beat," Jordan said. "I stock shelves at a grocery store. Most days I have to be there at four."

"Four o'clock in the morning?"

Jordan nodded. "It's not so bad. I have more time in the afternoon for the group of young boys I mentor."

Sierra tilted her head. "You work with kids too?"

"Yup. Boys who don't have dads. They're a great bunch. A little attention goes a long way with them."

"I know what you mean." Sierra pulled breakfast fixings from the refrigerator. "I loved working with the girls at the school. That was the program I told you about that was cancelled. I wish I could keep working with them or even start a new program at another school."

"Why can't you?"

Sierra hesitated. "I guess the best way to say it is that I've been offered a different position. A new ministry. I need to decide if I'm going to take it before I return to Rio."

Jordan noticed how she had turned her face away from him as she revealed this information and how her shoulders had dropped. He walked into the kitchen and poured milk in a mug while waiting for the coffee to finish brewing. What he really wanted to do was get a better view of Sierra's face to figure out why she seemed to have taken such a dip. He leaned against the counter as she cracked eggs into a bowl. "I have the feeling you're not real excited about the new position."

"It's a big change." She didn't look at him. With small movements she scrambled the eggs with a fork.

"What can I do to help?" Jordan asked.

"Nothing. I need to think and pray this through myself."

"I meant how can I help with breakfast."

"Oh. I thought you meant . . . never mind. You could make the toast, if you want."

In an attempt to be clever, Jordan lifted his coffee mug and in a grandiose voice said, "I'd like to make a toast to our morning chef."

It took Sierra a moment to get his joke, but when she did, a sunshine sort of smile lit up her face. She lifted an empty mug from the counter and clinked it with his.

The drip coffeemaker stopped dripping right then so Jordan filled his mug half full with the fragrant brew and looked toward the window. Daylight was lifting the dark veil of night. An idea came to Jordan. He put down his mug, went to the other side of the room, and turned the sofa toward the front window.

"Front row seats," he announced. "And this morning our feature film is *The Dawn.*"

"Nice." Sierra finished up their food and joined him on the tropical print sofa where they sat comfortably close, watching the morning come slowly. The light came in long stretches across the sand and the water, illuminating the horizon. On each thunderous wave a cap of crystallized white foam appeared and a feather of silver spray curled off the top like a rooster's tail.

"Two days ago at this time we were floating and swimming

in calm waters, watching the whales," Jordan said. "What a change a couple of days have made."

"Hard to believe, isn't it?" Sierra said. "You know, this upstairs location gives you an ideal view of the waves. Too bad you can't get up on the roof to take pictures right now."

Jordan went for his camera. Even though the window was dirty after the storm, he wanted to see what he could line up. He clicked a couple of shots and checked them.

"It's no good. I need to be outside. The glass in this window is distorted." He turned to Sierra and was struck by her clear expression and the way the light was hitting her. "Do you mind if I take your picture?"

"Now?"

"Yes. You look great there in the filtered light. The crazy colors in that sofa make the perfect contrast."

She looked at him with a skeptical gaze but tilted her head in a way that he had learned was a universal "yes" and an invitation to capture the shot. He liked that she didn't put up her hand or turn away. Her relaxed posture in front of the camera was an indication to him that she had a solid self-image. It would say a lot about her if she protested too much or insisted on fixing her hair or posing in what she would consider a more flattering way. Her natural posture and sleepy morning expression were perfect in his eyes.

He clicked four or five more shots and put down the camera.

"So, are you going to send Derek the photos?"

Her question surprised him. Jordan had to admit that the idea had crossed his mind. It would be great fun to show Derek the gorgeous woman with whom he was apartment marooned. "Why do you ask?"

"I have four brothers, remember? I know how these things work for you guys. Plus, I admit I picked up on what you were saying to Derek on the phone last night."

Jordan gave Sierra a half grin. "It sounds like both of us

could give our friends something interesting to speculate about."

"Are you saying that your social life is about as active as mine and that's why our friends would be shocked to know we were hanging out together?"

"Pretty much." Jordan joined her on the couch. "Is that what we're doing? Hanging out together? I thought we were starting Day Two of our apartment captivity."

Sierra laughed. "True, we have been house-wrecked, as opposed to shipwrecked."

"That's a good one. House-wrecked. Even if we weren't marooned here, my answer is yes. We are hanging out together, and I'd like it if we could keep hanging out together for the rest of our time here."

"So would I."

"Good."

"Good."

They exchanged the warmest sort of smiles. Everything inside of Jordan made him want to reach over a few more inches and finger the ends of her hair.

She pointed at his camera. "May I take a picture of you? Will you show me how?"

"Sure." Jordan gave her a mini-course in adjusting the lens and setting up the shot.

Sierra stood and held the camera steady as Jordan struck a relaxed pose. It felt odd being on this side of the viewfinder. He felt self-conscious and adjusted his position as Sierra clicked a string of eight or nine shots.

"Let's see how they look." Jordan held out his arm.

"Not yet. I'd like to try something, if you don't mind."

"Sure, go for it." Jordan leaned back and tried to look comfortable as Sierra backed up and took a long shot of him from the backside of the couch.

She took her time and seemed to be having fun. A few

minutes later she handed over the camera and asked, "So tell me how they look."

Jordan pulled up the string of photos as Sierra leaned over the back of the couch and looked over his shoulder. She critiqued the shots before he had a chance to make any comments.

"Too much light. Hazy. Too close. Not bad. That one's okay."

Jordan agreed with her assessments. He clicked back to the one she called "not bad." It was actually pretty good.

"If I give you my e-mail address, would you send me that one?" Sierra asked.

"Sure." He turned and looked at her over his shoulder. "What are you going to do with it?"

With a flippant grin, Sierra came around to the front of the sofa and took a seat at the other end. She leaned her elbow on the back of the couch. "I thought I'd send it to my friends when you send my picture to Derek. Or, you know, I could always use it as my screen saver."

Jordan's eyes widened. "I take it you saw the mermaid shot on my laptop."

"Mermaid shot?"

"That's what you looked like to me. And I'm sure you figured out that I took that before I knew who you were."

"Yes."

For a moment the two sat looking at each other. Jordan tried to read Sierra's thoughts. To him it seemed as if the shadows were being siphoned from the room and light was filling the space between Sierra and him. He felt rocked in the deepest part of his soul.

"How about some more coffee?" Sierra sprang from the couch.

"Sure." Jordan handed her his mug. To his slight embarrassment but not surprise, he saw that his hand was shaking. Then he noticed that her hand was shaking, too.

CHAPTER TWENTY-TWO

Sierra carried the two empty coffee mugs to the kitchen and hoped Jordan hadn't noticed the way her hand trembled. She couldn't believe the rush of emotion that had come over her when Jordan called her picture the "mermaid shot" and then had looked into her eyes so deeply it seemed he could see all the way to her heart.

No guy had ever looked at her like that before.

The intensity and honesty that she saw in his expression and that she knew he could see in hers was too much. That was why she stood and pulled herself away. She had to figure out what was going on.

As Sierra poured the coffee, she told herself it was impossible to feel this drawn to someone in such a short time. And yet, why not? She couldn't say she ever truly had been in love. Was this what the first blush of love felt like?

Sierra remembered that Jordan liked his coffee with milk and poured some in, preparing his coffee with care before returning to the sofa.

"I have to ask you something," Jordan said.

"Okay." Sierra settled at the end of the couch and took a sip of her coffee, trying to keep her feelings hidden and her heart calm.

"I just wondered if you and Mariana have plans for tonight. Once we're sprung from our house arrest, I need to get down to the beach. I'll be taking pictures most of the day. But I'd really like to have dinner with you. And Mariana."

"I'll ask her. It should work out unless she has plans with the friends she stayed with last night. If she does, then it would just be me."

"That would be fine." Jordan's expression was warm and easygoing.

Sierra looked away. Part of her wanted to give in to the strong feelings growing inside right now. Another part of her warned that she should be on her guard and not open up too much or come across too eager or available. What could come of their relationship since they had such a short time together?

Just then they heard the squeak of car brakes and the sound of a car door slamming.

"Sounds like we have company," Jordan said. He and Sierra went to the door and both leaned out to see who would come around the side of the house.

"Who do you think it is?" Jordan asked. "Mariana or the Island Fix It Man?"

Before Sierra could make a guess, she saw Mariana coming around the side of the house and stopping in front of the collapsed stairs. She looked up and shouted, "Sierra!"

"Hello! Right here." Sierra waved.

Jordan was standing next to Sierra on the landing. He waved.

Mariana's mouth opened, but no words came out. Sierra wished she had a camera to capture the moment. Mariana had often made Sierra speechless, but Sierra couldn't remember a time she had had the same effect on her friend.

"Sierra, what are you doing?"

"Waiting to be rescued."

"There's a guy up there with you."

"There is?" Sierra playfully looked around.

"What are you doing? How did you get up there? Who is this guy?"

"This is Jordan. Jordan, this is Mariana."

"Nice to meet you," Jordan said.

Mariana wasn't polite in her response. She stood with her hands on her hips, staring up at them with her sunglasses on top of her head. "Jordan, whoever you are, and whoever you think you are, you need to know that this is no ordinary woman you lured to your penthouse."

Sierra turned to Jordan. "Did you lure me?"

"No. Absolutely not."

"He didn't lure me," Sierra replied to Mariana.

"As a matter of fact, she was the one who knocked on my door."

"I did," Sierra added.

Mariana looked as flustered as Sierra had ever seen her. "And then the stairs fell off?"

Jordan and Sierra looked at each other. Turning back to Mariana they nodded.

"And the electricity went out." Jordan's expression made it clear that he was having as much fun with this as Sierra was.

"Sierra, why didn't you tell me last night?"

"Because I knew you would try to come back in the storm. And besides, telling you like this is way more fun."

Sierra loved being the one who had the chance to drive her friend a little crazy.

"I'm going to look in the garage for a ladder. That's what I'm going to do." Mariana bustled off as Jordan and Sierra stood at the open door, peering down, sipping their coffee.

"Nice day," Jordan said.

"Yes, it is." Sierra was still in her playful mood. "It's a very nice day."

They could hear the sound of the rickety garage door rising. At the same time, the sound of a motor scooter coming their way grew louder. As Jordan and Sierra watched, an older Asian man on a bright yellow scooter came around the side of the house where the broken stairs gathered in a heap and made a roadblock. He came to a stop and used his flip-flop–covered feet to balance the small scooter as he surveyed the mess.

His back was to them, and Sierra noticed that he wore his T-shirt tucked into his tighty-whitey underwear that rose above the edge of his elastic-waist shorts. Sierra thought that was a peculiar way to wear his clothes, but not half as odd as what she spotted next. The man carried a red flyswatter with the long wire handle tucked into his tighty-whitey waistband. The flyswatter sprouted from the back of his shorts like a monkey's tail.

"Morning," Jordan called out.

The man climbed off the scooter, and as he walked toward the garage, the flyswatter whacked his back in an uneven rhythm with the slapping of his flip-flop sandals.

"Hello!" Jordan said.

The man turned around. "Oh, there you are. Aloha. Hey, you got big trouble here."

"Yes, we do. Are you the Island Fix It Man?"

"Yes, yes. My son is on his way with the truck. We can fix this. We fix everything. One time we got a cat out of a dryer vent and even the tail that was caught. But the vet couldn't sew it back on."

"So you fix everything but cat tails," Jordan said.

"Yeah, pretty much."

Mariana appeared from around the corner, hauling a dented aluminum ladder. "I found one."

The three observers watched as she set the ladder in place

and discovered what Sierra had already guessed when she saw Mariana carrying the ladder. It was too short. The ladder rose halfway to where the stairs had snapped off. She looked disappointed and then noticed the Island Fix It Man.

He gave her a nod and, without saying anything, collapsed the ladder, tucked it under his arm, and carried it back to the garage. With every step the flyswatter slapped his back, and his flip-flops slapped his feet.

Mariana looked up at Sierra and Jordan with amusement on her face. She held out both hands, palms up. "What's going on here? This is nuts. Is this some sort of American television show? Is the joke on me?"

"No," Sierra said. "The joke is not on you. That's our Fix It Man. His backup support is on the way."

In a low voice, Jordan said, "It looks like his backup support is following him."

Sierra and Jordan exchanged grins, and Mariana said, "Do you two know each other? I mean, from before yesterday?"

"Yes," they answered in unison, and then they both laughed.

"We went whale watching on Maui," Jordan said.

"He was the photographer at the wedding," Sierra added.

"Then, what? You decided to bring him back here with you?" Mariana asked.

"No, he followed me."

"Actually, you followed me. I arrived first."

"That's right. He was here first. He's on assignment to take pictures at the surfing competition."

Mariana looked more confused than before. "How did you know you were both staying at the same place?"

"We didn't," Sierra said. "It was a God thing."

Mariana's expression didn't change. She looked at them without blinking. "You say that all the time. Sierra, but this time I almost believe it."

"Believe it," Jordan and Sierra said in unison again.

They turned to each other and gave a funny sort of team victory gesture that was a cross between a high five and a knuckle bump. Sierra laughed at her own awkwardness. She didn't know what the current expressions or gestures were in the US.

All she knew was that Jordan was grinning at her, and she was feeling pretty happy.

CHAPTER TWENTY-THREE

Jordan's cell phone rang halfway through the stairway repair project. He had ignored it the first time it rang earlier that morning. This time it occurred to him that it might be Derek calling with an update on whether he had caught a flight that morning and was arriving in time for the competition.

Leaving Sierra by the front door, Jordan grabbed his phone and saw that the call was from Derek, as he had suspected.

"Hey, what's happening? How's Mindy?"

"She's about the same."

"So you're still in California."

"Yeah, I can't leave her. Not like this. She kept telling me to go and get on the plane this morning, but her mom can't come to be with her, and I don't think I should leave. She has a couple of friends who have been checking in on her. One of them called a few minutes ago and said she could stay with her starting tomorrow. That means I could try to catch the first flight out of LAX in the morning. All this depends on how Mindy is doing."

"I really feel for you, Derek. I know I keep saying the same thing every time I talk to you, but I'm so bummed this is happening to you guys."

"I know. Worst timing ever. But it is what it is, right? I'm going to make some calls and see if I can be a late arrival and still make the lineup for tomorrow. The big storm you guys had over there delayed everything a day; so that's in my favor. If you could manage to brew up another storm today, that would buy me some more time."

"The skies are clear. Another storm doesn't seem likely, but I haven't checked the weather report."

"I did. No storms are predicted. I was just hoping."

Jordan glanced out the front window at the sun-filled morning. The sky was a primrose shade of blue with only a few floating whiffs of clouds. The waves rolled in with thunderous curls, cresting at about twenty feet in his estimation. "I probably shouldn't tell you this in case it bums you out even more, but the waves are monstrous."

"I know. I've been watching the online feed. You guys have perfect conditions today. It's killing me not to be there. Are you getting some good shots?"

"I haven't gone down to the beach yet."

"Why not? Competitions started almost an hour ago."

"I know. The storm took out the staircase to this second-floor apartment. The repair guys are here now."

"Well, I guess I'm not the only one missing the big event, then. And by the way, what was with the girl last night? Sarah? Was that her name?"

"No, Sierra. Her name is Sierra." Jordan glanced at the door and noticed that Sierra turned and smiled at him when she heard her name.

"And? Come on, details, bro."

"Sure. Okay. I'll do that. I'll talk to you later."

"Oh, so you're back to code-speak. She must still be there."

"Exactly."

"That's all I'm going to get out of you?"

"Yes."

Derek let out a huff of air into the phone. "All right. Later, then. I have some calls to make. I'll talk to you when you're able to use full sentences."

"Sounds good. Say hi to Mindy for me."

"I will."

Jordan hung up and packed his camera and equipment. The minute he could clamber down those stairs, he knew he needed to be on the beach. His first stop would be the judging stand. If he could find the right person to talk to, he might convince the guy to let Derek come a day late and still compete.

"Is everything okay with your friend?" Sierra came over to where Jordan was carefully packing his camera case.

"Mindy still isn't doing well."

"She hasn't miscarried, though, has she?"

"No, she hasn't."

"That's encouraging."

"Yeah, but it's not so great that Derek is missing his big shot at this competition."

"But the baby is what really matters."

Jordan looked at Sierra and felt a twinge of irritation at her comment. "Of course." He knew he wasn't trying to diminish that part of the complicated situation. Was that what she thought?

"I'm not saying the baby doesn't matter," Jordan said. "Of course the baby matters. But you have to understand that Derek has been working for this opportunity for years. And here it is, first day of the competition, perfect conditions, and he's not here."

"I understand." Sierra lowered her chin and looked at Jordan without blinking. "But the baby is what really matters."

"Right. I just said that." Jordan's twinge of irritation grew into exasperation, and he knew it showed in his voice. After all the warmth and compatibility he had felt toward Sierra last night, he hadn't expected those emotions to be overshadowed by a burst of irritability. "You don't have the whole picture."

Sierra didn't look away or retreat in response to his sharp words. That surprised him. She seemed to take in his last comment and consider it before she said, "You could be right. I don't have the whole picture. But to my way of thinking, people are always more important than projects."

Jordan stood and gave her a careful look. "Of course they are. But what's the point in having a goal or a longtime dream, only to find that you're blocked before reaching it? Wouldn't you fight your way through the obstacles to make it happen?"

Sierra looked down for a moment as if his words had struck a sore spot.

"I'm just saying, sometimes you have to press forward and fight for your goals," Jordan said.

"And sometimes you have to let them go without a battle and move on to whatever is next, whether it's your dream or not."

Jordan saw a flicker of sadness cross Sierra's expression, and he realized she must be projecting this discussion about Derek onto her situation in Brazil He knew she had had to give up the afterschool program with the teen girls. Was that what this conversation was about for her?

"Why?" he asked. "Why would you give up and do something that's not your dream?"

"Because . . ."

Jordan noticed that her eyes were filling with glimmers of tears.

"Because why?" he asked.

Her voice rose. "Because sometimes you just have to. You have to change and be willing to let go of what you want to do in order to help other people." Sierra blinked and looked away. Jordan felt comfortable pressing the topic. He could tell that it had triggered something in Sierra and that she wasn't the type of woman who would shut down and hold it inside. She seemed to like the challenge of a debate and that made her even more attractive to him.

"Is that what you've had to do in Brazil? Let go of what you want to do so that you can help other people?"

A hint of surprise brushed over Sierra's expression. "Why are we talking about this?"

"You said that people are more important than projects."

"They are." Sierra folded her arms and stood with her shoulders back, communicating an air of assurance.

"What if the people are the project?"

Sierra's eyes narrowed.

"Isn't that how it was for you with the afterschool program with the girls? And all the other projects you've taken on over the last four years?"

Sierra looked at Jordan as if he had just pulled back a curtain and seen something in her heart he wasn't supposed to see.

"I didn't think we were talking about me," Sierra said quickly. "I thought we were talking about your friends."

"We were."

"So why are you bringing my situation into this?"

"Because I'm trying to make the point that every situation is complex with lots of different sides. You can't always make a blanket statement and assume it applies to every circumstance."

Jordan could see Sierra's jaw tightening by the slight twitch on her face. He had a few more points to make about Derek and Mindy but chose to back down. He knew this could easily turn into a circular argument with plenty of misunderstandings. It was best to pull away and not risk the possibility of another jab at her vulnerable spot. Jordan had a feeling he could easily jeopardize this barely begun relationship and demolish it. He had managed to do that more than once with his friendships.

Just then the son of Island Fix It Man called to them from

the bottom of the staircase. "Hello up there! Can you come to the landing?"

Jordan made his way to the open door. He was aware that Sierra hesitated a moment before she followed him.

"Let me throw this rope to you," the repairman said. "You need to anchor it to something steady up there."

The man tossed up the rope, but Jordan missed it. He tossed it again, twice, but both times Jordan missed it. On the fourth toss Jordan caught it and was aware that Sierra had watched his fumbling attempts. She didn't tease him, though. Clearly their earlier lighthearted spell of bantering had passed.

What impressed him, though, was that she stepped in and worked alongside him to anchor the rope. Most women he knew would have pulled back after the sort of conversation they just had. Sierra clearly wasn't like most women.

And at the moment, he wasn't sure if that was a good thing or not.

CHAPTER TWENTY-FOUR

Sierra watched as Mariana opened the small refrigerator in their downstairs apartment and pulled out two bottles of water. Their apartment was the same floor plan as Jordan's. The living room and kitchen were one open space with a long counter and three bar stools separating the two rooms. Jordan's apartment had less furniture and a round kitchen table. This apartment was more nicely furnished with a rectangular table along the far side of the room. Plus this apartment had two bedrooms instead of one with a bathroom between the two.

Sierra accepted one of the waters that Mariana offered her, twisted off the top, and took a long drink. She had been talking nonstop for the past twenty minutes, ever since the stairs were bolstered back in place and she had left Jordan's apartment with her luggage. She and Mariana had made it as far as their kitchen before Mariana insisted that Sierra tell her the whole story.

"If it were anyone other than you, Sierra, I would say this couldn't happen. I mean, who meets a guy like that, swimming in the ocean, and then finds out he's the wedding photographer?"

"I know."

Mariana continued to list the coincidences. "And even though it makes sense that we ended up at the same beach house because of the connection with the airline his friend had, this is still so unusual."

"I know." Sierra headed for the wicker chair by the sliding glass door that led out to the front patio. She positioned the chair so that she could see Mariana, who planted herself on the sofa, but also so Sierra could easily gaze beyond the patio to the beach where Jordan had joined the other photographers.

Turning to Mariana, Sierra asked, "Do you think it's creepy unusual or cool unusual?"

"It doesn't matter what I think. You're the one who has to decide that. Didn't you say a little while ago that this was one of those 'God things' you always talk about?"

"Yes, I did say that, didn't I?" Sierra gazed at the rolling surf and the blue skies. "I think it is a God thing. A huge God thing."

"And you really like him, don't you?"

Sierra turned back to Mariana. She felt a smile warming her face. "Yes, I really like him."

"Well."

"Yes, well."

"So what happens now?" Mariana asked.

"Dinner," Sierra said. "Tonight. He invited both of us. Do you want to go?"

"No, of course not." Mariana uncrossed her bare legs and tugged at the hem of her short denim skirt. "I'm not going to get in the way of your love life now that it's finally starting. I'll do something with Tianna. She and I need to find some guys to start our own island romances with. I can't believe you're the one who met a guy first. That was my goal for this trip, not yours. Tianna and I have some catching up to do."

Through the open slatted windows on the side of the house, Sierra could hear someone walking up to the front door. A quick rap followed. She hopped up and opened the door to see Jordan.

"I thought you would be out on the beach by now," she greeted him.

"I did too. But I have a problem."

"Come on in." Sierra held open the door as Jordan said hi to Mariana and walked over to the sofa. The downstairs portion of the beach house had a sand-colored sectional that was in much better shape than the couch in Jordan's apartment. Instead of a coffee table, they had a rectangular hassock.

Jordan had barely sat on the couch's edge before he said, "I received a call from the property management company that rented the apartment to my friends. I had called them yesterday to report the broken stairway. They said I need to vacate the apartment until an inspector comes. Also, since they didn't approve the repairs by Island Fix It Man, they won't cover the charges."

"That's ridiculous," Mariana said. "What did they expect you to do?"

"They expect me to move out and stay in one of their other units. The problem is that the only other place they have available is in Waikiki. That's too far for me to go and still do what I came here to do." Jordan rubbed the back of his neck. "I started looking for other places available here on the North Shore and haven't had any success. I wondered if you might have any leads, Mariana. You said you have friends staying farther up the coast. Do you remember the name of the place they're staying at?"

"Turtle Bay. But it doesn't matter. You don't have to find another place to rent. Just stay with us," Mariana said.

Jordan looked at Sierra and back at Mariana. His expression made it clear that wasn't the solution he had been looking for, but the possibility intrigued him.

"You're not going to find anything else. We have two

bedrooms. Stay here." This time Mariana's words carried an air of finality.

Sierra wasn't sure how she felt about this sudden decision that Mariana was making for all of them. But it made sense for Jordan to stay at this house on Sunset Beach to complete his photo assignment. She thought for a moment that she and Mariana could move to the place at Waikiki, but then she would be far away, and she didn't want that.

"Are you sure?" Jordan asked. "I'll move back upstairs once the inspector shows up and gives a clearance on the stairs."

"I don't think you should hold your breath until the inspector arrives," Sierra said. "And once he does come, those stairs aren't going to get a quick approval. The one right in the middle did a lot of groaning when I came down it a little while ago."

"It cracked some more when I came down," Jordan said. "It's reinforced, but you're right. I don't think the stairs will pass inspection."

"It's decided," Mariana said. "You're staying here. And Sierra told me about your friend. If he shows up tomorrow, he can stay here too. We have two rooms and two beds in each room. It's not a problem."

Sierra noticed that the pinched lines in Jordan's forehead eased. "If you're both sure that's okay with you, then that would be great. Thanks."

"To pay us back for the kindness, we'll let you cook for us." Mariana grinned and turned to Sierra. "Is he a good cook?"

"I'd rather not say." Sierra gave Jordan a teasing grin.

He folded his arms. "You haven't given me a chance yet to demonstrate my skills in the kitchen. How about if we have a friendly little competition this week and let Mariana decide who is best?"

"You have to buy all your own groceries," Mariana said.

"Of course."

"Then it's agreed," Mariana said. "This arrangement is turning out in my favor. I'll have not one chef but two. Now, which of you is going to take out the trash and do the dishes?"

Both Jordan and Sierra looked at Mariana as if the answer to that should be obvious.

"Okay, fine, we'll take turns," Mariana said diplomatically. Quickly changing the subject she asked, "Jordan, do you need help to move your things down here?"

"Sure, thanks."

The three of them took it one step at a time up and down the stairs as they transferred everything, including the food in his fridge. The move took twenty minutes, and as soon as they were done, Jordan grabbed his camera and equipment to head for the beach.

"There has to be something wrong with him," Sierra confided in Mariana after he left. She was feeling even more enamored with Jordan and could hardly wait to change clothes so she could get down to the beach to join him.

Mariana laughed at Sierra's comment as if it were blissfully naïve. Sierra knew she was inexperienced and far behind Mariana's sophistication when it came to romances, but she still wanted what she felt for Jordan to be real and lasting. It still seemed too good to be true.

Mariana replied, "Plenty of things are wrong with him. Why go looking for all the flaws now? You can make a long list after he breaks your heart. For now, have fun. Enjoy the attention while it lasts."

Mariana's words echoed in Sierra's thoughts half an hour later as she meshed her bare feet in the warm sand and headed for the gathering of photographers along the shore's edge. She remembered how Mariana had been partially correct about Tawni wanting Sierra to come to the wedding to baby-sit Ben.

Could Mariana be right again? Would Sierra find herself back in Brazil a week from now making a long list of Jordan's flaws after he broke her heart?

She hoped not. She really hated it when Mariana was right, but she especially didn't want Mariana to be right this time.

Sierra convinced herself this was different. Mariana didn't know how well Sierra and Jordan had hit it off last night or how natural it had felt to be around each other. Even the debate that morning about people over projects felt like a natural conversation to her. Sierra believed she had every reason to nurture this new relationship. The feelings were there on both sides. She was sure of it.

Approaching the photographers gathered on the beach, Sierra looked for Jordan. A couple of the guys glanced at her. One gave her a nod. They were more focused on the rising and falling waves and the two surfers who were paddling out to take their runs.

Continuing down the beach, Sierra enjoyed the warm breeze as it whipped her hair in every direction. Hundreds of spectators spread across the sand in front of the tall judges' booth that had been constructed at the top of the beach where the sand met the walkway and parking area. Weaving through the crowd to the judges' booth, she looked for Jordan but didn't see him. She walked to the far end of the beach where only two photographers had their cameras propped up on tripods. Jordan wasn't one of the two.

After almost an hour of hunting for Jordan, Sierra gave up and headed back to the beach house. That was odd. Very odd. He said he was going to the beach to take pictures; yet he was nowhere to be found.

When she entered the house, Sierra called out for Mariana. She wasn't there. Going back outside and checking the driveway, Sierra noticed that Mariana's car was still there, but Jordan's car was gone.

Sierra felt as if her emotions were ascending a staircase as unreliable as the one along the side of the house. At any moment it could all give way.

CHAPTER TWENTY-FIVE

The first thing Jordan did when he left the beach house was to make a call to Bill at the magazine and give him an update on how the storm had taken out his stairs and delayed his arrival on the beach.

"I'm on my way now. I should catch enough good shots for you before ten o'clock my time tonight."

"That's not what I was hoping to hear. We need to have at least a dozen edited shots from you uploaded by six o'clock our time."

"That's four o'clock here." Jordan tried to calculate how much longer he would have on the beach to take shots before he had to start editing.

"Are you saying you don't think you'll have what we need by then?"

Jordan hated being caught in this position. He wanted to deliver, especially since this was his first day on assignment. What Bill was asking was way more ambitious than Jordan thought he could pull off. Nonetheless, he knew he needed to come through for the magazine.

"That's a tight schedule, but let me give it all I've got."

"You're not convincing me, Jordan. Listen, I have some photos that came in already from an amateur who is on the beach there at Sunset. I can use those for this first round today. I would rather put up some subpar shots early than wait for yours. We can edit these shots here and upload them in the next half hour."

Jordan stopped walking and tried to think how he could convince Bill not to give the opportunity to some rookie who showed up first with the goods.

"I can step it up," Jordan said. "Give me an hour. I'll have what you need."

"No. Changed my mind. I have another assignment for you. How about if for today only you cruise down to Waimea and take some shots for us of the winter swell? We've had unconfirmed reports of twenty-foot waves coming in later today. If that's true and if it holds, The Eddie could be on tomorrow. Can you do that?"

"Sure. Absolutely." Jordan didn't hesitate even though he wasn't sure how far away Waimea was or how heavy the North Shore traffic would be. He also didn't know what Bill meant by "The Eddie," but he knew Derek would know.

"Have those shots of Waimea to us, edited, by six o'clock our time, and we'll be squared for today."

"Okay, I'm on it." Jordan picked up his pace. Instead of returning to the beach house and getting in his car, he headed for the judges' booth at the center of Sunset Beach. He went up to the first official he found and asked questions about entries in an attempt to find out if Derek could compete if he arrived tomorrow.

It took Jordan twenty minutes and the repetition of his question to four officials before he found someone who was familiar with Derek and his entry application.

"You know, it's not the best for him because he'll show up behind by one heat, but if he's here by two o'clock tomorrow, I'd say sure. Why not? Give it a shot. He should be able to make the lineup. Tell him to call me directly and let me know if he's coming." The man pulled a flyer from the table and wrote his number on the back.

"Great. I'll let him know. Thanks, man."

"Sure."

Jordan rushed back to the beach house, grabbed his car keys, and took off for Waimea. He had hoped Sierra would be at the house so he could see if she wanted to go with him. But when he arrived, neither Sierra nor Mariana were at the house and Mariana's rental car was gone.

Taking off on his own, Jordan pulled the map of the island of Oahu from his glove compartment and saw that Waimea was located only a few miles south of Sunset Beach. Turning onto the Kamehameha Highway, he slid into a backlog of slow-moving traffic on the two-lane road.

Jordan was wishing he had had the free car upgrade on this island instead of on Maui where he hadn't done much driving. Today was the perfect day for a convertible. Taking advantage of the time in the car, Jordan called Derek to update him on the competition status for tomorrow.

"Thanks for checking into it, Jordo. I'm thinkin' I'm going to try. I have a seat on the 6 a.m. flight out of LAX, and Mindy is insisting I go."

"That's great news. I take it she's feeling better?"

She says she is. I'm thinkin' she's being brave for me. We'll see how she does tonight."

"Here's the number you need to call to let them know you're coming." Jordan gave Derek the phone number and then said, "One more question. What is 'The Eddie'?"

"You honestly don't know?"

"No."

"You didn't let Bill know that, did you?"

"No. What is it?"

"It's an elite Quicksilver competition named for Eddie Aikau. He was the first lifeguard at Waimea and surfed thirty-foot waves back in the seventies. They have only held the competition like eight times in the last twenty-five years because the waves have to be over twenty feet with a thirty-foot face before they go out. Only twenty-eight surfers are allowed to compete, and they have to swim out. There are no jet ski tow-ins."

"Bill said the reports were coming in that the waves might be big enough this week, and The Eddie would be on."

"You're kidding. I hadn't heard. That's even more reason for me to get over there."

"I'm on my way to Waimea now to take some pictures for Bill."

"Is Sierra with you?"

"No."

"All right. So? Tell me what's going on. How did you meet this girl?"

Jordan gave a shortened report to Derek of how he and Sierra had met and concluded with, "She's not like other girls, you know? She's her own woman."

"How serious are you about her?"

"Serious? I'm not serious about her. How can I be? She lives in Brazil. I'm just enjoying the chance to hang out with her." Jordan knew that if he were honest with Derek he would admit he was infatuated with Sierra. Talking about her made him feel self-conscious. He didn't want to build up anything that was only going to dissolve by the end of this trip.

"You sure about that?"

"It's different, you know? The way we connected was unique. We had a great time last night. The best part was keeping you guessing as to why I had a woman in my apartment."

"Yeah, you had Mindy and me guessing, that's for sure. You

know, Jordo, they need photographers in Brazil too. Surf photographers, even."

"Yeah, well, they need photographers in Santa Barbara. And at the moment Bill needs a photographer at Waimea Bay, and I just got here. It's a zoo. I need to hang up and find a place to park."

Jordan drove around for fifteen minutes before locating someone who was pulling out of a parking spot. He inched his way in and gathered his camera equipment. Trudging down toward the beach, he stopped at a lookout area to stare in awe at the huge wave that rose like a giant's fist, curled its ominous blue knuckles, and smashed the water with a thunderous pounding. He thought the waves at Sunset were big. These waves were even bigger and carried an even louder crash and roar.

Jordan found a great spot to the side where he could shoot down on the bay and catch the rolling blue fists as they punched their way toward the shore. Within the first twenty minutes he knew he had captured some decent shots. Not to be overly confident, though, Jordan took the long walk down to the beach and set up his tripod and telescopic lens camera in the center of the beach. He wanted to catch the waves front-on in full force as they came bullying their way to the shore.

The white sandy beach was wide and curved in a large crescent. A huge, dark lava rock formation rose on the shore like a petrified pirate ship. What made the mass so unusual was that it wasn't connected to the rest of the land. It sat by itself, marooned at the water's edge.

About ten minutes into his shoot, a man came up to Jordan. "Sorry to bother you. May I ask a question?"

Jordan kept his camera steady and looked over at the man who was wearing a red shirt and wraparound sunglasses.

"I was wondering if you're doing freelance or if you're already with a sponsor for The Eddie."

"Neither. I'm on assignment for *Surf Days Magazine*."

The man looked impressed. He held out his hand. "Scott Wallford. I'm with Moana Ali'i."

Jordan shook his hand, gave him his name, and repeated "Moana Ali'i" with what he was sure sounded like a question at the end.

"Moana Ali'i Surfboards," Scott added.

"Yes. Of course." He had heard of that line of surfboards from Derek.

"Are you exclusive with *Surf Days*?"

Jordan wasn't sure how to answer. He knew Derek hoped to pick up sponsors if he did well in the competition. Jordan hadn't expected to be courted, though, as a photographer. That is, if that was what Scott was doing. It surprised Jordan; yet his being on assignment for *Surf Days* must have been significant enough to put him in the running.

"I'm open to discussion," Jordan said carefully.

"How about if we talk over dinner tonight? Six o'clock? Ted's?"

Jordan really wished Derek was here to help interpret this offer. Was Moana Ali'i a sponsor Jordan wanted to talk with? And who was Ted? Why did Scott assume that Jordan would know where Ted's place was?

"I have plans for dinner tonight. Tomorrow night maybe?" Jordan's thoughts had gone to how it would be ideal for Derek to be the one to take this meeting. If the dinner was moved to tomorrow night, both of them might be able to go.

"Can't do it tomorrow. I'm booked the next four nights and then I'm going to be off island for two weeks."

Jordan was starting to think he better not brush this guy off.

Scott pulled a business card out of his pocket. "How about if you give me a call after you're done with your dinner tonight? I can come meet you wherever you are. Let me know."

"Okay. Yes. I'll do that. Thanks."

They shook hands again, and Scott made his way down the beach where he struck up a conversation with another photographer. Jordan clicked through another ten minutes of shots and checked his watch. He had a little more than an hour and a half to drive back to Sunset Beach, edit the photos, and send them off to Bill. It still seemed doable.

As soon as he was back in the car, he called Derek and gave him the rundown on meeting Scott.

"Jordo, you gotta do it. What are you doing talking to me? Call the man back right now and tell him you'll meet him at Ted's like he asked. This is what we've been after, man. Don't blow this one off."

"Okay, okay. But tell me, who is Ted?"

"It's a place. Ted's Bakery. It's the place to go on the North Shore. You gotta take this meeting, Jordo. You really do. Give him a call right now before he books dinner with some other photographer at Waimea."

"All right. Okay. I will." Jordan hung up with Derek, and as Jordan sat in traffic, he placed the call to Scott and said he would be able to meet Scott at six after all.

"Great." Scott said. "I'll see you at Ted's. Six o'clock."

"Okay, I'll see you there."

As the rush of what had just happened dissipated, Jordan thought about Sierra. She was the reason why he had told Scott he couldn't meet with him. He slammed his palm on the rim of the steering wheel.

As much as he wanted to spend more time with her, Jordon knew Derek was right about not passing up this business opportunity. She would understand. Wouldn't she? The two of them could have dinner the following night. And this time he wouldn't invite Marianna to join them.

Jordan inched his way toward Sunset Beach feeling the stress over how things were shaping up for the rest of the day. This day had begun with such a grand, front-row view of the dawn and Sierra beside him. He wanted to be near her again. To see her face. To watch the sunlight in her exotic long curls.

A sharp thought came to Jordan. This was the time in his life when he needed to focus on his career, not on a relationship. As mesmerizing as Sierra was, Jordan didn't want to start anything long distance that he couldn't maintain now that his career was opening up.

He spent the rest of the drive to the beach house convincing himself that Sierra already had come to the same conclusion. The timing just wasn't right for their relationship.

CHAPTER TWENTY-SIX

Sierra heard a car pull into the beach house's driveway and went to look out the bedroom window. It was Mariana's.

Sierra opened the front door and tried to sound lighthearted. "Where did you go?"

"To the store. Why? What are you so uptight about?"

"I didn't know where you were."

"I wasn't gone long. You were headed to the beach to be with Jordan. I didn't think I needed to leave you a note."

"I didn't find Jordan."

Mariana looked confused. "He said he was going to take photos on the beach with the other guys. I heard him."

"I know. So did I. But he wasn't there. I looked everywhere. And when I got back here, I saw his car was gone."

"Are you worried about him?" Mariana asked. "Worried that he wasn't being honest with you?"

"No, not at all. I'm sure something came up or changed with his schedule. It's not a big deal." Sierra watched Mariana as she unloaded nail polish, sunscreen, and a six-pack of diet soda from her grocery bag. "He didn't happen to leave a message on your cell phone, did he?"

Mariana pulled her phone out of her bag. "No." She looked at Sierra with her concerned mother expression. "He's a guy. He's working. When you're around, he's interested. When you're not around, he's going to focus on his work. That's how it goes."

Sierra scowled at Mariana.

"It's true. Once you go through a few more relationships, you'll learn this. This is going to be a good experience for you. Good practice." Mariana walked away and went into the bathroom, closing the door behind her.

Sierra didn't like Mariana's assessment. Jordan wasn't just any guy. What they had shared was over-the-moon amazing. The more she had thought about how they had connected in such an extraordinary way and how things had been so natural for them last night, the more convinced she was that something strong and important was going on between them. Jordan wasn't just "practice" material for her to expand her experiences with guys.

Sierra leaned against the kitchen counter and folded her arms. She was stuck. If she went out to the beach again, she might miss Jordan when he came back to the house. If she stayed at the house, he might end up being gone for the rest of the day, and she would have forfeited a significant portion of her Hawaiian vacation.

"Mariana?" Sierra headed for the bedroom and called out to the closed door. "What are you doing the rest of the afternoon?"

"I'm going to Tianna's. We're going to Ted's for dinner."

Sierra didn't know who Ted was, but she wished Mariana would stick around with her for a while instead of running off to Tianna's again.

"What are you going to do?" Mariana asked.

"I'm having dinner with Jordan, remember?"

"I meant, what are you doing now?"

"I don't know."

"Do you want to come with me to Tianna's?"

"No. I think I should wait here. I'm not sure what time we were going to go to dinner." Sierra added, "You know that Jordan invited you to come, too."

"Yes, I know. That's why I'm leaving."

"You don't have to do that. I mean, you don't have to leave. Not this early, especially." Sierra hated talking to a closed door. She also hated sounding so pathetic, as if she didn't know what to do with herself if her playmates went off with someone else.

"Sierra, will you relax? You have your guy. Now have a good time with him. That was the point of this vacation, remember?"

"For you, maybe. That wasn't my purpose. This vacation hasn't exactly gone the way I thought it would."

The bathroom door opened, and Mariana emerged with her hair up in a twist and her makeup freshly applied. "Well, guess what, Sierra? This vacation hasn't exactly gone the way I thought it would, either."

"What does that mean?"

"Think about it." Mariana brushed past her, smelling of sweet vanilla and guava from the lotion she had bought. "I'll see you later."

Sierra followed her to the door. "Are you saying you're upset because I met a guy before you did? Is that what you're saying?"

"No, of course not." Mariana gave her a look that communicated her anger and frustration, but Sierra wasn't sure what she had done to upset Mariana.

"What is it, then? The fact that I went to Maui and left you here alone for two days?"

Mariana narrowed her eyes. "Do you remember what I told you when you asked why I didn't invite Aleen and my other roommates to come on this vacation?"

Sierra thought back. "You said they went to Paris with you and now you wanted me to come to Hawai'i with you."

"I also said I would rather have you come with me because I knew I would have more *fun* with you. So far, Sierra, I have to tell you, even starting with the ride to the airport in Sao Paulo, you have been anything but fun. It's like we're not even on vacation together."

"But you said it didn't bother you that I went to Maui."

"I know."

"And you are the one who is always saying we're supposed to be meeting guys."

"I know. Good for you."

Sierra tried a different approach based on how upset Mariana sounded. "Listen. The storm changed everything for us yesterday. That was nobody's fault. You and I haven't even had a chance to do anything together yet."

"Oh, so you noticed."

"Mariana. Be fair. How is that my fault?"

"I didn't say anything was your fault. I just said it wasn't fun. Try to see my side."

Sierra had never felt this frustrated with Mariana. "I do see your side. Try to see my side."

"I see your side. I understand. I just want to have a vacation, too. I want to have some fun. I'm going to Tianna's. I'll see you later." With that, Mariana left.

Sierra stood by the door of the beach house alone, frustrated, and confused.

Unfortunately, she remained in that same mental state for the next few hours as she took a shower, made a snack, and ended up trying to nap on one of the lounge chairs on the front patio. Being caught in the middle was torture.

When she finally heard a car rolling into the driveway, Sierra hopped up and went inside. Deciding she shouldn't appear too eager when Jordan walked in, she went to the fridge and pulled out a can of something Jordan had bought called "POG." She looked closely at the label as she heard his footsteps approaching the door. It was a drink made from passion fruit, orange juice, and guava juice. Sierra popped the top and took a sip.

Jordan entered, and she greeted him casually. "Hi there."

"Hey. How are you doing?"

"Great." It wasn't the truth, but she didn't want any of her floundering emotions to show through.

Jordan went directly to his laptop on the kitchen table and pressed the ON button. He pulled a few cords out of a bag and went to work, plugging things in.

"Did you get some good shots?" Sierra asked.

"I hope so." Jordan looked at his watch and then glanced at Sierra where she stood by the refrigerator. "Listen, I have a deadline I'm trying to hit in sending these off, and I have a meeting I need to go to."

"Oh. Okay." Sierra maintained her smile.

"The meeting is a dinner meeting. It's at six o'clock. So I apologize, but it looks like we'll have to move our dinner plans to tomorrow night. Is that all right with you?"

"Of course. Sure. That's fine." Sierra kept her demeanor up, as she headed for the front door. "I'll give you some space," she said, trying to sound as upbeat as possible. "Hope it all goes well. See you later."

Making her exit with almost as much of a decisive closing of the door as Mariana had given, Sierra headed for the beach with the can of POG in her hand. She didn't want to cry. She didn't want to be upset. She didn't want anyone to see her or talk to her right now. This dip in her emotions had to be due to jet lag or the convoluted argument she had had with Mariana. It couldn't be related to Jordan or that Mariana was right about his not keeping his word—both when he said he would be on the beach and when he said he would take her to dinner.

For the second time that day Sierra meshed her feet in the warm sand. This time, instead of heading for the crowds, she headed the other direction, away from the beach house and away from the few dozen spectators left on the beach now that the day's competition was done.

She walked to the water's edge. The enormous waves were still rising and falling far out in the water, at least twenty yards from where Sierra pressed her feet into the firm sand. Once the waves made their white, foaming dive, the liquid splinters calmed down to a manageable slosh and raced to shore where the water slid across the sand at only a few inches' depth before rushing back out to sea.

Sierra could feel the power of the waves even though she was only ankle-deep in the blue-and-white foaming saltwater. All that roaring power seemed to calm the intensity that had been roaring inside her. The late afternoon sun warmed her right arm. She drew it behind her back so that it wouldn't get sunburned. The wind picked up the ends of her hair and twisted them every which way.

Drawing in a deep breath, she tried to be understanding about Jordan's need to work and to keep up with his important meetings. That was why he was here.

She thought again of how Mariana was here to have fun; she was out doing her best to make sure that happened.

Then Sierra reminded herself why she had come. It had nothing to do with Jordan. It had nothing to do with having fun with Mariana. Her future needed to be decided. And the time had come for her to give that important detail her full attention.

Now, if only she could do that without chiding herself for giving in to such infatuated fairy-tale thoughts about Jordan. What was it Mariana had said about Jordan being a good experience for her? Good practice?

Maybe that was all that her time with him had been. A good experience. Practice.

But nothing more.

CHAPTER TWENTY-SEVEN

Working as quickly as he could, Jordan clicked through the photos he had taken at Waimea and moved the best ones to a new folder. He checked the time and went even faster through the last two dozen shots. Then, selecting the top ten, he went to work editing the shots for clarity and composition. He heard his phone buzzing from inside his camera bag, but he let it go, staying focused on the project and the deadline that was less than ten minutes away.

The clock on his computer showed the time as 3:59 when Jordan hit SEND, and the e-mail went to Bill, letting him know the photos had been posted to Bill's password-protected photo site and were ready for his review. Leaning back, Jordan stretched.

"That was too close," he murmured. Looking around, he half-expected Sierra to be there. He knew she had gone out when he was in the heat of his deadline. Now that he had a little time before his dinner meeting, he wished she were here so he could spend that time with her.

Jordan went to the fridge and pulled out a bottle of water. He carried it out to the patio and surveyed the wide beach. The late afternoon sun broke through the clouds on the horizon and spread a golden blanket of light over the white sandy beach. The colors were like nothing he saw at sunset in Santa Barbara. This amber glow of enchantment was what made Hawaii distinctive and also made for breathtaking pictures.

Within a few minutes Jordan had scooped up his camera and was on the beach, his feet wedged into the sand, as he captured a dozen shots of the ocean, beach, and sky. He edged his way toward where a few of the event photographers were still hanging out, packing up their equipment and talking about how the competition had gone that day. Jordan didn't know any of them.

He gave a friendly nod to one of the guys, who looked up and acknowledged him. In the morning Jordan would be on the beach with these guys, like the new kid who starts school a day late. He didn't know how competitive the men were or if they were a tight circle. But then he realized that it didn't matter if he felt welcomed. He had a job to do, and he intended to do it to the best of his ability. The last thing he wanted was for an eager amateur to supply Bill with photos that should be coming from Jordan's camera.

Walking farther down the beach, Jordan took some shots of the judges' booth and the banners advertising the event's sponsors. He kept an eye out for Sierra but didn't see her. The way she had slipped out when he needed to concentrate and had been so understanding of his deadline impressed him.

Jordan wished again that she were here, walking along the beach with him. He knew this was an important season and that he needed to concentrate on his career. Hadn't he already coached his thoughts and emotions to accept that this wasn't the time to enter into a long-distance relationship?

Still, he had to admit, he missed her.

Jordan found himself once again thinking of Sierra at six o'clock when he drove into the crowded parking area next to an unassuming building that matched the address for Ted's Bakery. Clearly, this was the place to be. Beachgoers stood in line waiting to get inside. Jordan joined them next to a wall that was painted with a bright blue surf scene that included a long wave curling across the wide space. Several dozen surf logo stickers were affixed around the front door in a way that reminded him of how a teen would decorate his closet door. To his right were round picnic tables covered by bright blue umbrellas.

"Is this the line?"

Jordan turned to see a young woman with long, dark hair dressed in a bikini top and a colorful piece of tie-dyed fabric knotted low around her slim hips. "Yes."

He quickly turned forward and looked for Scott, not sure if they were supposed to meet inside or at the picnic tables.

"What time is it?" The young woman touched his arm as if trying to get his attention.

Jordan checked his watch. "It's six o'clock exactly."

"Do you live here?"

"No."

"Where do you live?"

Jordan hated to be rude, but he was here for an important business meeting, not to be chatted up by a scantily clad teenager who was asking too many questions.

"I live in Santa Barbara." He was turned only halfway toward her and didn't make eye contact as he gave his clipped answer.

"Hey, I live in California too!" This seemed to be enough of a connection for the gregarious young woman to wrap her arms around Jordan, cuddle up under his arm, and give him a big side hug.

Caught off-guard by her sudden expression of affection, Jordan raised his arm and looked down at her. She clung to him like a koala bear with her head pressed against his chest.

"Great," he muttered, trying to pull away.

She held on to him and looked up at him with her wide

brown eyes. That was when Jordan could see that she wasn't sober.

"Okay. Great. Come on." He stepped out of line and headed for the nearest picnic table with her arms still around him. "How about if you sit over here? That's it. Right here."

She reluctantly took the only open seat beside a tall girl with red hair who was in the middle of a conversation with her group of friends.

"Someone is sitting there," the redhead said.

"She'll only be here a minute," Jordan said, walking away. He didn't want to get tangled up in any sort of mess right before meeting with Scott. Instead of slipping back in line, Jordan slid past the people at the front of the line. "I'm just going inside to look for someone."

As soon as he entered, he saw that it wasn't a restaurant but rather a well-organized deli where diners ordered their food and then took it to go or to eat out at the picnic tables. The air-conditioning inside felt invigorating after being in the hot weather all day. Jordan spotted Scott and went up to him, feeling relieved that he didn't have to go back outside.

"Did you already order?" Scott asked.

"No, not yet."

Scott nabbed the attention of the guy behind the counter. "And add whatever he wants to my check."

"I can get it," Jordan said.

"No, my treat. And if you like sweet stuff, you should try their chocolate *haupia* pie or the pineapple macadamia cheesecake."

Jordan kept it simple and ordered a sandwich and a soft drink. He followed Scott out to the crowded picnic tables and was glad to see that the koala-bear girl wasn't waiting for him. She seemed to have found someone else to latch on to and was now standing in line with two surfers, who were checking out the tattoo on the back of her neck as she pulled her hair to the side and bent her head so they could take a closer look.

Scott led the way to the farthest table and asked the guys sitting there if they minded Scott and Jordan joining them. The guys made room, and Jordan wedged onto the seat across from Scott. This wasn't what he had expected for a business meeting. How could they talk privately with so many people around?

"Tell me about your assignment for *Surf Days*." Scott jumped right in. "Are you just tracking The Eddie?"

Jordan kept his voice low. "No, I'm covering Sunset this week. Waimea was a side trip today."

"Have they made the decision yet?" one of the guys at the table asked. "Is The Eddie on?"

Scott seemed a little surprised at Jordan's question. "You know how it works. They say that 'the bay calls the day.' It's up to the waves to decide."

"So, we'll know tomorrow." Jordan took a bite of his sandwich and wished Derek were there. He'd be knowledgeable about all things surf culture related. All Jordan knew were effective shutter speeds at midday.

Scott leaned in. "Are you looking for assignments from sponsors, or do you want to stay exclusive with *Surf Days*?"

"I'm open to what comes along."

"Have you given any thought to going exclusive with a company like Moana Ali'i?"

"Not a lot of thought," Jordan said honestly. "I mean, again, I'm open to other opportunities."

Scott didn't appear impressed with Jordan's less-than-enthusiastic response. Jordan realized he should have replied more like he had seen Derek interact with the reps from the companies he really liked. Derek would have been positive and would have started to talk about contract points right up front. However, It struck Jordan as odd that as far as he knew, Scott hadn't seen any of his work. Why would he be ready to talk about going exclusive?

Jordan took another bite of his sandwich and tried to recalibrate his thoughts so that he could find a natural way to ask the right questions and not blow this conversation.

Just then, a slim young woman in a wraparound beach dress came up to him and said, "Jordan, why didn't you call me?"

He pulled back and gave her a startled look. He had never seen her before. She had short, dark hair, dark skin, and an accent. He didn't recognize anything about her.

"I'm sorry to embarrass you like this," she said. "But you said you were going to call, and you never did. I've been waiting. We had such a great time together." She reached over and ran her fingers through his hair as all the guys at the table watched.

Jordan pulled back even farther. "Hey, I don't know what's going on, but you obviously have me mistaken for someone else."

"Jordan, how can you say that to me? You're breaking my heart! Don't you remember what you told me last night on the beach? You said we were meant to be together. I believed you." She reached for him as if she were going to pull a koala-bear move like the woman in line.

Jordan jumped up and put his hands in front of him on the defense. "I am not who you think I am. I don't know how you know my name, but I don't know you. Nothing happened between us."

"You call last night nothing?" The woman burst into tears and ran off.

Jordan slowly sat down, stunned. He cautiously made eye contact with Scott, who looked humored at what had just happened, as did the other guys around the table.

"Cold," one of them said.

"Dude," another guy said, shaking his head.

"I was telling the truth. I don't know her. I've never seen her before in my life."

"If you say so."

Jordan couldn't believe this was happening. What a crazy mess! He looked down at his sandwich, but his appetite was gone.

"So, tell me what you've done so far for *Surf Days*." Scott returned to their conversation as if nothing out of the ordinary had happened.

"I did a shot they're planning to use for the cover of the February issue." Jordan pulled out his phone and quickly scrolled through his favorites file in order to show the image to Scott.

Scott looked impressed.

"That picture was my big break, I guess you could say. This is the first time I've been on assignment for them. I'm pretty much a rookie." Jordan knew that if Derek were here he would be kicking Jordan under the table for talking himself down. This was his one chance to make an impression, and he was undercutting himself big-time.

Just then all the guys at the table looked past Jordan to someone who had apparently come along and was standing next to him. By the inquisitive expressions on the guys' faces, Jordan had a feeling the mystery woman had returned. He didn't want to look, but he seemed to have no choice.

Slowly turning, Jordan saw Mariana's face light up with a big smile, as if the fun part of her vacation had just begun.

"Hi, Jordan."

"Hi."

All the guys at the table stopped eating, waiting to see how this episode was going to play out.

Mariana seemed to enjoy all the attention. "Do you want to introduce me to your friends?"

With a sweeping hand gesture around the table Jordan

pointed at Mariana and said, "This is Mariana. She's from Brazil, and we're renting at the same beach house."

The guys all said their hellos, and then Mariana said, "And this is my friend who is also from Brazil, Tianna."

The woman with the short, dark hair who had just put on such a convincing show for them reappeared and leaned over to give Jordan a tiny kiss on the cheek.

"Sorry. She put me up to it."

"We saw the girl in line who was all over you," Mariana said. "I knew it was the perfect chance to play a little joke on you. You should have seen your face!" Mariana imitated Jordan's stunned expression, and everyone laughed.

Mariana's joke went over much better with the guys at the table than it did with Jordan. Within a few minutes, she had commandeered the table along with Jordan's conversation with Scott.

"I have to catch up with some other people," Scott said before he had finished eating. "You're on my radar now, Jordan. I'll be watching for your work. Maybe we'll have a chance to talk later in the week."

"I hope so." Jordan stood when Scott rose to leave and decided to go, too. That way he thought he could at least walk Scott out to his car.

"Are you going back to the house?" Mariana asked.

"You can hang out with us," Tianna added. "Maybe Sierra wants to come, too."

"Yeah. Maybe." Jordan tried to make his exit but by the time he managed to get away from the table, it was too late for him to casually catch up with Scott and try to talk to him some more.

Jordan's car was at the far end of the parking area. The majority of people hanging out seemed to have gathered here in search of directions to a party.

That was the last thing Jordan was looking for tonight.

CHAPTER TWENTY-EIGHT

As Sierra walked along the beach alone at sunset, she felt the restlessness in her spirit dissipate. It was as if the ferocious waves had challenged her to a contest to see which of them was the most agitated, and the roaring waves won. As her bare feet left their mark in the cooled sand along the shoreline, she felt little bits of her frustration being left behind with each step.

She drew in deep breaths, tasting the salty air as she exhaled. She sent whispered prayers into the wind and felt her thoughts refocusing. In a small way the ocean water's churning reminded Sierra of the way their old washing machine used to twist and chug in the basement of her grandmother's one-hundred-year-old house where they lived in Portland.

During Sierra's high school days, she used to go on a search for her mother when Sierra returned home from school. Often she found her mom in the damp, quiet basement sorting laundry. Sierra would review the daily drama, as her mother calmly folded towels and listened. Her mother rarely gave advice. Sometimes she offered suggestions. Mostly she listened. And that was all Sierra needed to make sense of her life.

Sierra's memories of that dank, musty place were vivid as she watched the clouds turn the shade of apricots. The sun cast glittering spears of golden light into the ocean, and the waves continued to foam and rage and throw themselves at the shore. She decided what she liked the most about those times with her mom in the basement was that she knew she had her mother's full attention. In a family of six children, that was a rare occurrence.

Multiplying that feeling many times over, Sierra felt as she walked along the beach that she had God's full attention, in spite of the millions of children He kept an eye on day and night. It wasn't as if she sensed Him giving her any advice or specific direction for the future. But she was okay with that. What she felt was that her dilemma mattered to Him, and eventually everything would work out.

Sierra strolled back to the beach house, trying to picture herself living in a Brazilian village. It could be a once-in-a-lifetime experience. She might love the simplicity of it all. Life in its most elemental form without all the confusing influence of modern Western society. No one in the village would care that she didn't have a cell phone. No one would ever show up for a wedding wearing the same aqua dress.

And no one in the village would say that I reminded them of a mermaid.

She put that thought aside as she approached the beach house. Dusting the sand off her feet, she entered and called out, "Hello, anyone else here?"

No reply echoed her call. She was alone.

A wash of unexpected emotion came over her. She thought she had just calmed all those churned-up feelings.

"That's it," she muttered to herself. "I'm going to call my mom."

Sierra went to the bedroom and borrowed Mariana's laptop so she could log on to the online phone service she used. A moment later she heard her mother's voice answer the phone, and when she did, Sierra leaked tears.

"Are you all right?" her mom asked.

"Yes, pretty much. Do you have a few minutes?"

"Of course."

Sierra took advantage of talking freely without anyone overhearing her. She gave her mom all the details about the wedding, talking to Paul, meeting Jordan, ending up at the same beach house with him, the storm, and the collapsed staircase. Sierra concluded with a summary of how she knew she needed to be objective. Jordan had work to do, and she was pretty sure he was over her already, if he ever had been intrigued to begin with. What mattered now was that she focus on her decision about whether to take the position in the village.

"I just took a long walk on the beach and prayed about everything, and I'm okay. Really. It's beautiful here, and I'm glad I came. I just wanted to talk to you and tell you what's been happening."

"I'm so glad you called. I've been wondering how things were going for you." Her mother paused and then asked, "Sierra, do you have any sort of peace about taking the position in the village?"

Sierra heard herself say, "Yes."

She wasn't sure that's how she really felt or if that's what she thought her mom expected her to say. Backtracking she said, "Actually, I don't know. I think so. I'm willing. It seems to be what's next."

Her mom paused again and then said, "Sierra, you are a woman of options. You know that, don't you?"

"Yes." Again she wasn't sure if that was a true answer or an expected answer.

"As you were talking I was thinking that there is an option you should consider."

"What's that?"

"I think you should come back to the States for a while."

"Why do you say that?"

"I'm not sure. A mother's intuition, perhaps. I know you can live in a village and do a lot of good there. But it's not really you. You didn't grow up longing to live in the jungle. You love to help people and to start new projects. You can do that anywhere. I just think you should look into using your gifts somewhere in the US for a few years. If your heart still tugs for you to return to Brazil, then you can always return. For now, think about coming home."

Sierra felt her teeth clenching. The last thing she wanted to do at her age was to go home and move in with her parents. That would be like admitting defeat. She could never live at home again. Not after all the independence she had experienced over the years.

"I'll think about it."

"Good. That's all I want you to do. Just think about it. Consider all your options."

"Okay. Thanks, Mom." Sierra felt herself shutting down. This wasn't what she had expected to hear and certainly not what she had wanted to hear. She had called because she was hoping for a listening ear, the way her mom had listened back in high school. She wasn't looking for direction.

"Let me give you one more thing to consider."

Sierra felt her defenses go up even higher.

"I know that you have been deliberate and diligent in seeking whatever it is that God wants for you. Your father and I think that's wonderful. We admire your determination. You have always had a strong spirit. Now, consider asking yourself a simple question. Ask, 'What do I want?' and then listen to your answer."

"Okay," Sierra said automatically.

"The reason I'm suggesting this is because, in this case, I think you'll find that what you want is exactly what God wants."

Sierra immediately thought that wouldn't be true.

"You know how God tells us to delight ourselves in the Lord, and He will give us the desires of our heart? Well, you have been delighting yourself in the Lord for many years, Sierra. I honestly think that, if you take a close look at the desires in your heart right now, you will see that's what God is leading you to do."

Sierra found herself disagreeing with her mother, which didn't happen very often. To her way of thinking, she would be selfish to ask herself what she wanted. All she wanted was for her life to count for God, and that meant doing what God wanted her to do, even if it was something she didn't want to.

After Sierra ended the call, she stretched out on the bed and listened to the clucking of the geckos as their gentle sounds floated through the open window. Outside the sky had darkened, but the air still was warm, and the sound of the crashing waves continued like the steady beat of a tribal drum. The sound calmed her down and helped her to lower her defenses.

In the darkened room, Sierra thought about her mother's line that Sierra was a woman of options. What were the options that were available to her? She knew she could go back to school. She hadn't finished college yet. That would be a good option—that is, if she could decide on a major.

Another option was to try something different and do a search for ministry opportunities in different places of the world. What if a ministry in Africa needed someone with her skills? Or Switzerland? She had visited there with her friend Christy when she was in high school. Sierra loved Switzerland. Why couldn't she go there to do something meaningful?

Because you don't really want to go there.

Overhead the ceiling fan moved the air without making a sound. Inwardly she felt as if all her thoughts were being moved around. Even though she couldn't hear the sound with her ears, it seemed as if she could "hear" dreams crashing and breaking into pieces as her hopes bumped into reality and her feelings collided with the facts.

Her idealized memory of how her mother had always been there to listen but kept her opinions to herself was now crumpled up and ready to be tossed away. What her mother had said really messed with her mind.

Finally, Sierra gave in and asked the question her mom had suggested.

Okay, so what do I want?

The answer made a grand entrance into her thoughts.

I want to move to Santa Barbara and continue this relationship with Jordan until it comes to a natural conclusion. That's what I want.

Sierra hopped up and exited the bedroom. She went to the kitchen and turned on the light. Knocking some pots and pans around, trying to decide what to make for dinner, she concluded that her mom was way off track this time. She had to be. Her advice was just bad. Moving to Santa Barbara couldn't be the answer for Sierra's future. Chasing Jordan was definitely not a godly goal. That was something other women did. She had more substance than that.

Just then someone rapped on the door. Sierra tried to pull herself together. She turned on the porch light and looked through the slatted windows on the side. She could see the profile of a guy she didn't know.

"Are you looking for Mariana?" Sierra asked without unlocking the door.

"No, I'm looking for Jordan."

"He's not here. Do you want to try calling his cell to see when he'll be back?"

"I called him a couple of times and left messages. He hasn't called me back."

Sierra noticed that the guy had a surfboard in a travel cover with him.

"By any chance, are you Sierra?" the guy asked.

"Yes. Who are you?"

"I'm Derek."

CHAPTER TWENTY-NINE

Raindrops as fine and small as a sprinkling of dust particles managed to find their way to Jordan's camera lens. The unpredictable wind that twisted the rain and deposited the droplets on his lens had already knocked over one photographer's tripod. The weather acted like an unruly child, picking up handfuls of sand and throwing it at Jordan's back so that his bare legs felt as if they were being pelted and left with tiny pock marks.

Last night had been one crazy night. The sort of night he hoped never to repeat.

Jordan looked at the other photographers up and down the beach. They weren't deterred by the change in weather. They were hungry for the shots. They were eager to prove themselves to the sponsors in the same way the surfers were pulling out all the stops and performing on the fifteen-foot waves in view of a large audience on the sand and a lineup of sponsors in the raised booth.

And Derek was one of those competitors.

After Jordan's call to him the day before, Derek had checked into afternoon flights, found a seat on a flight that, with the time change, got him into Honolulu at 5:30. He caught a bus to the North Shore and ended up at the beach house a little after seven. Fortunately, Sierra was there to let him in.

Jordan was so frustrated over the meeting with Scott from Moana Ali'i surfboards and the way Mariana's practical joke had sabotaged it that he drove all the way into Haleiwa to find something to eat where, hopefully, no one would hassle him.

He had briefly considered going back to the beach house to see if Sierra wanted to go with him to Haleiwa, but it seemed like a bad idea considering his attitude. Aside from the two bites of sandwich, he hadn't eaten since their breakfast that morning by the window. That had been such a beautiful time with her. He didn't want to ruin it with a venting session about the immature antics of her best friend.

Jordan worked through a new way of how he would present himself to the next potential sponsor that came along. Better yet, he decided he would be the one to pursue the next sponsor. He would get an overview of which key sponsors were at the meet and then formulate a strategic plan to connect with the ones he wanted to work for. That's how Derek had been going about his search for a sponsor as a surfer. Why couldn't the same strategy work for a photographer?

An air horn sounded, signaling the end of the ten-minute heat. In a few minutes the next two competitors would be up. Derek was one of them. This was his first run. Jordan planted his feet, lowered his baseball cap, and lined up Derek in his lens as Derek paddled out toward the fifteen-foot blue beasts.

"This is it, Derek. You can do it."

Jordan had been so focused on the ocean he didn't think anyone was close enough to hear him.

Sierra's voice spoke up from his left side. "Which one is Derek?"

Jordan turned, surprised to see her. "Hey. How long have you been there?"

"Just a few minutes. I told Derek I'd watch when he was up."

Sierra wore her Rancho Corona sweatshirt and had the hood up, protecting her from the rain that was now coming down at a steady pace. Her blond curls seemed to be trying to escape the hood's restriction and tumbled out both sides. She had on a pair of shorts, and to Jordan's surprise, she was wearing cowboy boots. It was one of the most unexpected combinations he had seen on a girl, but somehow it made him want to stare at her.

Last night Sierra had ducked into her room and closed the door as soon as Jordan arrived back at the beach house. At the time he thought she was being considerate in leaving the room so that Jordan and Derek could have the chance to talk, that is, after Jordan recovered from the surprise of Derek arriving when he did. Mariana wasn't back yet when Jordan and Derek turned in for the night. As far as he knew, she stayed out all night.

"He's in the green rash guard." Jordan dragged his attention back to his camera and to Derek, who was now getting in position, waiting for just the right wave. He had only ten minutes to wow the judges.

"Sorry," Sierra said. "What's a rash guard?"

"A shirt," Jordan said without looking away. "Sort of like a sleeveless wet suit top." He focused the lens and put all his concentration on Derek.

The next wave swelled, and the other surfer who had gone out with Derek made a move for it. Derek hung back and rode over the top of the bronco as his competitor got up on his board and showed the audience why he was a favorite to take sweeps. Out of loyalty, Jordan didn't shoot the competitor. Then he realized that, if this guy did win and Jordan turned in his frames for the day without including any of what could be the winning ride, he would jeopardize his position with the magazine.

Jordan caught three crisp shots as the competitor came out the other side of the barrel with his hand gracing the wall of the wave. The guys who had the sophisticated cameras in the water were the ones who could nail those inside shots. Still, Jordan was pretty pleased with what he got.

The ocean seemed to be calming down as the rain pelted the sand, leaving tiny polka dots all around. Jordan had rigged an umbrella-like covering over the end of his lens, but the wind had torn it up. He steadied his tripod and pulled a cloth from his bag so that he could use the lull to make sure the lens was clear. In the middle of this process he realized Sierra was gone. He didn't blame her for taking off. The wind and rain didn't make for enjoyable conditions on the beach.

Just knowing she had been there beside him earlier had made Jordan happier than he would have thought it could. And now he couldn't believe it, but he missed her. He wished she was still there by his side. At the same time, he was impressed by how sensitive she was to give him space when he was working or, as she had done last night, take her leave so he and Derek could talk privately.

Jordan got his eye back where it belonged and focused the camera on Derek as the next set lined up. The waves came in an odd assortment of undesirable swells. These waves weren't at all like the ones that had been breaking yesterday and most of the morning. The storm that was rolling in was having an effect on how the deep water was behaving beyond the coral reef. Time was getting away. Derek needed to make a move, or he would be shut out of the entire session.

His competitor tried one of the inconsistent waves and took a dive off the top before the beaut crested. Derek let one more fickle wave pass, and then he took his shot. By the limited time left on the clock, Jordan knew what Derek had to know also: This was his one shot. He had to make it.

Jordan snapped photos the minute Derek got up on his board. He was leaning farther forward than Jordan had remembered seeing him lean in before. But then, Derek never had ridden such a big wave before. He kept his balance, bobbing the nose of the board up and down in an effort to keep control as the top of the wave closed over him like a giant, foaming fist.

For a moment, Jordan couldn't see Derek. He knew this was where so many of the surfers lost it, inside the curl. The more experienced surfers knew how to get low to increase their speed and maximize the wave's force on the back of the board. The ones who could hang on in that tunnel of unstable power were the ones who shot out of the open end of the barrel with a blast of white sea spray chasing them as they flew along the face of the diminishing arm of the wave.

Jordan held his breath. He kept shooting, watching as two and then three seconds passed. If Derek was going to make it out, it had to be now.

There he was! The flash of green from his rash guard was the first thing Jordan saw through the sheet of white ocean spray. The tip of Derek's blue board blended with the water and wasn't recognizable until he was all the way out. Derek went for a risky turn, and as he did, the irregular wave seemed to lash out with a watery whip and flipped the board from the backside up. Derek shot straight up above the wave and did a duck and roll sort of plunge into the water with his surfboard still attached by the ankle strap.

Jordan captured it all on film. Pulling away, he tried to focus his eyes for long distance, waiting to see Derek and his board as they rolled toward shore. Jordan also knew that this was one of the most treacherous parts of the runs at Sunset Beach. He had heard the other photographers talking about the undertow in the deep water. He had also heard a lot about the coral reef. It was what kept the big waves out to sea and away from the shoreline, but it was one of the worst on Oahu for surfers and responsible for serious injuries and even deaths over the years.

All Jordan could see was the expanse of feisty white water churned up where the wave had come down with great force. One of the jet skis was heading out to the site. Derek's competitor was lined up to take the next wave that was about to crest. Again, Jordan felt torn. He needed to do his job and take the important shots of the day. But he wanted to rush down to the water and watch as the jet skis pulled Derek in.

First they had to find him.

Jordan took one shot of the competitor as he rose to his feet at the top of what had to be one of the biggest waves of the day. He kept clicking as the experienced surfer took his position and then found he couldn't hold it.

While the crowd on the beach watched, the surfer who was favored to win took a dive down a twenty-foot wave. His ankle strap broke loose, and his surfboard shot into the air like a rocket ship, spinning as it flew over the waves backside.

Jordan snapped all the way through the moment until neither the surfer nor the board could be seen. Then he left his camera and ran to the shore where he saw the jet ski coming in with Derek in tow.

Sierra was already at the shore. "They have him," she said.

Jordan felt frantic. If Derek came out of this mangled in any way, what would Mindy do? Derek needed to go home in one piece. He was going to be a father. He had a lot of responsibility waiting for him at home. This was insane. What had they been thinking?

The jet ski did a turn in the shallower water. Two lifeguards went over to the stretcher that was rigged to the back of the jet ski. For a moment the lifeguards bent over Derek, and nobody moved.

"Is he okay?" Sierra asked.

"I can't tell. Why aren't they bringing him on shore?"

Sierra stepped closer and slid her hand into Jordan's. He was surprised at what a difference her soft and comforting closeness made in calming him down. He gave her hand a squeeze and then, because he couldn't stand not knowing, he let go of Sierra's hand, threw his baseball cap on the sand, and ran into the water.

CHAPTER THIRTY

Sierra drew both her hands to her mouth as she watched Jordan plunge into the water. He swam toward the jet ski where Derek was laid out on the stretcher at the back. Two lifeguards were bent over him, and she couldn't tell if Derek was even moving.

A second jet ski with an attached stretcher had been dispatched to rescue Derek's competitor. He was towed in to the shallow water and managed to slide off the stretcher and make his way to shore without assistance. His board, it seemed, was on its way to the nearest neighboring island.

Sierra thought she saw Derek's head come up just about the time that Jordan reached him. They were in shallow enough water and, while it was churned up and not desirable for an afternoon swim, it seemed safe for them to stay where they were and assess the situation.

"Can you tell if he's okay?" A man wearing a straw beach hat came up alongside Sierra and dipped his chin toward Derek.

"I can't tell." She went over and scooped up Jordan's baseball cap from where he had tossed it on the sand.

The man followed her. "Was that your boyfriend who went out in the water after him?"

"No, he's a photographer. He and Derek have been friends since college. This was their dream. Jordan is here on assignment for *Surf Days*, and this was Derek's first run. His wife was hit by car a few days ago on her bike. They almost lost the baby she's carrying, but for the moment she's okay. Derek just got here last night."

Sierra suddenly stopped her nervous rattling and put both her hands over her mouth again. She knew the anxiety of the moment had released the floodgates of information, but that was no excuse. She should never share so many personal details with a stranger.

"Sorry," she said quickly. "I'm just nervous."

The guy nodded. "It's okay. I understand. Hey, look. They have him up."

Sierra saw Derek heading toward them with his board. Jordan was right beside him. As they made their way to shore, Sierra said, "It looks like he's all right!"

"Do you know if either of your friends is sponsored? I mean, aside from the magazine?"

"No. They're hoping that might happen while they're here. It's super-competitive, from what I understand. Jordan had a meeting last night that didn't go well with a sponsor he was hoping to impress; so I think they're both a little discouraged about that."

Sierra realized that, once again, she was saying far too much. She pressed her lips together and watched as Derek and Jordan emerged from the water and walked toward her. She went to meet them holding Jordan's baseball cap for him. It relieved her that the guy in the straw hat didn't follow her.

"Are you okay?" she asked.

Derek nodded. He coughed and shook the water from his ears.

Sierra looked at Jordan, expressing her relief. He gave her an appreciative nod and took his baseball cap, which she held out to him.

Derek said, "Thanks, man," and gave Jordan a slap on the back.

"You sure you're okay?"

"Yeah, I'm good."

The three of them headed back to where Jordan had abandoned his camera. Fortunately, everything was as he had left it. The wind hadn't toppled the stand, and no one had walked off with any of his expensive equipment.

Sierra pulled a beach towel from her shoulder bag and offered it to both of them. Not that it made much difference since the rain was still coming in at an angle. Neither of the guys had much to say. They patted their faces dry. Jordan put on his cap and went back to work, putting all his attention onto his camera.

Derek hung around for a little while and then said he was going to the booth to see if he had made the lineup for the afternoon heat. She could tell that he would be content to sit out the next heat. Whatever happened out there had shaken him deeply.

After Derek left, Sierra wondered what she should do. It wasn't pleasant being out in the rain and wind with the heart-stopping life-and-death moments playing out in front of her. But she had nothing to do back at the beach house. Mariana hadn't come home all night. Sierra guessed she was having fun with Tianna after making her declaration yesterday about how un-fun Sierra was.

That morning Sierra had woken up before Derek and Jordan. She had made coffee for all of them, and that's when she heard Jordan's account of what had happened at Ted's with Mariana and Tianna. Sierra felt like apologizing for her friend's actions but knew she didn't need to. Mariana was who she was. Sierra wasn't responsible for anything Mariana said or did.

Sierra also picked up how discouraged Jordan was after he had missed out on making a good connection with the guy from the surfboard company. Jordan didn't make any suggestions about the two of them connecting for dinner that night. Nor did he seem to remember the cooking competition they were supposed to be having. Sierra had made a comment about how, if they did manage to set up a night to show off their culinary expertise, Derek would have to be the judge now since Mariana seemed to be spending her vacation elsewhere. Jordan's expression made it clear that he had traveled miles in his thinking since that playful challenge had been made.

So now that she was standing in the rain-tossed weather, she tried her mother's recent remedy for indecision. Sierra asked herself, *What would I like to do right now?*

The surprising answer was to go shopping. That was Mariana's cure-all for boredom, not Sierra's. What made the difference this time was that Sierra had noticed a number of little huts alongside the road that sold gauze skirts and wind chimes made from shells. That was her kind of shopping. Not high-end designer wear and shoes with impossible heels.

"I'm going now," Sierra said softly, hoping not to disturb Jordan's concentration.

He pulled back from the camera and looked at her with surprise. "You are?"

She nodded. "I'll see you later."

"Are you sure you need to go?"

Sierra hesitated. It was nice of him to come across so interested all of a sudden. But she didn't see any point in staying. It wasn't as if they could talk while he worked.

"I'll see you back at the house later."

"Okay."

As Sierra walked away, she could feel Jordan watching her. This was more attention than he had shown to her last night and this morning combined. But she knew he had a lot going on. She didn't expect to be his top priority. It was nice, though, to feel noticed.

Once Sierra was back at the house, she saw Mariana's car in the driveway. Sierra entered quietly, guessing that Mariana would be asleep, and she was right. Sierra tried to gather her things. She left her heavy sweatshirt at the house and slipped her shoulder bag across the front of her. If she got wet in the rain, she got wet. She didn't care. It was warm rain. Her plan was to ride one of the beach cruiser bikes she had seen in the garage, and that meant she wanted to be unencumbered as she pedaled.

Mariana didn't move from her splayed-out position on the bed. She was wearing her ruffled eye mask and her purple earplugs. Sierra guessed it had been a long night and her friend had partied hard. She would probably sleep until sunset.

Maneuvering the bike out of the garage, Sierra realized it had been a long time—a very long time—since she had ridden a bike. She took her time, checking the tires, moving the handlebars, making sure the seat was firmly in place. Swinging her cowboy-booted leg over the low center bar, Sierra got back in the saddle and rode that two-wheeled pony out of the driveway and onto the long walkway that went up and down the coast for miles. Lots of people were out walking and riding in spite of the drippy, windy weather.

Sierra loved the feeling that came with riding a bike again. She had forgotten how this felt, like a slice of one of the best parts of childhood. It represented a sense of freedom and independence. That was how she had always felt when she climbed on her bike and took off to a friend's house as a child. She pretended she could go wherever she wanted to, including to the moon and back. Sierra realized how much her sense of independence had been wired in her from early on.

The first shop she saw across the road was painted a rainbow of bright colors. Sundresses on wire hangers flapped in the breeze like banners. Two young women sat out front in white plastic patio chairs as one of them braided the other's hair.

Sierra crossed at the crosswalk and leaned her bike against a palm tree next to the shop.

"Aloha," one of the women said. "You're welcome to go on in. If you see anything you like, let me know."

Sierra entered the small shop that was part manufactured home and part add-on creative construction. She had seen plenty of structures like this in Brazil, but it was odd to see one on American soil. Clearly the building inspector hadn't been out here for a while.

Inside the shop was a display case with gorgeous silver jewelry for reasonable prices. On every inch of wall space there hung either a painting, a hook with a variety of scarves, or a peg with small purses made from coconuts. One wall was covered with frames made out of Hawaiian license plates and hand painted T-shirts with dolphins and sea turtles. From the ceiling hung long beaded necklaces and strings of pastel-colored pearls.

Sierra loved everything about this shop. She took her time examining all the clever works of art. One pair of earrings caught her attention. They were made from small shells that hung in three dangling strings like tiny wind chimes.

Poking her head out the door, Sierra called out, "I found some earrings I'd like."

The woman who had greeted her stood up and smoothed out her wraparound skirt before taking the stairs up into the shop. "Which ones did you find?"

Sierra pointed to them in the case, and the woman took them out. "These are the smallest puka shells I've ever seen. A local woman collects shells on the beach and then makes them into jewelry for me. She just brought these in the other day. I think the storms are bringing up a lot of treasures from the sea."

Sierra loved the earrings. She loved that they were made

from "treasures from the sea" right here on the island. The price was more than she wanted to pay out of her limited funds, but for these earrings from this place, it was worth it.

"How do you say 'thank you' in Hawaiian?" Sierra asked the woman.

"*Mahalo*. Or, *mahalo nui loa,* which means 'thank you very much.'"

Sierra went for the shortened version and repeated "mahalo," which was about as ambitious as she thought she could be considering her challenge with languages. Slipping back onto her bike, she stayed on the inland side of the road and pedaled her way to two more shops where she enjoyed just looking.

The rain had stopped. The sun felt warm on her head as she pedaled her way back to the house. She was thinking of what a pleasant day this had ended up being. It wasn't because she had her future figured out, because that certainly wasn't true. It wasn't peaceful because she and Mariana were getting along so great, because that relationship still felt like a time bomb waiting to go off. And it definitely wasn't because she felt as if she and Jordan had a future just waiting to open up for them with a dazzling display of fireworks.

What Sierra felt good about was being in the moment.

Her mom's reminder to delight oneself in the Lord had stuck with Sierra, and she had decided that morning she was going to find ways to experience that delight while she was in Hawaii. It was working. She was thoroughly enjoying what she had in front of her right now, as she rode the bike under the gorgeous palm trees and felt the wind on her face. This was her vacation.

Right now. Today. She felt protected by God and very much loved by Him. All her life He had led her in paths of righteousness for His name's sake. Sierra had every reason to believe He was going to continue to lead her.

The best part was that she felt confident she was going to like whatever it was He led her to next.

CHAPTER THIRTY-ONE

Jordan missed Sierra.

He knew that was crazy. She had only stood by him for a bit, yet he missed her presence.

Shaking away thoughts of her, he went back to work. The competition went into the late afternoon, and Derek didn't come up again on the roster. Depending on how the scoring went tomorrow morning, he could have another chance at the lineup in the afternoon. If he didn't make that cut, then he was out.

As soon as Jordan heard that and took a look at the lineup for the remainder of the day, he headed back to the beach house with Derek so Jordan could edit and upload his quota of shots on Bill's site. He knew it was going to be a lot of work, but at least he could do it sitting down.

"Did you connect with any sponsors?" Jordan asked Derek as the two of them trekked slowly through the sand. Derek had his board under his arm, and Jordan carried his heavy camera bag over his shoulder. They were both moving a lot more slowly than they had that morning when they headed out for their big day.

"I was pretty much shut out," Derek said. "I think it's all locked in for this year. I didn't think the competition would be this tight. I'm not trying to be negative about it, just realistic. It's not lookin' good."

"Then we go with what we have, and we do what we can." Jordan stopped walking through the hot sand and turned to the ocean. "Look at this. All this. We made it this far, didn't we? We never thought the day would come, but it did. This was our day. You had an epic ride, Derek. I have it all on film. Wait till you see. Even you won't believe it's you. You did it. You surfed Sunset."

Derek stood next to him and nodded slowly. "You're right. I haven't even stopped to think about that."

"Like I said, wait till you see the photos. Mindy is going to love it. She'll be so happy for you."

Derek began walking again, slowly. "You know the saying they have about this place? They say that the North Shore will make you or break you."

"I'm glad it didn't break open your head today."

"Yeah. Although, I think I might have cracked a rib. "I'm hurtin' pretty bad."

"Do you think you should have it looked at?"

"No. I think I need to call my wife, eat something, have a look at your photos, and then sleep."

Jordan was glad to see Sierra's car in the driveway when they returned to the house. He wasn't so thrilled when he saw Mariana's car there as well.

The two guys used the garden hose to wash the sand off their feet and the saltwater off Derek's surfboard. Jordan had a look around the other side of the house and noticed a strip of yellow guard tape had been placed across the bottom of the stairs. Apparently the inspector had been there and condemned the stairs. That meant he and Derek couldn't retreat to the upstairs apartment if things turned uncomfortable with Sierra and Mariana. He wasn't too worried, but after Mariana's prank last night, he was prepared to move back upstairs—rickety staircase or not—if he needed to.

The guys entered the house and heard the shower running. Jordan looked around. One of the women was showering, and one of them was probably out on the beach. He decided to get moving on the editing and uploading while Derek went hunting in the refrigerator.

"We need some food here," Derek said. "Who bought the carrot sticks? That's not food. We need to go to the grocery store."

Jordan ignored his friend and went to work transferring the photos from the camera to his laptop. As soon as all of them were safely uploaded and saved, he went searching for the shots of Derek. "Do you want to see these?"

Derek came over, chomping in an exaggerated way on a handful of carrot sticks.

"Dude," he muttered.

Jordan smiled. "That's you, dude. See what I mean?"

"It doesn't feel like it looks when you're out there. It doesn't seem like a sheer cliff. Wait, go back. Look at that one!"

"I know, That's you, Derek. These turned out good."

"You have the skills, man."

"So do you, Derek."

"Whoa! Look how clear that one is. Perfect." Derek had stopped chomping. He leaned in closer. "That really is me, isn't it?"

"Yup."

"I did it, didn't I?"

"Yes, you did."

"Have you sent these to Mindy yet?"

"No. I have to send them to Bill first. Then she can go on *Surf Days'* site and see them as soon as he uploads the ones he wants."

"You can't just send them to her like you always do?"

"Nope. It's part of my agreement."

"That's a bummer. I'm not going to ask you to cheat for me though."

"That's good," Jordan said. "Because you know I wouldn't do it. I can't. My word has to mean something." He was talking more to himself than to Derek. What he didn't expect was the response that came from behind the closed bedroom door.

"That's interesting," Mariana's voice called out. "So, if you give your word that you're going to take my friend to dinner and then you end up going out with a bunch of guys, that's not because your word doesn't mean anything?"

Jordan froze. He had explained to Sierra that he had a meeting last night She said she understood. Did she say something to Mariana about his going back on his word? Was that why Mariana played the prank on him?

"What are you and Sierra doing for dinner tonight?" Jordan hoped to quickly smooth over whatever misunderstanding had taken place.

"Wouldn't you like to know?" Mariana answered.

"Yes, as a matter of fact, I would like to know so that I can arrange to have my business meetings elsewhere." As soon as the words were out, Jordan wished he could reel them back in.

The bedroom door opened, and Mariana came out in a short, strapless dress with her long hair hanging over her shoulders and still dripping from the shower. Derek's mouth dropped open, and he put the bag of carrot sticks on the counter.

"Hello," she said, giving Derek a sweet smile. "Who are you?"

"Derek. Jordan's friend."

"Are you single?"

"No, I'm very happily married."

"I thought you might be. Well, welcome anyway." Turning to Jordan she said, "So you're saying that was a business meeting last night at Ted's?"

"Yes, it was. I told Sierra. She understood. You don't need to worry about her feelings being hurt or anything, if that's what's going on here."

"The only thing I worry about with Sierra is that she's too serious. She needs to lighten up. Maybe you do too, Jordan. I was only having a little fun last night."

He couldn't tell if her soft words were sincere.

Mariana came over to him smelling of fragrant island flowers. She put her hand on his shoulder. "Jordan, I'm sorry. I really am. I didn't know. I thought you would enjoy the joke."

Before Jordan could reply, the door opened, and Sierra stepped inside, her face glowing. "Aloha," she said when her gaze fell on Derek in the kitchen. Derek's gaze went to the kitchen table, and Sierra followed his line of sight. Jordan watched as Sierra's countenance fell when she saw Mariana in her short dress, standing so close to him.

Instead of removing her arm from where it rested on Jordan's shoulder, Mariana turned to him and said, "I hope you'll forgive me, Jordan. Sometimes I go just a little too far." With that, she went over to her purse and shoes on the bar stool, picked them up, and slung the strappy black shoes over her shoulder.

"Don't wait up," she said.

"Where are you going?" Sierra asked as Mariana brushed past her.

Mariana paused on the doorstep to strap on her sandals. "Waikiki Do you want to come with us and have a little fun?"

Sierra didn't answer.

"I didn't think so." Marian pressed the clicker on her car locking system and left.

CHAPTER THIRTY-TWO

For a moment, Sierra stood by the open front door of the beach house debating if she should go after Mariana and try to convince her not to go to Waikiki.

She knew her independent friend would resist. This was how Mariana spent her vacations. After a trip, she would tell Sierra crazy stories about parties with new friends she had met at dance clubs. Whenever Sierra would scowl, Mariana would assure her that she knew her limits and was a good judge of character. Those two qualities kept Mariana from getting "sucked under," as she called it. She could flirt, have fun, go just a little crazy, and leave before a party went bad.

Sierra hoped Mariana's formula for avoiding trouble would work once again. She really wished the two of them had been able to talk today. After Mariana's accusation about Sierra not being a fun companion, Sierra felt she needed to defend herself or at least prove they could do lots of fun things together. She knew the vacation hadn't gone the way Mariana had hoped. But to Sierra's way of thinking, Mariana hadn't given Sierra a chance to show that she was fun to be around. The bike ride would have been the perfect way for Sierra to make her case. At least it would have been Sierra's idea of fun.

"Are you okay?" Derek asked from the kitchen.

Sierra broke away from her contemplation. She could hear Mariana's car exiting the driveway and released a wobbly breath. "Yes, I'm okay. I'm concerned for my friend."

"Is she going to be all right?" Jordan stood from the table and went over to Sierra by the open front door.

"I hope so. She knows her limits, and she's a good judge of character." Sierra knew she was repeating those two points to convince herself, not Jordan.

"Is there anything we should do?" Jordan asked.

"No. I don't know. She will probably be fine. She always is." Sierra closed the door and pulled off her cowboy boots and socks so that she could feel the cool tile floor on her bare feet. "Mariana is determined to make her own decisions and live life her way."

"Aren't we all," Derek said.

The three of them stood quietly in a triangle, exchanging half glances.

"I'm going to grab the shower," Derek said. "Unless you were hoping to get in there right away, Sierra."

"No, go ahead. How was the rest of the day for you guys?"

"Good," Jordan said. "I took some great shots of Derek. Would you like to see them?"

"Sure."

Sierra followed Jordan to the laptop, relieved that the awkward moment with Mariana was put aside and that it didn't dominate the conversation. She hoped that when Mariana returned that night, the two of them could have a heart-to-heart talk and settle their tiff. The best way Sierra saw that happening was by the two of them making a plan to do some fun things together during the few days they had left. Sierra was thinking that going for a sunset cruise might be fun. She had seen a flyer advertising cruises, whale-watching excursions, and a snorkeling sail during which they could see turtles and tropical fish. She and Mariana needed to book something like that. Then the fun would begin.

Sierra leaned in behind Jordan as he clicked through a set of photos that caught every second of Derek's impressive ride on the monster wave. "Wow. Those are amazing, Jordan. You really are gifted at catching just the right angle."

"It has a lot to do with the light."

"I was meaning to ask you. Do you have a website?"

"Yes, but it's outdated. I need to overhaul it."

"What about a brochure or a flyer or something? Do you have something printed that you can hand out to people when you meet them? That way they can see some of your work immediately, and they'll have your contact information. Then they can go to your website for more pictures."

"That's a great idea. I've never had anything like that. A flyer would have been helpful with the sponsor I met with last night. I felt so unprepared. I didn't know how to make a pitch to him the way I've seen Derek do with sponsors. He's a natural at it."

"Well, let me know if you need any help with doing something like that. One of my first office positions in Brazil was helping the graphic designer who did all the visuals and printed materials for the mission and the church we went to. He was good. I learned a lot."

Jordan looked up at Sierra. "Thanks. I just might take you up on that. Although, it could be challenging to communicate about details like that via e-mail. I suppose I could find someone where I live who could pull together something for me. It's a great idea. Thanks, Sierra."

"Sure." She pulled back and headed for the kitchen, processing his response. It made sense for him to work with someone local, but was he trying to say that he didn't plan to stay in touch with her after they went their separate ways?

She didn't want to read too much or too little into Jordan's comments. That had been one of her biggest problems way back in her fledgling relationship with Paul. She didn't want to operate now under a teenage set of relationship evaluation points. The only problem was her relationship with Paul was her sole reference point.

"Are you hungry?" She hoped the change of topics would keep her emotions buoyant. She had been so happy that afternoon on her bike ride. All her feelings about Jordan and her future had been hopeful. Now she was concerned about Mariana, frustrated about their lack of communication, and reading finality into Jordan's comments about their brief connection. It wasn't looking good on any front.

"Yeah, but I can wait," Jordan said. "I have to edit and upload these photos for Bill at the magazine."

"Okay." Sierra closed the refrigerator door.

"Do you want to go out later?"

She looked over at Jordan and saw that he was watching her, eyebrows raised, waiting for a reply.

"Do you mean go out somewhere to eat?" Sierra wanted to be sure she understood him correctly.

"Yes. I need to make up for the way I flaked on you for dinner last night."

"Don't worry about that."

"What do you think? As soon as I'm done here, we can go."

"Sure." She looked at the clock. "Do you think you and Derek would like a snack before then?"

"I wouldn't mind. Thanks, Sierra."

She pulled a variety of potential ingredients out of the fridge and used her creative energy to whip up some deviled eggs and a chopped salad with lettuce, olives, oranges, and carrots.

Derek and Jordan made the food disappear in minutes. Derek went out on the front patio to call Mindy while Jordan kept at his project. Sierra cleaned up the kitchen and then retreated to the bedroom where she closed the door all but a crack and stretched out on her bed.

A familiar melancholy covered her like a thin blanket. Outside the evening sounds of the geckos eclipsed the constant chatter of the tropical birds. Sierra felt this semisweet sadness every time she started to feel at home somewhere in Brazil. She would put down roots, and then something would change and she would have to move again. It didn't seem logical that she should feel that same way about being at a beach house with these guys she had just met.

Yet being in the kitchen, being in the rhythm of everyday living with them, felt strangely normal. It was as if this was what she was supposed to do, and these were the people she was supposed to be doing life with. It made no sense.

Sierra prompted herself not to analyze any of her feelings.

After all, they were only feelings, and she knew how unreliable they could be.

Drifting off for a short nap, Sierra hoped the sense of bliss she had experienced that afternoon would return when she awoke. She wanted to enjoy her time with Jordan that evening and not think about what was next.

When Sierra awoke, it was dark. The ocean waves' constant thunder was the only sound she heard. Getting up, she opened the door, expecting to see Jordan still at the table, working on his laptop.

But Jordan wasn't there. The only light came from under the hood over the stove.

Sierra squinted as she tried to read the clock on the microwave. It was still flashing all eights since it hadn't been reset after the power outage. She turned on a light and went over to Jordan's laptop since it was the only place she could think of to find the correct time. When she lifted the top, the screen lit up, and she saw that her mermaid photo was back as his screen saver. That made her smile.

10:47 was the time on Jordan's computer.

Oh no! How did I sleep that long?

Sierra didn't remember hearing a thing. If Jordan had tried to wake her to go to dinner, she hadn't heard him. She didn't think she had moved once. Now that she was awake, she wasn't sure what to do. Had the guys gone to dinner without her? Were they still out? She knew that Mariana hadn't returned.

Opening the front door, Sierra padded outside under the gently swaying palm trees. By the pale blue light coming from over the neighbor's garage, Sierra could see that Jordan's car was there. The guys were probably asleep. She still couldn't believe how deeply she had slept. She had to admit it was the best rest she had experienced since she had arrived.

The cool night air felt good as she wrapped her arms around her middle and looked up at the sky. Above her a half moon, looking like a surfboard wedged in the sand, jutted up from behind a silver cloud. It wasn't golden as she would have expected a Hawaiian moon to be. This midnight moon had a pale ivory tone and seemed far away.

Sierra kept her face to the heavens and whispered a prayer. This time the prayer wasn't about herself and her future. Her prayer was for Mariana.

Padding back inside, Sierra went hunting in the fridge for something to eat. She saw a pizza box and discovered two remaining slices of takeout pepperoni pizza. It had been a long time since she had eaten cold American pizza. The guys wouldn't mind if she ate their leftovers, would they? They had no idea what a big treat this was for her.

The first bite was in Sierra's mouth and she was enjoying all the old familiar flavors along with memories of high school days and her favorite breakfast after Friday family pizza night, when she heard a cell phone buzz.

From behind the closed door of the guys' room she heard Jordan's groggy voice. "Hello?"

She swallowed the bite of pizza and listened, hoping this wasn't an emergency call about Derek's wife.

"Yeah, she's here. Where are you? Are you okay?"

Sierra heard footsteps as Jordan stumbled out of bed. The door opened, and he squinted in the light that Sierra had turned on over the counter. Jordan looked up, surprised to see Sierra standing there.

"Mariana, she s right here." He handed the phone to Sierra, clearly concerned.

"Mariana, are you okay?"

"Sierra." Mariana's voice came out low and raspy through the phone. She said only three words, but they were weighted with deep fear. "I need help."

CHAPTER THIRTY-THREE

Jordan was bummed that he had missed the deadline to send the photos to Bill. He had missed it by only five minutes, but still, in this competitive business, five minutes provided enough of a wedge for an amateur to slide in and win the vote for what would be displayed on the website's home page. Jordan knew he would have to step things up if he wanted to maintain his position. He never expected this much pressure when he agreed to the assignment. He loved capturing memorable moments in photos, but he didn't love feeling as if he had to continually compete for his position. It was the nature of the business, and he knew that and knew he was in no position to complain. He was living his dream.

Derek had stretched out on the lounge chair on the patio and was zoning out after his call to Mindy. Jordan guessed that Sierra had fallen asleep as well, based on how quiet things were after she went to her room.

Jordan made his way to the shower, hoping he still had a clean shirt to wear. He grabbed one of his least crumpled T-shirts and a pair of shorts and knocked softly on the closed bathroom door. When no reply came, he opened it and entered. The adjoining door on the other side of the bathroom opened to the room where Sierra was.

Carefully reaching to close the door, Jordan caught a glimpse of Sierra asleep on the bed. The fading peach-colored light from the sunset illuminated the room, providing a natural spotlight to hundreds of floating dust particles in the air. They seemed like tiny dancers sprinkling her with broken bits of dreams. He wondered if that was what life had been like for her. That was what he had picked up from what she had shared about her time in Brazil.

Jordan knew he should look away and close the door, but he felt captivated. Sierra's back was to him, and her wild, blond curls cascaded over her shoulder like the foliage he had photographed on the sea cliffs on Maui. Her slim legs and bare feet curved gracefully across the bedspread, reminding him once again of a mermaid.

Jordan knew it would be too invasive to take a picture of her, but he wished he could capture her lovely position. The light would be this soft for only another few moments. If he set the aperture right, he might even catch the dust particles as they floated above her.

He quietly closed the door and took his shower, trying to think about something other than Sierra. It was difficult.

Jordan figured he had made enough noise with the water running in the shower to awaken Sierra so that once he was out of the shower and dressed they could go to dinner. He was surprised to find that she wasn't in the kitchen when he emerged. Derek was still asleep in the lounge chair on the patio. He stirred, though, when Jordan opened the screen door and went outside.

"What's the plan?" Derek asked.

"I think Sierra is asleep. She didn't come out here, did she?"

"No. Are you going to wake her?"

Jordan debated. "No. I think I'll pick up a pizza and a few things at the grocery store. We can all eat here. I'll take her to dinner tomorrow night."

Derek turned in the lounge chair and seemed to be trying to get a good look at Jordan's face. He lowered his voice. "So what do you think?"

"What do I think about what?"

Derek gave him a smirk, "Come on, Jordan. You haven't said a thing about what you think about her." He emphasized the "her" and pointed toward the bedroom with his thumb.

"Her, huh? Is that what I should start calling her? The Great 'Her.'"

"You're not ready to make a declaration about her. Interesting. I know you. You'll avoid the topic as long as you can. To honor your cold feet, I won't ask again. You can tell me what you want, when you want."

"Cold feet? I just met her."

"So?"

"So, she lives in Brazil."

"That's why they invented e-mail, Skype, and airplanes."

Jordan shook his head. "The timing isn't right."

Derek nodded.

"It's too bad." Jordan rubbed his hair with the palm of his hand, sending the last drops of water from his shower into the air. "She's pretty amazing."

"And gorgeous."

Jordan gave Derek a surprised look. "You're married, dude."

"I still have eyes." Derek leaned back in the chair and folded his hands behind his neck. "And so do a whole lot of other guys. You should have heard what they were saying about her on the beach today."

Jordan pulled a lawn chair around to face Derek. The light had faded so Jordan had difficulty making out Derek's expression. "What did they say?"

“Some of the other surfers asked who she was when they saw that she was down at the water.”

“What did you tell them?”

“I said she was from Brazil. There’s a big group here from Brazil. You know their homeboy won The Eddie a few years ago. It’s a big change from a couple of decades ago when the locals smashed up the boards of the Brazilian surfers and sent ’em home. They exacted their revenge in the best way.”

Jordan wasn’t interested in surfing history at the moment. He was more concerned with what Derek had told the guys about Sierra. “You didn’t tell them her name or where she was staying, did you?”

“Look at you, going all Homeland Security.” Derek laughed. “Why should it matter what I told them? You haven’t made your move on her. From what it sounds like, you don’t plan to, either.”

Jordan rubbed the back of his head, feeling frustrated with the direction this conversation was going. He didn’t know how to respond. True, he did feel irked that other guys were asking about Sierra. She was too good for them. But Derek was right. Jordan hadn’t indicated to Sierra that he wanted to pursue anything with her.

Derek was watching Jordan, and Jordan could feel his gaze even though he was looking down.

“Wow.” Derek swung his legs over the side of the lounge chair and stood up. “I hadn’t expected this. You got it bad, bro.”

“What? For her?”

“No. For your career. You have the dream by the tail, and you’re not letting go for anything or anyone.”

“Is there something wrong with that?”

“I don’t know, man. We’ll see how it goes. It’s not over till it’s over, right?” The light coming from the kitchen caught the side of Derek’s face, illuminating his expression so that Jordan could see that he was serious.

"Right," Jordan agreed.

Derek headed for the screen door and stopped before he went inside. "But then, when it's over, I'm tellin' ya, the only thing that's going to matter is who's going to be there waiting for you at the end of the dream."

CHAPTER THIRTY-FOUR

Sierra looked at the clock on the dashboard of her rental car. It was 11:53. She had been driving around the same city block in Waikiki for ten minutes. If Mariana didn't show up in the next few minutes on the sidewalk where she said she would be, Sierra was calling the police. That was what Jordan had told her to do, and that was what she was going to do.

In the wake of Mariana's late-night SOS call, Jordan and Sierra had made some quick decisions. One of those decisions Sierra regretted. She had insisted that she go to Waikiki by herself to pick up Mariana. Now she wished she had agreed with him when he had pushed to come with her.

"I can handle this, Jordan." Sierra had tried to sound as forceful as she could. "I've managed to take care of myself all these years in the barrios of Brazil. I think I can handle driving to Waikiki to pick up my friend."

Jordan had backed down, which she appreciated. But his response to her was much more firm than she expected. "Fine. Go. No one is questioning your strength and independence here, Sierra. You don't have to prove anything, you know. No one is passing out gold stars for your good works and bravery."

She remembered the way his jaw flinched in the light of the kitchen. Then he added, "I can't stop you. So I'm not going to try. But here, take my cell phone. And if you have any problems, call the police immediately. I'm serious. Call the police."

"All right. I will." She had marched out the door, as if she were sure of what she was doing. Now, once again, she wished Jordan were with her.

Sierra slowly made the turn on Kalakaua Avenue and stayed in the lane close to the curb. After being on the North Shore and navigating Kamehameha Highway with ease, the contrast she discovered when she entered Waikiki was unnerving. Buses, cars, and trucks all jockeyed for position on the wide multi-lane boulevard. Tall buildings rose on either side of the street, and even though it was midnight, masses of people were strolling past high-end shops, restaurants, and entrances to hotel lobbies. This felt nothing like the five-star hotel she had stayed in on Maui. Nothing about this main drag in Waikiki felt like any of the other places she had been to on the two islands.

Sierra had her windows rolled down as she scanned the hundreds of people on the sidewalk and went as slowly as she could so that Mariana could spot her. The traffic fumes, humidity, and heat were getting to her so she turned on the air conditioner, just to breathe.

One more time around, Mariana. That's it. Then I'm calling the police.

Clutching the steering wheel, Sierra felt her anger rise again, as it had ever since she had put Jordan's phone to her ear and Mariana said, "I need help. Can you come get me?"

"What happened? Are you okay?"

"Tianna met a guy, and she wants to stay with him. We brought her car, and I don't have a way back. I'm not going to stay here. These aren't respectable guys. I'm so sorry to do this to you, Sierra, but I need you to come get me."

Sierra had jumped into fix-it mode. She grabbed a pen and wrote down the restaurant's name and address where Mariana said she was. Jordan's phone had directed her into downtown Waikiki where she was now circling the block. Sierra had called Mariana when she entered the Waikiki area, and all Mariana said was, "My battery is almost gone on my phone so listen. Don't park. Just drive by the address I gave you, and I'll come out and jump in the car."

Taking a chance that she might squeeze in one more call before Mariana's battery went dead, she had tried the number again about five minutes ago. No answer.

And no Mariana on the curb waiting.

Sierra inched her way around one of the thirty-story-high hotels and one of the many ABC stores she noticed along the way. She turned the air conditioner to the highest setting as she waited at what felt like an extremely long light that she had waited at multiple times. Drumming her thumbs on the steering wheel, she waited, she tried to pray, tried not to panic, tried to think through what to do next.

All that she could think of was Jordan's statement that nobody was giving out gold stars for good works and bravery. That really got to her. His comments about her independence and stubbornness weren't new. She had heard those descriptors many times. But the gold stars made it seem as if she were trying to prove something.

So what am I trying to prove?

She wasn't sure she wanted to know the answer to that question, and she definitely didn't want to know it now. Nudging her rental car to make the turn back onto Kalakaua Avenue, Sierra was about to pass the restaurant one more time. She drove slowly behind the truck ahead of her and continued to glance out the open passenger window. She thought she saw a raised hand in the crowd and slowed down to almost a stop.

The car behind her honked, but Sierra stayed where she was, trying to get a good look. She called out, "Mariana!"

From out of the crush of pedestrians, Mariana emerged with a tall guy right beside her, his arm was leaning on her shoulder.

What is she doing? Who is that guy?

Mariana pointed toward the crosswalk at the light. Sierra scooted ahead and stopped at the red light. The driver of the car behind her wasn't happy that he missed his chance to go through this time around. Mariana hurried to the car with the guy still keeping his hand on her shoulder.

Mariana opened the door.

"Hey," The guy said, leaning in to check out Sierra.

Mariana's expression was one Sierra hadn't seen before. She yelled over the noise around them in an overly enthusiastic voice. "This is Beau. He's from North Carolina."

Sierra couldn't believe Mariana was standing there, making introductions. "What's the deal? I've been circling the block and calling you!"

Just then the light turned green and Mariana made a lightning-fast entry into the passenger's seat, disconnecting herself from Beau. She slammed the door shut, locked it and yelled, "Go! Sierra, go!"

Sierra hit the gas pedal. She drove through the light and made the same turn she'd made five times that night.

Mariana looked over her shoulder "He's coming. Drive faster. Get us out of here!"

Sierra heard Beau's large hand thump on the side of the trunk as she coasted through a yellow light and made another turn.

"Mariana! What is going on?"

"I didn't think I'd ever get away from him. What a night. I

don't know what is wrong with Tianna. These guys were rough, you know what I mean? And so big."

"No, I don't know what you mean." Sierra made a quick turn and headed away from the hotel row and toward the freeway. She kept her temper to a simmer and looked for the sign for H-l so she could turn to enter the freeway.

"Mariana—"

"I know what you're going to say."

"No you don't.'

"Yes I do. You're going to tell me I'm irresponsible and flirting with disaster and that you're very angry with me."

Sierra had calmed just enough to respond with, "I would have started with the angry part first and yelled a little before moving on to the irresponsible part. But you know what? You're an adult. You're responsible for your own decisions. You don't need me to tell you anything. And I want you to know that, from here on out, I'm not coming to get you. This is your one-time pass. After this, you can take a taxi. Or rent another car. Or grow up."

"I've decided to grow up."

Sierra didn't add another comment. She was still angry.

For the next five minutes the two of them didn't talk. Sierra turned off the air conditioner and rolled her window halfway down to feel the breeze on her neck.

"You don't think I'm serious, but I am," Mariana said. "You can still be mad at me, if you want. I don't blame you. But I made my decision tonight. I don't want this sort of craziness anymore. Not like Tianna. That's why I didn't invite her to stay with us at the beach house. When I found out she was coming to Oahu at the same time, she asked to stay with me, but I said no. I told her I didn't want her to bring the guys home."

Sierra wanted to calm down and listen, but she was having a hard time. It was easier to stay mad.

"Tianna gave me a hard time, saying that I wouldn't let her

stay with me because of the guys, and yet you brought a guy home, and he's even staying with us. I told Tianna you were sleeping in the same room with me, not with Jordan, She didn't believe me."

"I don't care if she believed you."

"I know. And that's the thing about you, Sierra."

"The thing about me?"

"Yes. It's the good thing. You know who you are, and no one can convince you to think or do something different. You don't give in. It's the right kind of stubbornness. You have the right kind of morals, too. And look how happy you are."

At the moment Sierra felt like she was anything but happy.

"I was so jealous when you came back to the house glowing after your bike ride this afternoon. You didn't need a guy to make your day fun. You didn't need to get high. You just have this thing about you."

Again Sierra repeated, "This thing about me?"

Mariana let out a huff. "Okay, I'll say it. God. You have God. He's all over you. Or in you, or whatever it is. It's obvious. It's always been obvious, even when you're at your worst."

In a smaller voice Sierra said, "And you have certainly seen some of my worst moments these past few years."

"You've definitely seen some of mine. And . . ." Mariana paused. "You're still my friend."

The remaining fire in Sierra's emotions smoldered to gray ash. She felt her spirit calming. Over their years as friends they had had deep discussions about God as well as fiery arguments about religion versus relationship. Mariana ended each talk with the declaration that she was too young to give over the control of her life to Christ. But she would do it when she was an old lady. For now, she wanted to have fun.

"Thank you, Sierra, for coming all this way to get me."

"You're welcome. But I meant it when I said this is the only time I'm doing it."

"I know. And it will be." Mariana drew in a deep breath. She reached over and put her hand on Sierra's arm. "Sierra, I want what you have."

"What do you mean?"

"I want God. I want Him back in my life. Like He was when I was a girl. Before my mother died."

Sierra had waited a long time to hear Mariana say anything remotely close to the words that spilled out just now. She found that, now that this moment had come, she didn't know how to reply.

"I've seen how it is with you, Sierra. God has His hand on you. I want that. You don't have to say anything. I think you're still mad enough at me that you might try to talk me out of repenting."

"Well, actually—"

"No," Mariana interrupted. "Don't say anything. I know what to do. I know what to say. I'm going to pray. And I'm going to pray aloud because I want the demons to hear it and know they have lost one of their faithful subjects. You just drive. And don't try to stop me."

Sierra kept her blinking eyes on the well-lit highway and drove through the darkened night. As she drove, Mariana prayed in Portuguese. She prayed with such fire and fervor, Sierra felt every word burn inside her, even though she couldn't understand many of them.

After Mariana's prayer came a calm between them like an evening breeze. And after the calm came many tears, washing away all that had come before and making Mariana's overturned heart ready for what was yet to be.

CHAPTER THIRTY-FIVE

For the past two and a half hours Jordan had been looking at his computer screen, editing wedding photos and then looking out the open side window to see if any headlights were turning into their driveway. It seemed the best way to keep awake and yet not appear that he was waiting for Sierra to come back, even though he was.

I'm never going to forgive myself for not going with her. How could I have done that? If anything happens to her . . .

Jordan rose and went to the refrigerator. One slice of pizza remained. He took a bite and could hardly swallow it. He hated cold pizza. Sticking the rest of the slice in the microwave, he warmed it and ate it in four bites.

He had estimated how long it should take Sierra to drive to Waikiki and back and knew that if she hadn't encountered any problems she should have returned by now.

He had also considered driving to Waikiki. But without a cell phone to connect them, or any idea where Mariana had told Sierra to meet her, he doubted that he'd be able to find them. It was torture to sit there and do nothing.

Through the open window he saw the flash of car headlights

illuminating the room with a beam of heavenly hope. Jordan didn't bother to wait until the women came in. He charged out the door and went to them just as Mariana was opening the passenger door. She handed him a grocery bag.

"Here, can you take this?" Mariana said.

"Why did you guys stop for groceries?" Jordan knew his voice was louder and sounded more irritated than he intended. "We have food here."

"We don't have birthday cake and ice cream here," Mariana said.

Jordan looked over the top of the car at Sierra as she climbed out of the driver's side. In the pale illumination of the mixture of moonlight and glow from the lights he had left on inside the house, he could see that she was smiling. She came closer and grinned.

Jordan was mystified. Sierra had been furious when she had left to pick up Mariana. She had been gone hours, and now they arrived with birthday cake? Was it Sierra's birthday? Mariana's?

He waited until Mariana had passed by, and then he drew closer to Sierra, trying to gauge her expression. "Everything okay?"

"Yes." She was still smiling broadly. This was a huge difference from the expression she had worn earlier that evening.

It must be her birthday! Why didn't she say something?

As soon as they were inside and had shut the door on the bugs that were congregating around the car's headlights, Jordan put the grocery bag on the counter. "I wish you would have told me it was your birthday, Sierra."

"It's not her birthday," Mariana said brightly. "It's mine."

Sierra lifted the cake and the carton of ice cream from the bag.

"It's not my welcome-to-the-world birthday," Mariana said. "It's my welcome-to-the-Kingdom-of-God birthday."

Jordan scratched his eyebrow. He was trying to track with

what was going on here. He looked to Sierra for some support and a few more details. The bedroom door opened, and Derek came out, squinting in the light.

"Are you guys okay? What's going on?"

"Sit down, sit down." Mariana pointed to the sofa. "We're going to celebrate. Think of this as our fatted calf. I'm the prodigal who came home."

Jordan thought he was putting the pieces of this crazy puzzle together, but he wasn't going to say anything until he was sure he understood. He sat on the sofa. Derek sat next to him with his arms resting on his thighs like a basketball player waiting to be called into the game.

Mariana explained how her mother was a strong Christian, an evangelical, and that she took Mariana to Sunday school and prayed with her every night when she was a little girl.

"I loved Jesus back then, like my mother did, and I wanted to be just like her when I grew up. Then, when I was eleven, she died. It was a terrible, terrible death. I don't want to talk about that. I was so lost that I decided, if there was a God and if He was so cruel as to take my wonderful mother when I needed her most in my life, then I didn't want to have anything to do with Him. And that's how I lived. Until tonight."

Sierra came over to the couch and handed Jordan a plate with a slice of chocolate cake and a generous scoop of ice cream. The look on her face was still one of contentment.

Mariana handed a plate of birthday cake and ice cream to Derek. "So tonight I repented. I came back to God. I knew for a long time this was what I needed to do, but tonight it was unmistakable. It was time. I want to love Him and live for Him the way I have watched Sierra do all these years. What she has, what you have, Jordan, it's irresistible. Really. You don't know. I have seen it all on the other side. All of it. It's so empty. And there is no happiness there."

She lifted her fork and gave an indication that the three of them should do the same. "Here I am. Back on the right side, on God's side at last. Happy birthday to me!"

Sierra lifted her fork and gave a cheer.

Jordan followed Sierra's lead. "That's incredible, Mariana. Really. Wow!" He wished he had better words for her.

Derek found strong words of affirmation and spoke between bites.

It was slowly coming to Jordan what a significant moment this was for Sierra. He couldn't imagine what it would be like if Derek and Mindy had been his close friends all these years and yet didn't share his same core beliefs. His admiration for Sierra rose even higher as he realized the sort of challenges she had faced in Brazil. She had told him how difficult the language was for her. Not having the ongoing support of Christian friends and family nearby had to be even more difficult.

"So what happened in Waikiki?" Jordan asked. "Is your friend okay?"

Mariana's expression turned somber. "I hope so. Sierra and I prayed for her on the way back here. If Tianna is anything like I am, I know she's going to have to figure this out for herself. It does no good trying to convince someone that what she is doing is destructive until she is ready to hear it."

"Her life isn't in danger or anything, is it?" Jordan asked.

Mariana looked down. "I'll call her in the morning. It's like Sierra told me. Tianna is an adult. She's responsible for her own decisions. If she wants me to come rescue her, I'll do it once."

Mariana told about how she and Tianna had met a group of guys at the beach and how Tianna wanted to stay with them and go clubbing, but Mariana didn't want to go. They had an argument, and Tianna took her car keys and left with one of the guys.

"I was stuck there. What was I supposed to do? I'm sorry I had to call you on Jordan's phone, Sierra. I saw no other solution."

"I'm glad you called," Sierra said.

The birthday party wound down, and Derek was the first to meander back to bed. "The sun is coming up in just a few hours. I hope you guys get some sleep too."

"We will," Mariana said.

Jordan delayed going back to bed. He helped to clear the plates and stalled further by taking out the trash to the bin by the garage. When he returned to the kitchen both Mariana and Sierra had gone to their room and closed the door.

He wanted to say something to Sierra. He didn't know what. Something about how concerned he had been for her and how sorry he was about the comment he had made before she left about her Independence and trying for gold stars.

It was too late. But he could tell her in the morning. Or rather, later that day. Maybe by then he would have a better idea of what he wanted to say.

Jordan turned off the light and stumbled back to his room. His stomach was tightening. He didn't know if it was the cake or the thoughts he was trying to process. He knew he wasn't willing to step up to the plate and take a swing at what an ongoing relationship might look like with Sierra.

And yet, he didn't want anyone else to even get near that plate.

CHAPTER THIRTY-SIX

Sierra heard someone rumbling around in the kitchen about the same time the first birds started in on their chorus of jubilee for the new day. She groaned and turned over but knew it was useless to try to sleep any more.

Mariana appeared unaffected by the morning sounds and kept sleeping as Sierra pulled on a long, flowing beach skirt and a sleeveless, gauze top. She opened the door quietly and shuffled into the kitchen.

"You guys are sure up early. Did you get any sleep?"

"Couple of hours." Jordan gave her a smile. "How 'bout you?"

She covered her mouth as a yawn came out. She figured it was the only answer needed.

Derek put down his coffee mug and looked at the time on the microwave, Someone had reset it to the correct time. "We have to get going. The Eddie could be on. They had reports of closeout sets at sunrise."

Sierra had picked up enough talk from the people she was around at the beach to know that this elite surfing competition only happened when the waves reached a certain height. She didn't remember what it was, but apparently the magic number had been hit and the word had gone out that today was the day.

"Are you competing?" she asked.

Derek laughed. "Not in this one. It's by invitation only. Surfers are nominated by their peers. I'm not one of the big wave surfers. Don't ever plan to be."

"You were yesterday." She reached for a mug in the cupboard.

"And apparently, that was my only day. I didn't make the roster for the next heat."

Sierra paused before pouring herself a cup of coffee. "So that's it? That's as far as you can go?"

Derek nodded.

She caught a hint of disappointment, but he didn't seem as bummed as she thought someone like Derek would be after working so hard and then only getting one good run.

"I'm really sorry to hear that, Derek. I know this was important to you."'

"I'm okay with it."

"Are you really?" Jordan leaned in and reached for the milk carton that was on the counter beside Sierra. "I mean, I thought you would be a lot more upset. You seem pretty calm. Hasn't it sunk in?"

"No, it's sunk in. But I'm okay with it. I mean, I'm old, Jordo."

Jordan laughed.

"We knew it was a long shot. I went as far as I could. This is where the dream ran outta steam, man. My semi-pro surfing career ends here."

"That's not necessarily true," Jordan said.

Sierra poured her coffee and stepped to the side where she leaned against the counter and watched the concerned look on Jordan's face.

"Yeah, it's true," Derek said. "You know it's true. We have to look at this for what it is. I had a good run. It's over."

Sierra felt Derek's words go deep. She had had a good run in Brazil. Was that dream out of steam for her?

"You know what I realized?" Derek asked. "I realized that what I want in life more than anything is a good wife, some healthy kids, and food on the table. That's it, man. I don't need whatever it was I've been chasing all these years. Don't get me wrong; I love surfing. I'll always love it. I'll probably be one of those old guys out on his board when I'm seventy. But for now, knowing that Mindy is all right, and that we have our first baby on the way, that's it. That's my life right there. That's my real dream."

Sierra felt her throat tighten at Derek's words. She sipped her coffee again and stole a look at Jordan. He was looking down and had his lips pressed together.

The fact that Jordan's dream was coming along nicely while Derek's had come to a halt had to impose some sort of weight on Jordan. She thought about all the dreams she had that were connected with Brazil. Many had been fulfilled. She had had a good run, as Derek had said. And now? Was that it? Was she done?

Sierra opened the cupboard and pulled out a box of cereal. She picked up a bowl from the dish rack. She saw that her hand quivered as it had the day after the storm when she and Jordan were sitting close on the couch and had an intense moment of gazing at each other. Sierra felt then that Jordan had been able to see all the way to her heart.

Now it seemed that Derek's words had gone all the way to that same deep place. Sierra didn't think she had ever admitted it to anyone, but her deeply rooted dream was for a loving spouse and a healthy family as well. It was a dream she didn't dare to acknowledge for fear that it might be asking too much of God to fulfill.

"Do you want to come with us?" Derek asked.

Sierra looked up. Both Jordan and Derek were looking at her

with expectant expressions. As she fixed her gaze on Jordan, Sierra thought she saw something hopeful in his eyes. She wondered if she was reading into the moment because she wanted something to be there. She had tried not to let herself build up fanciful scenarios about him. But now she was at the point where she couldn't deny her attraction grew each time she was around him.

Even though Jordan hadn't given a solid indication that he was interested in her, she needed to finally admit to herself that she was interested in him. Very interested.

"You know," Sierra said cautiously. "I told Mariana I'd do something with her today. But, since she's still asleep, maybe I could follow you guys in my car, hang out for an hour or so and then come back when she's up and ready to go."

Jordan was still looking at her with a hopeful expression. "I have to come back here around ten. We could all go to Waimea together, and then you and I could come back here."

"Sure, that sounds great."

"You can leave me at Waimea Bay all day," Derek said. "I don't want to miss any of it."

"I'll get a few things together." Sierra ducked into the bedroom and saw that Mariana was awake.

"Are you guys going somewhere? I heard you talking."

"We're going to Waimea. Do you want to come? The guys want to get there early. Jordan's coming back here in a few hours."

"Of course I'd like to go." Mariana stretched leisurely. "How much time do I have to get ready?"

"They want to leave right away."

"Can we meet them there in a little while?"

Sierra hesitated. She would rather go right now. But she gave in. "Sure, we can do that. I'll go tell them."

It took Mariana a full hour to get ready. Sierra knew it would. Mariana was the only person Sierra knew who would take a shower and straighten her hair before going to the beach. While Mariana prepped, Sierra made sandwiches, cleaned up the kitchen, and washed two of her shirts in the sink.

Once they were finally on their way with towels, beach chairs, and a picnic lunch stuffed into the backseat of Mariana's convertible, they were stunned at all the traffic. The highway was packed. Their trek to Waimea Bay was slow going, but it gave them time to talk, and that was what Mariana seemed most interested in.

She talked about her childhood and her relationship with her dad. She told Sierra some stories she never had shared before about old boyfriends and lost friendships. It seemed to be a purging session for Mariana.

"God's grace for you covers everything," Sierra said. "It's all fresh starts from here."

"Yes!" Mariana shouted out the open top of the convertible, "I love my new life!"

Sierra smiled. She still couldn't believe the way Mariana had prayed last night, and the way even her countenance appeared different.

As they entered the area where the competition was being held, the bottleneck of cars became ridiculous.

"We'll never find a place to park," Mariana said. "How badly do you want to see the monster waves? Haven't we been looking at huge waves all week?"

Sierra wanted to see Jordan, not the waves. But he was only going to be there another hour or less before he went back to Sunset Beach.

"I guess we could call Jordan and tell him we're not coming."

"Yes, do that. Call him. I found out about a good beach not far from here that is calm enough for swimming. You and I can go there instead. I haven't been in the water since I got here. What's the point of going to Hawaii if you don't plunge into the water?"

Before Sierra could pull Mariana's phone from her purse, Mariana stopped her and added, "That is, if you want to do this. Go swimming, I mean. I didn't give you much of a chance to have a say in this."

"I'm okay with swimming. We weren't going to find parking, and even if we did, it would have been hard to find Jordan and Derek with so many people on the beach."

"Okay. Good. Call Jordan. And tell him I haven't forgotten about the cooking competition. You and he were supposed to be having a challenge in the kitchen. Do you remember? I was going to be the judge."

"Yes, I remember."

"Tell him that we should do that tonight. The two of you can cook for Derek and me."

Sierra called Jordan, and he answered right away. She explained the change in plans and then added Mariana's reminder about the cooking challenge.

"What do you think? Would you like to demonstrate your culinary skills tonight? I can tell you right now that I'll win. I mean, just in case you feel intimidated and want to back out."

Jordan laughed. "I do have to back out, but not because you've intimidated me out of the competition."

"Then what's your excuse? It better be a good one."

"It is. I just made dinner plans five minutes ago."

Jordan explained that he had had a conversation with a scout for a huge company that sponsored all the major surfing competitions. If Jordan were picked up as one of their exclusive photographers, this massive corporation would send him all over the world to shoot surfing competitions. The way he explained the opportunity, it sounded as if it were the very best of the best photography positions he could have in this industry.

"That's great!" Sierra hoped she sounded positive. Jordan sounded very excited.

"The guy's name is Zach. You met him."

"I did?"

"He said he talked to you on the beach yesterday, and you told him about Mindy and the accident and how I was a photographer and this was my dream."

Sierra remembered the guy in the straw beach hat who had come to the water's edge asking if Derek was okay.

"I may have gotten a little too chatty with him."

"No, it was perfect. You paved the way for me. I know he wouldn't have sought me out this morning if you hadn't talked to him. Thanks, Sierra."

"You're welcome." She hung up and felt a window of hope closing. Jordan was on his way to the sky's-the-limit future he had been working toward. Any inklings and nudgings she had felt in the kitchen that morning about Jordan seeing into her heart were destined to end right where they started.

In Derek's words, "This is where the dream ran outta steam, man."

CHAPTER THIRTY-SEVEN

The moment Jordan hung up the phone after talking to Sierra he felt a sharp twinge of sadness. It seemed odd, since he was still amped up over the conversation he had had with Zach. What impressed him most was the way Derek had entered into the conversation with strong support and affirmation for Jordan. Zach was from the sponsor corporation Derek had dreamed about being in partnership with once he garnered enough titles on the surfing circuit.

That opportunity would never be there for Derek, and yet he rallied around Jordan with the same enthusiasm as if he were the one being courted and invited to dinner.

"Your life is about to change big-time," Derek said. "Are you ready for it?"

"Let's wait and see what Zach has to say tonight before making predictions like that. It's a volatile business. You've taught me that."

They were standing in the sand watching the enormous waves curl and crash, curl and crash. None of the competitors had gone out yet. Spectators were still arriving in a steady stream, and it seemed some of the competitors were still coming as well.

"Do you wish you were going out there?" Jordan nodded at the ferocious wall of water that had just crested.

"No way." Derek folded his arms and shook his head. "That stuff is way beyond my skill set. Yesterday, that was my wave. That'll always be 'the one.'"

"I'm glad you were able to get over here," Jordan said. "I'm glad you surfed your wave."

Derek bobbed his head. "I am a blessed man. Very blessed. And I know it."

Jordan had his camera out and took photos even though no one was in the water yet. "Did you hear that guy talking as we were walking down here from the parking area? He said this bay is like a big swimming pool in the summer. Completely calm. No waves."

"That's what I've heard."

"It's hard to believe when you're standing here and you can feel the sand under your feet practically vibrate with the pounding force of those waves."

Jordan kept checking his watch. He realized he needed to get a running start on the traffic if he was going to make it back to Sunset by ten o'clock. After he had taken about a hundred frames of the surf at Waimea, he said, "I'm going to hit the road. Are you okay getting back on your own?"

"Yeah, it's only a couple of miles. I'll walk or catch a ride. Don't worry. I'll be fine."

Jordan thought he caught a hint of extra courage in Derek's words. He had been doing a great job of saying the right things all morning on how he had had his chance, his wave, a shot at his dream, and now he was content to go home to his wife and baby-on-the-way. As admirable as Derek's words were, Jordan couldn't help but feel that his friend had to be more torn up inside than he was letting on.

Remembering how he had told Sierra last night that no one was passing out gold stars for bravery, Jordan wished that weren't true. He wished he had some sort of gold star he could give his friend for his bravery.

The traffic wasn't as bad as Jordan thought it would be going north. He arrived on the beach, set up his camera, and talked a bit with some of the other cameramen. One of them asked about Jordan's girlfriend with the long, golden curls. "Is she coming out here today?"

"No." Jordan left it at that. He didn't want to explain that Sierra wasn't his girlfriend because he didn't want the other guy to get any ideas about pursuing her. Not that Sierra would respond to just any Joe. She was reserved, inexperienced, and had high standards.

Jordan thought about how reserved and inexperienced he was, and how he, too, had high standards.

How many women like her are left out there?

As the meet continued and Jordan snapped photos, he thought about what it was going to be like traveling around the world, flying first-class, staying at top hotels, and capturing surfing photos in exotic locations.

Then he thought about what it would be like to come home to the image that he saw through the partly open bathroom door last evening. He remembered how Sierra looked, stretched out under the floating particles of dust. He thought about the mermaid picture on his screen saver. Then he remembered the way her eyes looked like aquamarine stained glass the afternoon when he tried to open her hotel room door by mistake and she was standing there with her bare-bottomed nephew in her arms.

She was going to be hard to shake. He knew that. But he had found himself enamored with a few women in the past whose images and memories faded as soon as he put some distance between himself and them. Jordan believed that was how it would be with Sierra. She would go back to Brazil and only be a pleasant part of his memories from this trip.

Maybe, just maybe, he would see her again if the world surfing tour took him to Rio de Janiero. He would see Sierra while he was there, as well as the statue of Christ with His arms open over the city. Now, that would be something to look forward to.

An air horn sounded, and the other photographers packed up their gear.

"Is that it for the day?" Jordan had thought this heat was supposed to last until four o'clock.

"They officially called The Eddie. It's on," one of the guys said. "Everyone's going down there. They've got swells coining in with a fifty-foot face."

Jordan had realized that the swarms of people who arrived that morning were doing so in anticipation of the competition taking place, but apparently it was now a certainty. He made the trek back to the beach house and got in his car in order to join the masses on the narrow highway, slogging his way back down to Waimea. If he had thought about it and if he could have fit all his equipment in the basket, he would have taken the beach cruiser bike. He would have arrived sooner, that was for sure.

Mariana's tip about the quiet cove and good swimming beach turned out to be correct. The farther they drove from the massive crowds on the North Shore, the more the highway and the scenery opened up. It was fun riding around in the convertible. The beautiful surroundings seemed close enough to reach out and touch. Sierra was glad they had done this. She loved seeing other parts of the island.

The two of them hauled their beach gear to a spot underneath a gathering of six palm trees that provided a nice half-shade, half-sun spot on the sand. Sierra noticed that the sand wasn't as fine as the white-sugared sand at Sunset Beach. The reason, she guessed, was because this sand wasn't subjected to the same intense "spin cycle" as the sand churned up and spewed onto the beach at Sunset.

For the first half an hour both Sierra and Mariana napped, still tired after their late night and the emotional highs and lows they had been going through. They woke when a mom with two grade-school daughters walked up and talked to them as if they were awake and just trying to sunbathe.

"Would you like these? We're flying back to Oregon tonight." She held up two pink rafts. Mariana quickly snatched them.

"Come on, Sierra, let's go float."

Once they were out on the water, they experienced a welcome moment of hilarity trying to board the rafts. Sierra managed to wrestle the slippery beast first and was on her back with her head on the blow-up pillow as she watched Mariana flip over three times.

"Stop laughing!" Mariana said. "You looked just as ridiculous trying to get on."

"I'm sure I did, but you will notice that I'm the one who is on now."

"Ha! I'll show you." Mariana paddled over while holding on to her raft and tried to tip Sierra off her raft. She had no success.

"I had four brothers," Sierra reminded her. "I learned how to hold my own early in life."

"Yes, you did." Mariana remained determined to clamber onto her raft, and her efforts paid off. She mounted the pink pony, stretched out her legs, and put her head on the pillow. "There, not so hard after all."

"Right," Sierra said. "Not hard at all."

"Oh, be quiet."

They floated on the water, feeling the sun's reflection as it intensified.

"Can you believe that people live here and do this every day?" Mariana said.

"I doubt that people who live here get to do this sort of leisurely activity every day."

"Well, they should."

Mariana paddled closer to Sierra's raft. "I've been thinking about something. I think I made happiness and having fun my entire goal in life."

Sierra wasn't going to disagree with her friend there.

"And I think you have done the same thing with Christian ministry. You made that your goal for everything you do."

Sierra popped her head up. She hadn't expected Mariana's comment. "There's nothing wrong with that," she protested.

"There can be something very wrong with that. And you are the one who told me this. We are made to love God and serve people. If you start to focus on just serving God, then pretty soon you run out of love for people."

"I told you that?" Sierra felt unprepared for such a comment.

"Yes, a long time ago. Sierra, lately you have been too worried about how you can serve God better. I liked you more when I first met you and you just loved God. There were always plenty of service things for you to do."

Sierra remembered Jordan's comment about gold stars not being handed out and how she didn't have to prove anything. "Do you think I'm trying to prove something if I stay in Brazil and take that position teaching the children and living in the village?"

"Are you?"

Sierra didn't answer.

"We both know you can do it. That's not the question. You are capable of doing many things. But is that what you were made to do?"

"I don't know," Sierra stammered.

"I can tell you how to find out. You taught me this, too. You ask yourself, does this make my heart happy? Does it give me more energy and joy? Then that's when you know you are using the gifts God gave you and doing what He created you to do."

"Where did you get all this?"

"I told you. From you. You told me this."

"I did? When?"

"I don't know. Some time when you were talking. Sierra, don't you see? All these years you have put your words in me as your interpreter. Every word you put into me in English has gone through me before it came out in Portuguese. Every word. I heard it. I listened. I learned so much from you."

Sierra didn't know what to say.

"And now I think it's time for you to learn something from me. I have looked for love for a long time in a lot of places. I know many times over what love is not. And I also know what love is when I see it. You love God. I know that. Now, I think you will be able to love Him even better if you can stop trying to make God proud of you."

Sierra felt as if the world had come to a halt. All was silent. The only sound she heard was the whispered echo of Mariana's last sentence: *stop trying to make God proud of you.*

CHAPTER THIRTY-EIGHT

Jordan pulled into the driveway at the beach house a little past nine o'clock after his dinner with Zach. He sat for a moment in his rental car thinking about the big decision he had in front of him. It seemed best to get a good night's sleep and come to a conclusion in the morning.

The smell of wood smoke greeted him as he made his way to the front door. Someone must have lit a campfire on the beach. Jordan entered and discovered the campfire was on their front patio in the in-ground fire pit. He could see Sierra and Mariana on low beach chairs by the fire, but Derek wasn't with them.

Both the women looked up as Jordan pulled open the screen door.

"Hey, how did it go?" Sierra asked.

"Good." Jordan wasn't sure what else he wanted to say about his dinner with Zach. "Is Derek here?"

"He's in his room," Mariana said. "Packing."

"Packing?"

"He found a flight he can take home at midnight so he arranged for an airport shuttle to pick him up," Sierra explained. "We volunteered to drive him to the airport, but he insisted on taking the shuttle."

"I'll see how he's doing," Jordan said.

"Come back and join us," Mariana offered. "We have marshmallows."

"Okay," he said over his shoulder as he headed for the bedroom.

Jordan found Derek zipping up his small carry-on bag. "Hey, is everything all right? Is Mindy okay?"

"She's doing great. I decided I did what I came to do, and now I'm ready to go home. I left a message on your phone."

"I didn't check my messages. I had the ringer turned down. Are you sure you have to go?"

"I don't have to go, but I want to. I want to get back to Mindy."

Jordan sat on the bed's edge. "This sure wasn't what we expected it to be, was it?"

"Maybe not, but you won't hear me complain. I had the time of my life. It was a bonus hanging out all day at The Eddie. That was some meet today, wasn't it?"

"Yes. Amazing waves." Jordan knew that he still didn't have the same level of passion Derek did for the world of surfing or the surf community. He was impressed at how the competition had gone that day at Waimea, but not being a surfer, Jordan had never picked up the same enthusiasm and loyalty that Derek had for the sport.

"Don't look so down, Jordo. It was what it was. Everything got shaken up over the last week, and now what's left is what we go with. You don't have any complaints, do you?"

"No. But I'm bummed for you that things didn't go the way we had hoped they would. This was supposed to be your big break."

"And it wasn't. So what? I go on from here. It's okay. Really. Like I told you, this whole experience has made me shift my value system. I have a wife and baby to take care of. Those are the gold nuggets left in my life after this shake-up." Derek hiked his bag on his shoulder. "Walk with me to the highway. I have to meet the shuttle at the pickup point in a few minutes."

Jordan followed Derek back to the patio where he said his goodbyes to Mariana and Sierra. "If you decide to come to Santa Barbara, know that you will always be welcome to hang out at our place."

"Thanks," Sierra said with a smile. "I might have to take you up on that offer."

Jordan wondered for a moment if she meant that or if she was only saying what seemed natural in response to Derek's offer. When would Sierra ever be in Santa Barbara?

"I'm walking Derek to the shuttle pickup."

"We'll try not to eat all the marshmallows before you return," Mariana said.

Derek picked up his covered surfboard from where he had left it in the garage and carried it under his arm down the dark driveway as Jordan followed carrying his luggage.

"I still wish you weren't going yet. It's been too short," Jordan said.

"I know." Derek drew in a deep breath, as if trying to muster up some courage. "So tell me how your dinner went. Did Zach offer you the world on a silver platter?"

Jordan considered how to answer. He was hesitant to tell his friend how great the offer was. In an effort not to overdo the details, he skipped the description of the multimillion-dollar mansion where Zach and the rest of his staff were staying. He didn't describe the chef-prepared meal that was served to them on the oceanfront deck at sunset.

Instead he started with the downside. "I'd have to move."

"Where?"

"Here."

"Wow."

"It's an exclusive offer. They pretty much would own me and tell me where to go when. I'd be at their beck and call."

"And from the headquarters here they'll be sending you all over the world, right?"

"Mostly through the South Pacific with a lot of tournaments in Australia."

Jordan carefully watched Derek's expression in the glow of the streetlight overhead where they had stopped at the appointed pickup spot. Derek swallowed, looked across the street, and then looked at Jordan.

"You're gonna be livin' the dream, man. I'm really stoked for you."

"I didn't sign anything yet."

"You didn't?"

"No. The contract is something like thirty pages long. I told Zach I needed a chance to have my lawyer look at it, and I needed to think and pray about it."

Derek looked surprised. "You have a lawyer?"

"No. But apparently I need to get one. I didn't want to sign my life away without someone explaining the fine print to me."

"Sounds wise. You're going to take the offer though, aren't you?"

Jordan didn't answer. He didn't know. Something about it didn't feel right.

"You're not hesitating because of me, are you?"

"No. Well, possibly. It's such a shift in my thinking. You brought me into this whole surf scene. I've learned what I needed as I went along. I guess it doesn't feel natural going solo from here on out. It made sense and seemed clear when you and I started this project together. Now I'm not so sure this is my goal, if you know what I mean."

Jordan remembered what Sierra had said a few days ago about how people were more important than projects. Jordan's challenge to her had been, "What if the people are the project?"

That was how he felt about the years he had spent with Derek. The project hadn't been to get noticed as a photographer in the surfing world. The project had been Derek. The goal had been to get him noticed in the surfing world.

Now everything was upside down.

Derek seemed to be taking all this in as if it were the last thing he expected of Jordan. "What did Zach say when you didn't agree to sign over dinner?"

"He joked about how a dozen photographers were lined up behind me with a pen in their hand, ready to sign."

"I don't think he's joking."

A car passed them with all the windows down as loud music with a monotonous beat broke the pace of their conversation.

"Zach said something else."

"What?" Derek asked.

"He said, 'What's not to like about this offer? I'm promising you travel, money, and recognition in a highly competitive field. Are you afraid of success?'"

"Are you?" Derek asked.

"I don't know." Jordan knew he was tired from getting so little sleep the night before. The dinner with Zach had thrown him off balance. But it seemed something more was weighing on him. He just didn't know what it was. "I think I need to pray about this."

"Sounds wise. You pray, and I'll pray. I'd say don't overthink it, though, Jordo. Either it's the life for you, or it isn't. Simple as that. If you want it, then you can take it. It won't matter what an attorney tells you about the terms and conditions. You negotiate what you can, but basically you sign your freedom away in exchange for a huge, life-altering opportunity."

Jordan looked up at the night sky. Clouds gathered, creating a low ceiling and hiding the stars.

"Do you want it?" Derek asked.

"I don't know."

"It's not like you to be so indecisive."

"I know."

"I never would have guessed it. Here I thought you had it so bad for your career that you would have signed the minute Zach put the contract on the table."

They stood together silently for a moment, and then Derek said, "It's Sierra, isn't it? She's the wild card that has you all locked up so that you don't know what you want."

"No, it's not Sierra."

"Are you sure?"

At the moment Jordan wasn't sure of anything. He pulled out the same standard answer he kept giving himself. "She lives in Brazil."

Derek's expression changed. He looked surprised and humored at Jordan's response.

The shuttle bus pulled up to the curb and let out a hiss of exhaust. The driver opened the door. "It's extra for the board."

"Got it." Derek stuck his hand in his pocket and pulled out his wallet. Over his shoulder he said to Jordan, "You should talk to her. Ask her what she's gonna do when she leaves here."

Derek boarded the shuttle. "Call me tomorrow. Not too early, though."

The door closed, and Jordan waved as the driver pulled away from the curb.

For a few moments Jordan didn't move. He looked up at the night sky again and wondered if another storm was rolling in.

Jordan thought about how simple his life was when he arrived on Oahu a few days ago. He felt successful after shooting the wedding on Maui. In fact, he really enjoyed that. Probably more than he enjoyed the long hours he had stood in the hot sand today taking the same sort of shots he had taken the day before of curling waves and fast-moving surfers.

"What's my problem?" he muttered. "Why don't I know what I want to do anymore?" All Jordan knew for certain was that he would be crazy, absolutely crazy, to walk away from this opportunity.

Heading back to the beach house, Jordan thought about how Derek said he should talk to Sierra and ask what she was going to do when she left here. Jordan already knew. She was going to teach some missionary children in a jungle village. At least that's what she had told him when they were marooned during the storm.

He knew she wasn't excited about it, but it was what was next for her. Was that Derek's point? That even though Jordan wasn't excited about signing the contract, he should just go ahead, make the commitment, and move on?

Before he opened the door to the beach house, Jordan remembered how Derek had called Sierra the "wild card." She was. She was a beautiful, intriguing, captivating wild card, and she was throwing him off his game.

Jordan paused with his hand on the latch. The next step seemed clear. He needed to pull the wild card out of his winning hand and play with the other cards he had been dealt. The sooner this mesmerizing mermaid was out of his thoughts, the better.

CHAPTER THIRTY-NINE

Sierra was up before the dawn, before the birds and before her two housemates. She didn't risk the chance of waking them by making coffee. Instead, she pulled on a long skirt and her Rancho Corona hooded sweatshirt, and slipped out the door with a beach towel wrapped around her shoulders.

A single morning star sat on the dark horizon, just under the dense cloud cover, looking as if it were suspended in midair, waiting for the signal to drop into the ocean like a lone pebble. Sierra felt a certain sympathy for that star, hanging there, all alone. She, too, felt as if she were waiting for a signal.

Yesterday had been such an amazing, vision-adjusting sort of day. The sky had been clear, the weather perfect, and the afternoon at the beach with Mariana had been ideal. Yesterday morning Sierra's heart felt light after Mariana's big moment the night before and the way Jordan's gaze had landed on her as they stood in the kitchen. She started the day feeling hopeful about every area of her life. Derek's words about what he valued touched her deeply.

Mariana's words to her as they floated on the pink rafts had both unraveled and reknit all Sierra's thoughts about the future.

She realized how her heart had gotten off track. Her goal in life had somehow gone from loving God to trying to make Him proud of her. That all changed as she paddled and prayed alongside Mariana on the water. During that time, Sierra felt as if her life had been recalibrated.

On their drive back to the beach house, she and Mariana had stopped at a roadside stand to buy a plate of fresh-roasted shrimp. Sierra had stood there, looking at the long menu of options on the painted sign, and murmured to herself, "What do I want?" The answer, of course, was shrimp sautéed in garlic and butter.

But that simple question had triggered a memory, and her mother's words had come back to her. Mom had told her she was "a woman of options" and should ask herself a simple question, "What do I want?"

So Sierra had asked herself, and the answer was to go to Santa Barbara, find a job at the restaurant of her parents' friends, and follow this new relationship with Jordan until it came to a natural conclusion.

That was the answer. That was what she wanted. She wouldn't return to Brazil. That dream, like Derek's surfing dream, had gone as far as it was going to go. It was time for a new dream, and this was it.

Sierra had returned to the beach house with garlic breath and a grocery bag filled with graham crackers, peanut butter cups, and marshmallows. She wanted to show Mariana how to "pig out" with customized s'mores while they had all the right American brands to create the concoction.

That was yesterday. Clear skies, clear vision, and lots of emotional space opening up for a new dream.

This morning everything was different. Sierra pressed her feet into the cool sand. Tiny raindrops were falling, and the sky was lightening with shades of silver gray as streaks of rose pierced through the gathering of clouds. She felt as gray as the day and as confused as the wind that was coming in short gusts, spinning small tornadoes in the sand.

It was light enough for Sierra to see both ends of the long, wide beach. She stood in the middle, not sure which direction to walk. Even this moment of hesitation and indecision seemed to match everything else she felt this morning. She chose to go left, with the wind at her back, and took long strides through the firm sand at the shoreline while the snarling waves tried to reach for her ankles.

"Morning." A hooded jogger passed her, followed by a young couple with very pale skin who were walking with their arms around each other.

Sierra stopped her march, tossed her beach towel on the sand, and sat on it with her arms circled around her bent knees. She rocked back and forth slightly as the sky filled with its full light on this stormy morning.

Everything seemed so clear yesterday. I was all set to move to Santa Barbara, and then Jordan came back after seeing Derek off, and everything changed.

Bits of the conversation Mariana and Sierra had with Derek around the campfire came back. She had told Derek about her decision to not return to Brazil and how his words had helped her process that decision. Derek's concern had been for Mariana. How was she going to do without her best friend nearby?

"I'll come visit her every chance I get," Mariana had said. "She is supposed to find me a nice, Christian surfer in Santa Barbara. That's Sierra's new assignment."

Derek said he was going to have a hard time without Jordan if Jordan took the new assignment that was undoubtedly being offered to him at dinner that night.

"What assignment?" Sierra hadn't understood how the sponsorships worked. As Derek filled her in, her heart sank. What if she moved to Santa Barbara, and Jordan only used his place there as a home base while he flew around the world on assignment? Was she making a good decision to move to Santa Barbara?

In the same way that the storm clouds had gathered last night as they roasted their marshmallows over the open fire, clouds of doubt closed in on Sierra. When Jordan had arrived and she asked how the dinner went, his one-word answer was "Good." That's when Sierra felt her hopes drop into the ocean like a lone pebble.

More than anything she felt foolish for pinning her future on Jordan. She knew better than that. The only problem was that in her heart she was settled about the position in Brazil. That evening she had e-mailed Mark and Sara and told them she wouldn't be coming back to Brazil and that the position as a teacher wasn't something she felt called to do. Sending that e-mail had given her the strongest sense of peace and confidence she had felt in weeks. Sierra had no doubt that was the right decision.

But now what? Was Santa Barbara also the right decision?

Sierra watched the waves as they rose and crested. The white foam along the top looked like a row of chorus dancers, all kicking up their froth in perfect harmony and peeling down the line as if they had practiced this wave a thousand times before giving their audience of one this stunning performance.

The wave flattened out and rolled to the shore. She watched how the salty water went only so far and no farther.

God tells the waves how far they can go. He controls their coming in and going out.

She wondered if she had read that in the Psalms somewhere. The thought seemed familiar. Sierra tried to interject that thought into her discomfort. God was in control of her coming in and going out as well, wasn't He?

Her thoughts jumped back to the most painful words that had sunk into her yesterday during what had turned into a day filled with life-changing words. When Jordan returned from walking Derek to the shuttle stop, he had come out to the patio. Mariana offered him a wire coat hanger and marshmallows, but he turned them down.

Jordan had stood in front of them, and with his hands on his hips, said with firm conviction, "Looks like I'm going to take the offer. I'll be moving here to Oahu and traveling all over the South Pacific."

"Wow, congratulations!" Mariana said. "I might have to come visit you, or maybe you would like me to housesit for you while you're traveling."

Jordan had responded to Mariana with a cordial nod and a flat expression. He barely even glanced at Sierra before mumbling something about getting some sleep before he had to go back to work in the morning. That's when Sierra's star of hope dropped from her sky of possibilities.

Now that she was alone on the beach, staring at the vast horizon and the powerful waves, she felt an odd twinge of peace about her decision to go to Santa Barbara. Even though Jordan wouldn't be living there, Sierra still thought she should go. She didn't know why. It seemed random.

Maybe something important is there for me to do. Or maybe someone special lives there that I'm supposed to meet.

Sierra knew she didn't want to meet someone special. She already had met someone special. Very special. Jordan Bryce was about the most ideal guy she had ever met. But he obviously hadn't felt the same spark and magnetism. Even all the "God things" about their meeting apparently hadn't been enough to convince him to pay attention to her.

"Okay," Sierra whispered into the morning sky filled with dark clouds. "That's fine. I know I'm not leaving Brazil because of Jordan. That was a separate decision. I believe it's the right decision. I also feel directed toward Santa Barbara. Is that crazy? Lord, I'm trying to follow You with all my heart because I love You. I trust You. I know You're going to show me what's next."

Sierra felt the raindrops gently tapping on her sweatshirt's hood. Her years of living in Portland served her well at this moment; Sierra didn't mind the raindrops. She kind of liked the way they fell on her in a gentle rhythm.

With a deep breath of salty air filling her lungs, Sierra came to a conclusion. If God could direct the rhythm of the raindrops and tell the enormous waves where to stop before returning to the sea, He could lead her in this next phase of her life. And as far as her heart could see through the clouds of this decision, God was leading her to Santa Barbara.

"So be it," she whispered. Standing and shaking out her beach towel. Sierra walked toward the beach house, her face to the wind.

CHAPTER FORTY

"Are you sure you don't mind doing this?" Jordan asked Mariana as he handed her the grocery list he had just written.

"Are you kidding? I'm happy to do this and anything else you need. I'm especially glad that you're making good on your offer to make dinner. I'll tell Sierra when she gets out of the shower that the competition is on."

"No, don't tell her," Jordan said. "Let me make dinner tonight. She can make it tomorrow night for our final night here. You can compare the two and give your assessment after that. Sound good?"

"Okay." Mariana moved her empty cereal bowl to the sink. "You sure seem to have come alive this morning. You're in a much better mood than you were last night. How much coffee did you have?"

"None yet. By the way, would you mind making some? I need to pull my stuff together and get down to the beach early."

"Sure, I'll make the coffee."

Jordan dashed into the bedroom and unplugged his cell

phone from the charger. He grinned as he remembered how the buzzing of his phone had awakened him less than an hour ago. He had reached to turn it off, thinking the sound was coming from the alarm. It was an incoming call from Bill.

"Morning, Jordan. I wanted to check in and see how it's going."

"It's going fine." He sat up in bed and wondered why Bill was calling so early.

"I thought I'd let you know that the whole editorial team has been really impressed with what you've sent us."

"I'm glad to hear that."

"We've been talking, and we wanted you to know that if you're interested, we could keep you busy with more assignments."

Jordan leaned forward and tried to make sure he was catching everything Bill was saying. "Do you mean travel assignments?"

"Some. Not a lot. Mostly up and down the coast. We need a photographer down at Trestles in two weeks."

"I'll have to think about it and get back to you."

"Listen, Jordan, I'll be straight with you. We heard you've been pursued by several key sponsors there, and after seeing what you've produced for us, we understand why they're coming after you. We can't compete with their package offers. We don't have those deep pockets of revenue. But we can keep you busy and set up an agreement of some sort if you like. We're more on a handshake-basis here. You know that. We're not asking for an exclusive with you. Just a chance to keep working with you, if by any chance you don't sign with one of the big guns."

Jordan never expected such a call. He wasn't sure what to say. "I appreciate that, Bill. I'll give it some thought."

"You know my number. Looking forward to what you pull together for us these last few days."

After he hung up, Jordan meandered out to the kitchen to see if any coffee had been made. He definitely needed some this morning. The coffeepot was dry. Mariana was seated at the counter munching on a bowl of cereal. He heard the shower start and guessed that was where Sierra was.

That was when Mariana managed to elegantly unfurl the second unexpected wave of information on him that morning. "Sierra must have had an inspiring walk in the rain this morning," Mariana said. "She just came in and told me she's made her decision. She's moving to Santa Barbara."

Jordan froze. "Santa Barbara?"

"She came to the conclusion yesterday that her time in Brazil was over. Done. The dream ran outta steam, or whatever it was that Derek told her. She's certain that she's supposed to get a job at a restaurant in Santa Barbara that's owned by some of her parents' friends."

"Sierra just decided this?" Jordan asked.

"Apparently."

Jordan knew she couldn't have made that choice based on his living there. He had announced last night that he was moving to Oahu. What was going on?

"You can ask her yourself when she gets out of the shower."

"I have a better idea." Jordan grabbed a scrap of paper. That's when he wrote out the list of grocery items, which he asked Mariana to pick up for him.

Now that he was ready to head for the beach, he felt a little nervous about seeing Sierra on his way out the door. He didn't want to say anything to her. Not until dinner tonight. He knew if he saw her before then his plan might jump out and frighten both of them.

Sliding out the door, he made his way to the gathering of photographers whom he was coming to know on a first-name basis. He had heard them talking the last few days about whom they worked with and whom they wanted to be sponsored by.

None of the politics or competition of that part of the business appealed to him. Jordan just wanted to capture memorable moments in photographs. He wanted to work with guys who could accomplish their objectives with a handshake, not thirty pages of legal wording.

It was all coming into focus. He would stay in Santa Barbara and pick up assignments with *Surf Days* as well as any weddings that came his way. He enjoyed those. Sierra wasn't returning to Brazil. He had to keep repeating that to himself. Her living in Brazil had been his mantra from the beginning as the reason he couldn't consider continuing their relationship. Knowing that she was going to Santa Barbara changed everything.

Jordan wanted to surprise Sierra. He wanted to set up something special for her. That was why he had planned to cook for her tonight. He hadn't explained his entire plan to Mariana, but he hoped that he could find a way to be alone with Sierra. When he was, he would tell her that he wasn't accepting the offer from the big bucks corporate sponsor.

For the next few hours Jordan tried to concentrate on taking photos and not on all the places he wanted to show Sierra when she moved to Santa Barbara. He knew his friends would be nuts about her. He even had some ideas of places where she could stay for the first month or so without having to pay rent. It was as if the vista of his future had come into view, and all the details were coming into focus.

In the unfurling of his thoughts, Jordan finally gave himself permission to admit something that had been true from the first time he had seen Sierra.

I'm completely taken with this woman.

The only lingering question was whether she felt the same way about him.

~

Sierra and Mariana were riding the two cruiser bikes back to the beach house after going on an early afternoon run for shaved ice when Mariana told Sierra about the grocery list.

"I thought when we get back I'd take my car to buy the items he needs," Mariana said.

"Why is he doing all the cooking? I thought we were supposed to be competing." Sierra leaned forward on her bike and stood to pump the pedals so she could catch up with Mariana.

Mariana called over her shoulder, "He said you can cook tomorrow night, and I'll be the judge of which meal is best."

The sun had come out, and the rain clouds had fled. It had turned into a beautiful day.

Sierra decided she was going to do her part to make dinner fun. She didn't want to think about how the relationship with Jordan was about to hit a dead end in a day and a half when their lives would no longer overlap. Why couldn't it still be just as fun being around Jordan as it had been from the beginning? She smiled to herself thinking that Mariana would be happy to know Sierra was thinking of how to add a little more fun to her life.

Everything inside Sierra felt open and spacious. She felt peaceful about not returning to Brazil, and she had an equally settled feeling about going to Santa Barbara. It made no sense. She knew that. But she had already made some calls that morning on Mariana's cell phone and sent some e-mails. The waitressing job was looking good. Her mom's response on the phone had been, "I'm very glad to hear this, Sierra. This feels right to me."

Even though Sierra hadn't said anything to her mom about Jordan, she knew that a large part of her reason for selecting Santa Barbara was because of Jordan, even though he wasn't going to be there. He had been part of the catalyst to launch her into this wide open future. And who knew? Maybe someday down the road he would come back to visit his friends, and she could see him again. Who knew what might happen someday?

While Mariana was at the grocery store, Sierra spent a lot of time online arranging her flight and looking up information about Santa Barbara. When she heard Jordan come back from the beach and start to cook, she decided to let him work in solitude. Even though she was dying to work with him side by side, she opted for taking a shower and putting on her last fresh outfit. It was a summer dress with a flowing skirt and lace around the neckline. She put on her new shell earrings and took a little extra time with her hair.

Mariana came into the bedroom. "I'm going to meet Tianna for dinner. She called and wants to talk about what happened the other night."

"What about our dinner here?"

Mariana grinned. "Save me a bite of everything." She grabbed her purse and scampered out the door before Sierra could say anything.

Giving her arms and legs a good slather of her coconut-scented lotion, Sierra decided she had waited long enough. If Jordan didn't want her hanging around the kitchen while he finished cooking, that was fine. She would wait on the front patio like a woman of leisure.

The sight that met Sierra when she exited the bedroom took her breath away.

The patio beyond the sliding glass door had been transformed into a private dining room. Tiki torches flickered in the corners. A small table with a white tablecloth was flanked by two wicker chairs. A small fire glowed in the outdoor fire pit, and a dozen votive candles were set on the ground, the table, and the chaise lounge.

Beyond the patio, past the silhouetted palm trees, the picture-perfect white sand stretched out to where it met the foam-laced blanket of blue ocean. And beyond the sea was a twilight ablaze in streamers of orange, yellow, rose, and apricot. Sierra couldn't move. The golden sun was slipping into the sea.

"What do you think?" Jordan asked.

"I think that has to be the most amazing sunset I've ever seen." Sierra turned to face him and was surprised to see that he had on a button-down shirt and held a spatula.

"You look gorgeous." He focused on her and not the sunset out the window.

"Thank you," Sierra stammered. "So do you."

"Go ahead and sit down, I'll bring the food out to you."

She went to the sliding door, and when she opened it, she saw that the patio had been strewn with hundreds of petals from the tropical flowers that surrounded the beach house. On the table next to one of the plates was a single white gardenia.

Sierra took that seat and tried to figure out what was going on. She lifted the gardenia to her nose and drew in the heady fragrance. Then she tucked it behind her right ear, which she had learned was the side to wear a flower when you're single and available.

Jordan came out with a plate in each hand. "Chicken Parmesan, steamed zucchini, and jasmine rice." The presentation was beautiful.

"I'm impressed," she said.

"Wait till you taste it."

He sat and reached his hand across the table, offering for Sierra to slip her hand into his. When she did, he bowed his head and prayed a humble prayer of thankfulness for the food, the day, and Sierra.

"Amen," she agreed and lifted her head but didn't pull back her hand. "Jordan?"

He covered her hand with his other hand, and she felt like the sun must have felt tonight when it slipped through the beautiful sky to find blissful refuge in the powerful sea. "Jordan, what's going on?"

Jordan dipped his chin and looked into her eyes. "I'm not going to take the position with the sponsor I met with yesterday. I had what I consider to be a better offer this morning from *Surf Days Magazine*. I'm going to stay in Santa Barbara and do shoots up and down the California coast."

Sierra felt her eyes widen. "Did you know that I'm moving to Santa Barbara?"

"Yes."

Sierra looked at him without blinking.

Jordan grinned. "Do you remember how I said a few days ago that all the coincidences of how we met might not be so odd if God was trying to tell us something?"

Sierra nodded. She felt her heart pounding faster and her face warming.

"Well, I finally started to listen. I have no doubt. He's trying to tell us something."

They sat there, holding hands, gazing into each other's eyes in the candlelight, and this time Sierra knew Jordan could see all the way to her heart.

"Our dinner is cooling off," Sierra said.

Jordan didn't reply. He rose from the table, inviting Sierra to stand up with him. Then planting his two feet firmly, Jordan cupped Sierra's face in his hands, focusing on her lips.

Sierra held her breath and closed her eyes as she received the most perfect, tender, affectionate first kiss a young woman of options could wish for. Jordan drew back and let out his breath nice and slow. His eyes seemed to search Sierra's expression for a response. Her serene smile said it all, and she could tell he got the message.

This kiss at Sunset Beach would change everything for them.

Jordan slid his arm behind Sierra and held the back of her chair so she could be seated once again. He returned to his chair and picked up his fork. Before Sierra picked up her fork, she reached for the gardenia that she had put behind her right ear.

In one motion, Sierra transferred the gardenia to her left ear. She was taken. She knew it in her heart. This was so right. The most adventuresome, dream-filled season of her life was just about to begin.

Dear Beautiful Reader,

The first time my husband and I walked hand-in-hand on Sunset Beach was on our honeymoon many years ago. That was my first trip to Hawaii and the beginning of a lifelong affection for the Hawaiian Islands. We now live in Hawaii and the charm of this tropical paradise hasn't faded, nor has our love for each other. A kiss at Sunset Beach really can last a lifetime.

A few years ago we returned to the North Shore of Oahu for a visit in January. Sunset Beach was a completely different scene from what we first experienced during our August honeymoon. Instead of calm blue waters and gently rolling waves that were typical on this long stretch of white sandy beach during the summer months, the waves rose like great foaming beasts. We stood on the shore holding hands and staring in awe.

One of the many surfing competitions held at Sunset in the winter months was in full swing that day. Daring young men and women from around the world rode those giant waves with astonishing balance and grace.

One of the surfers lost his balance on the edge of a big wave and went catapulting into the deep water. His board shot straight up like a spinner dolphin, did a twist in the air, and dove in after him. We watched to see if he was all right. A few moments later he bobbed to the surface, got on his board, and paddled back out beyond the breakers, willing to give the next indomitable wave a try.

As I was writing this story, I thought about how overwhelming relationships can be during certain seasons of our lives. To conquer the wipeouts that come to all of us, we must paddle back out and be willing to give it all we have once again. But other seasons are like the summer months at Sunset Beach during which all the ocean has to offer is right there, calm and attainable. You simply need to step into the vastness and start swimming.

That's where I saw Sierra Jensen in my mind's eye as I

formulated this story. She was ready to be invited into love so that she could paddle her way into the next season of her life.

Sierra is a character I've "known" for many years. I started writing about her in the last Christy Miller book, *A Promise is Forever.* The twelve-book Sierra Jensen Series followed, focusing on Sierra's high school years. Sierra is one of the characters in the *Christy & Todd: The College Years Series.*

Are you curious about what happens to Sierra and Jordan after this story ends? You can find out when you read *Cottage by the Sea, Salty Kisses, Becoming Us* and *Being Known.*

Whether you are in a season of crashing waves and spinning surfboards or a stretch of calm breezes and swaying palm trees, my hope is that this story will provide you with a virtual getaway to Sunset Beach, Hawaii, one of the many beautiful places on God's amazing planet. May you feel encouraged to know that love is worth the risk and friendships are worth all your faithful efforts.

I'd love to keep in touch. Please come by my website for a visit: www.robingunn.com or visit www.christymiller.com.

Aloha,

Robin Jones Gunn

ABOUT THE AUTHOR

Robin Jones Gunn is the much-loved author of over 100 books with 5.5 million copies sold worldwide. She is best known for her Christy Miller Series as well as her *Father Christmas* novels that have been made into 3 Hallmark movies. Other bestsellers include the Sisterchicks Series and the Glenbrooke Series along with her memoir, *Victim of Grace.* Robin's other non-fiction books are *A Pocketful of Hope For Mothers, Praying For Your Future Husband,* co-authored with Tricia Goyer and *Spoken For,* co-authored with Alyssa Bethke.

Robin and her husband have two grown children and live in California. She travels extensively and is a frequent keynote speaker at local and international events. Robin also serves on the Board of Directors for Media Associates International, a nonprofit organization that provides training for writers and publishers in difficult places around the world.

www.RobinGunn.com

Christy Miller

The High School Years

Meet tender-hearted Christy Miller
and her Forever Friends in
this 4-book series

Christy and Todd

The College Years

See how Christy's
college years unfold
in this 3-book series

Christy and Todd

The Married Years

Follow Christy and Todd's first few years of marriage in this 3-book series

RobinGunn.com

Sierra Jensen Series

Join free-spirited Sierra during her high school years in this 4-book series

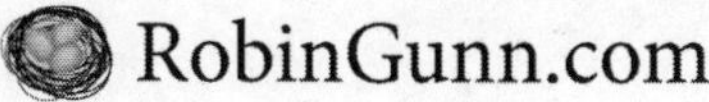